CROSS FIRE

Also by James Patterson

ALEX CROSS NOVELS

Along Came a Spider
Kiss the Girls
Jack and Jill
Cat and Mouse
Pop Goes the Weasel
Roses are Red
Violets are Blue
Four Blind Mice
The Big Bad Wolf
London Bridges
Mary, Mary
Cross
Double Cross
Cross Country
Alex Cross's Trial (*with Richard DiLallo*)
I, Alex Cross

DETECTIVE MICHAEL BENNETT SERIES

Step on a Crack (*with Michael Ledwidge*)
Run for Your Life (*with Michael Ledwidge*)
Worst Case (*with Michael Ledwidge*)
Tick, Tock (*with Michael Ledwidge, to be published January 2011*)

STAND-ALONE THRILLERS

Sail (*with Howard Roughan*)
Swimsuit (*with Maxine Paetro*)
Private (*with Maxine Paetro*)
Don't Blink (*with Howard Roughan*)
Postcard Killers (*with Liza Marklund*)

NON-FICTION

Torn Apart (*with Hal and Cory Friedman*)
The Murder of King Tut (*with Martin Dugard*)

ROMANCE

Sundays at Tiffany's (*with Gabrielle Charbonnet*)

THE WOMEN'S MURDER CLUB SERIES

1st to Die
2nd Chance (*with Andrew Gross*)
3rd Degree (*with Andrew Gross*)
4th of July (*with Maxine Paetro*)
The 5th Horseman (*with Maxine Paetro*)
The 6th Target (*with Maxine Paetro*)
7th Heaven (*with Maxine Paetro*)
8th Confession (*with Maxine Paetro*)
9th Judgement (*with Maxine Paetro*)
10th Anniversary (*with Maxine Paetro, to be published March 2011*)

FAMILY OF PAGE-TURNERS

MAXIMUM RIDE SERIES

The Angel Experiment
School's Out Forever
Saving the World and Other Extreme Sports
The Final Warning
Max
Fang
Angel (*to be published March 2011*)

MAXIMUM RIDE MANGA

Volume 1 (*with NaRae Lee*)
Volume 2 (*with NaRae Lee*)
Volume 3 (*with NaRae Lee*)

DANIEL X SERIES

The Dangerous Days of Daniel X (*with Michael Ledwidge*)
Daniel X: Alien Hunter Graphic Novel (*with Leopoldo Gout*)
Daniel X: Watch the Skies (*with Ned Rust*)
Daniel X: Demons and Druids (*with Adam Sadler*)

WITCH & WIZARD SERIES

Witch & Wizard (*with Gabrielle Charbonnet*)
Witch & Wizard: The Gift (*with Ned Rust, to be published November 2010*)

For more information about James Patterson's novels, visit **www.jamespatterson.co.uk**

James Patterson

CROSS FIRE

C

Century · London

Published by Century, 2010

2 4 6 8 10 9 7 5 3 1

First published in Great Britain in 2010 by
Century
Random House, 20 Vauxhall Bridge Road,
London SW1V 2SA

www.randomhouse.co.uk

Addresses for companies within The Random House Group Limited can be found at:
www.randomhouse.co.uk/offices.htm

The Random House Group Limited Reg. No. 954009

A CIP catalogue record for this book
is available from the British Library

Hardback ISBN 9781846054587
Trade paperback ISBN 9781846054594

The Random House Group Limited supports The Forest Stewardship Council (FSC), the leading international forest certification organisation. All our titles that are printed on Greenpeace approved FSC certified paper carry the FSC logo. Our paper procurement policy can be found at:
www.rbooks.co.uk/environment

Printed and bound in Great Britain by
Clays St Ives Plc

For Scott Cowen, the president of Tulane University
and a New Orleans hero, whose inspired leadership
and Herculean efforts helped secure a brighter
future for both Tulane and New Orleans after
the devastation of Hurricane Katrina.

Prologue

FINDERS, KEEPERS

One

IT HAD BEEN MONTHS since Kyle Craig had killed a man. Once upon a time, he'd been the type who needed everything yesterday, if not sooner. But no more. If years of hellish solitude in ADX Florence in Colorado had taught him nothing else, it was how to wait for what he wanted.

He sat patiently in the foyer of his quarry's Miami apartment, weapon cradled on his lap, watching the lights of the harbor and biding his time. He was in no particular hurry, enjoying the view, maybe finally learning to enjoy life. He certainly looked relaxed—faded jeans, sandals, a T-shirt that said CONSIDER THIS FAIR WARNING.

At 2:12 a.m., a key sounded in the lock. Kyle immediately rose to his feet and pressed his back against the wall, hanging there as silently as a piece of art.

The man of the hour, Max Siegel, was whistling as he came in. Kyle recognized the melody, an old snatch from his childhood. It was from *Peter and the Wolf.* The strings section—Peter's hunting theme. Ironically enough.

He waited for Mr. Siegel to close the door behind him and take a few more steps into the still-dark apartment. Then Kyle leveled his red laser site and squeezed the trigger. "Hello, Mr. Siegel," he said. "Good to meet you."

A stream of electrically charged saline solution hit Siegel squarely in the back, carrying fifty thousand volts with it. He grunted between clenched teeth. His shoulders seized up just before his body went completely rigid, and he fell like a tree to the floor.

Kyle didn't hesitate for a second. He quickly slipped a nylon cord across Siegel's throat, wound it around three times, and started to drag him in a small circle to sop up the saline solution on the floor, then yanked him straight through the apartment toward the master bath in the back. Siegel was too weak to struggle. Whatever effort he could muster was spent on the cord itself, trying not to be strangled.

"Don't fight me," Kyle said finally. "There's no point in it."

In the bathroom, Kyle lifted him into the oversize tub and tied off the ends of the cord to one of the chrome fixtures. It wasn't necessary, physically speaking, but it kept Siegel's head up where Kyle could see his face.

"You probably don't even know about these, do you?" he said, holding up the strange gun he'd carried in. "I know you've been underground awhile, but trust me, they're going to be huge."

The thing looked like a Super Soaker, which it kind of was. Regular Tasers could go for thirty seconds at best. This baby could *run* and *run,* thanks to a two-gallon wearable water pack strapped to his back.

"What...do you want?" Siegel finally choked out in response to the madness.

Kyle withdrew a small Canon digital camera from his pocket and started taking pictures. Full face, left profile, right profile.

"I know who you are, Agent Siegel. Let's start there, okay?"

A look of confusion crossed the man's face. Then fear. "Oh God, this is some kind of horrible mistake. My name is Ivan Schimmel!"

"No," Kyle said, snapping away—brow, nose, chin. "You're Max Siegel, and you're FBI. You've been deep undercover for the last twenty-six months. Worked your way up with the Buenez cartel until they trusted you enough to start making shipments.

"Now, while everyone's watching Colombia, you're running heroin from Phuket and Bangkok to Miami."

He lowered the camera and looked Siegel in the eye. "Never mind the moral relativism. It's all in the name of the big takedown at the end. Isn't that right, Agent Siegel?"

"I don't know who you're talking about!" he cried. "Please! Check my wallet!" He'd begun to struggle again, but another dose of voltage put a quick end to that. The electricity went right after the motor and sensory nerves. Siegel's pain tolerance was irrelevant. And the ammo, such as it was, ran right down the drain into Biscayne Bay.

"I suppose you might be forgiven for not recognizing me," Kyle went on. "Does the name 'Kyle Craig' mean anything to you? Or maybe the *Mastermind*? That's what they call me up at the Puzzle Palace in DC. As a matter of fact, I used to work there. Long time ago."

A flash of recognition came and went in Siegel's eyes, not that Kyle needed any kind of confirmation. His reconnaissance was still flawless.

But this Max Siegel was a pro, too. He wasn't about to stop playing the game now, *especially* now. "Please," he blubbered on when he found his voice again, "what is this? Who are you? I don't know what you want."

"Everything, Max. Every last little thing."

Kyle took another half dozen pictures and repocketed the camera. "You're actually a victim of your own good work, if that's any consolation. Nobody knows who you are down here, not even the local FBI. That's why I chose you. I selected you out of all the agents working in the United States. *You*, Max. Can you guess why?"

His voice had changed as he spoke. It was more nasal now, with the same shades of Brooklyn accent that laced the real Max Siegel's speech.

"This will never work! You're insane!" Siegel screamed at him. "You're fucking mad!"

"By some standards, I think that might be true," Kyle said. "But I'm also the most brilliant son of a bitch you'll ever have the pleasure to know." Then he pulled the trigger one more time and just let the thing *run*.

Siegel writhed mutely on the bottom of the tub. Eventually, he began to gag on his own tongue. Kyle watched, carefully noting every detail all the way to the end, studying his subject until there was nothing left to learn.

"Let's hope this works," he said. "Wouldn't want you to have died for nothing, Mr. Siegel."

Two

TWENTY-TWO DAYS LATER, a man bearing a striking resemblance to Max Siegel checked out of the Hotel Meliá Habana in the ritzy Miramar section of Havana, Cuba. Medical tourists were as common as pickpockets here; no one looked twice at the broad-shouldered man in the linen suit with bruises around his eyes and gauze over his nose and ears as he came through the lobby.

He signed the bill with a perfectly replicated signature and kept the charges on Max Siegel's brand-new American Express card. The surgeries, however, had been paid for in cash.

From the hotel, he caught a cab across town to Dr. Cruz's office, discreetly tucked into one of the city's endless neo-classic arcades. Inside was a full-service, completely staffed modern clinic that would have made a high-priced plastic surgeon in Miami or Palm Beach proud.

"I have to tell you, Senor Siegel, that I'm quite pleased

with this." The doctor spoke softly as he removed the last of the bandages. "It is some of the best work I've ever done, if I may say so." His manner was thoughtful but crisp and efficient—very professional. You'd never know he was willing to cut so many ethical corners along with the skin and bones of his clients' faces.

Dr. Cruz had performed seven separate procedures, something that might have taken months or even a year elsewhere. There was blepharoplasty for the eyelids; a template rhinoplasty for the nose, with a complete elevation of the skin and soft tissue in the nasal pyramid; new MEDPOR implants for more prominent cheekbones and chin; a sliding genioplasty of the jawbone; a little silicone augmentation for the brow; and, as a finishing touch, a nice little cleft in the chin—just like Max Siegel's.

At the patient's request, no electronic imaging had been taken before or after the procedures. For the right rate, Dr. Cruz had been more than willing to work from a series of digital blowups in hard copy, no questions asked, no interest in any biophysical detail.

Now, when he held up the large hand mirror for Kyle to see his reflection, the effect was stunning. The implants, especially, were like a miracle of change.

Max—not Kyle—smiled back from the mirror. He felt a slight sting at the corners of his mouth, which didn't move quite the same way as before. In fact, he didn't recognize himself at all. It was a total mind fuck, in the best possible way. There had been other disguises in the past, including some very expensive prosthetics that had gotten him out of prison. But they were nothing compared to this.

"How long will the bruising last?" he asked. "And this swelling around my eyes?"

Cruz handed him a folder of aftercare information. "With proper rest, you should be looking completely normal in seven to ten days."

The remaining changes, he could do for himself—shave and dye his hair down to a dark buzz cut and put in a simple pair of colored contacts. If there was any disappointment at all, it was that Kyle Craig had been so much better looking than Max Siegel.

But screw it. He needed to consider the larger picture here. Next time, he could be Brad Pitt if he wanted to.

He left the clinic in an excellent mood and took another cab straight to José Martí International Airport. From there, he caught a flight back to Miami, with a connection to Washington, DC, that same afternoon. For the main event.

Already, his thoughts had begun to coalesce around one idea: meeting up with his old friend and sometimes partner Alex Cross. Had Alex forgotten the promises Kyle had made to him over the years? That didn't seem possible. But had Cross grown just a little complacent in the meantime? Maybe so. In any case, the "great" Alex Cross was going to die, and die badly. There would be pain, but even more than that—regret. It would be a finale worth waiting for, no question.

And in the interim, Kyle was going to have some fun. After all, as the new and improved Max Siegel, he knew better than anybody that there was more than one way to take another man's life.

Book One

SHOOTER READY

Chapter 1

ANOTHER MANHOLE COVER had exploded in Georgetown, blowing nearly forty feet in the air. It was a strange little epidemic, as the city's aging infrastructure reached some kind of critical mass.

Over time, underground wires had frayed and smoldered, filling the space beneath the streets with flammable gas. Ultimately—and more frequently these days—the exposed wires created an electrical arc, lighting a fireball in the sewer and sending another three-hundred-pound iron disk flying up into the air.

This was the weird, scary stuff Denny and Mitch lived for. Every afternoon, they would gather up their papers to sell and hoof it over to the library to check the District Department of Transportation (DDOT) website for wherever rush-hour traffic was at its worst. Logjams were their meat.

Even on an ordinary day, the Key Bridge lived up to its

nickname, the Car Strangled Spanner, but today the M Street approach was somewhere between a parking lot and a circus. Denny worked his way up the middle of the traffic, and Mitch took the outside.

"*True Press*, only a dollar. Help the homeless."

"Jesus loves you. Help the homeless?"

They were an odd pair, to look at them—Denny, a six-feet-something white guy with bad teeth and stubble that never quite hid his sunken chin, and then Mitch, a brother with a boyish, dark black face, a husky body that topped out at five six, and stubby little baby dreads on his head to match.

"This is a perfect metaphor right here, ain't it?" Denny was saying. They talked to each other over the tops of the cars—or, rather, Denny talked and Mitch played a sort of straight man for the customers.

"You got pressure building, way down low where no one's looking, 'cause it's all just rats and shit down there, and who cares, right? But then one day—" Denny puffed out his cheeks and made a sound like a nuclear explosion. "Now you *gotta* pay attention, 'cause the rats and shit, they're everywhere, and everyone wants to know why somebody *else* didn't do something to stop it. I mean, if that ain't Washington to a tee, I don't know what the hell is."

"To a tee, bro. To a P, Q, R, S, *tee*," Mitch said, and laughed at his own dumb joke. His faded shirt read, IRAQ: IF YOU WEREN'T THERE, SHUT UP! His pants were baggy camos, like Denny's, only cut off around the calf.

Denny kept his shirt up over his shoulders to show off a half-decent six-pack. It never hurt to put a little eye candy on the table, and his face wasn't exactly his strong suit. "It's the

American way," he went on, loud enough for anyone with an open window to hear. "Keep doing what you always did, so you keep gettin' what you always got. Am I right?" he asked a pretty business suit in a BMW. She actually smiled and bought a paper. "God bless you, miss. Now *that,* Ladies and Gentlemen, is how we do it!"

He continued to fleece the crowd, getting more and more drivers to reach out their windows with cash in hand.

"Yo, Denny." Mitch chinned at a couple of street cops working their way over from Thirty-fourth. "I don't think these two are feeling us too much."

Denny shouted over before the cops could talk first. "Panhandling ain't illegal, officers. Not outside federal parklands, and last I checked, M Street ain't no park!"

One of them gestured around at the snarl of traffic, Pepco trucks, and fire department vehicles. "You're kidding me, right? Let's go. Clear out."

"Come on, man, you gonna deny a couple of *homeless vets* the right to make an honest living?"

"You ever been in Iraq, man?" Mitch added. People were starting to stare.

"You heard the officer," the second cop told him. "Move along. *Now.*"

"Hey, man, just 'cause you got an asshole don't mean you gotta be one," Denny said, to a few laughs. He could feel the captive audience coming over to his side.

Suddenly there was some pushing. Mitch didn't much like to be touched, and the cop who tried went down on his ass between the cars. The other one got a hand on Denny's shoulder and, like a lightning bolt, Denny knocked it away.

Time to go.

He slid across the hood of a yellow cab and started toward Prospect with Mitch right behind.

"Stop right there!" one of the cops shouted after them.

Mitch kept running, but Denny turned around. There were several cars between Denny and the officers now. "What are you going to do, shoot a homeless vet in the middle of traffic?" Then he spread his arms wide. "Go ahead, man. Take me out. Save the government a few bucks."

People were honking, and some of them yelled from their cars.

"Give the guy a break, man!"

"Support the troops!"

Denny smiled, gave the officer a crisp salute with his middle finger, and ran to catch up with Mitch. A second later, they were sprinting up Thirty-third Street and were soon out of sight.

Chapter 2

THEY WERE STILL LAUGHING when they got back to Denny's ancient Suburban, parked in Lot 9 by Lauinger Library on the Georgetown campus.

"That was awesome!" Mitch's doughy face was shiny with sweat, but he wasn't even out of breath. He was the type whose muscles looked a lot like fat. "*'What are you going to do?'*" he parroted. "*'Shoot a homeless vet in the middle of traffic?'*"

"*True Press,* one dollar," Denny said. "Lunch at Taco Bell, three dollars. The look on po-po's face when he knows you got him? Priceless. Wish I had a picture."

He plucked a bright-orange envelope from under his wiper blade and got in on the driver's side. The car still smelled of chain-smoked cigarettes and burritos from the night before. Pillows and blankets were bunched up in a ball on one half of the backseat, next to a lawn-and-leaf bag full of returnable cans.

Behind that, under a stack of collapsed cardboard boxes, a few old carpet remnants, and a false plywood bottom, were two Walther PPS nine-millimeter pistols, a semiautomatic M21, and a military-grade M110 sniper rifle. Also a long-range thermal-optical site, a spotting scope, a cleaning kit for the rifles, and several boxes of ammunition, all wrapped up in a large plastic tarp and bundled with several bungee cords.

"You did good back there, Mitchie," Denny told him. "Real good. Didn't lose your cool for a second."

"Nah," Mitch said, emptying his pockets onto the plastic lunch tray between them. "I won't lose my cool, Denny. I'm like one of them whatchamacallits. Cucumbers."

Denny counted out the day's take. Forty-five—not bad for a short shift. He gave Mitch ten singles and a handful of quarters.

"So what do you think, Denny? Am I ready or what? I think I'm ready."

Denny sat back and lit one of the half-smoked butts in the ashtray. He handed it to Mitch and then lit another for himself. While he was at it, he lit the orange envelope with the parking ticket inside and dropped it, burning, onto the cement.

"Yeah, Mitch, I think maybe you are ready. The question is, are *they* ready for us?"

Mitch's knees started to jackhammer up and down. "When do we start? Tonight? What about tonight? What about it, huh, Denny?"

Denny shrugged and leaned back. "Just enjoy the peace and quiet while you can, 'cause you're going to be famous as shit soon enough." He blew a smoke ring, then another, which passed right through the first. "You ready to be famous?"

Mitch was looking out the window at a couple of cute, short-skirted coeds crossing the parking lot. His knees were still bouncing. "I'm ready to start this thing, that's what."

"Good boy. And what's the mission, Mitchie?"

"Clean up this mess in Washington, just like the politicians always say."

"That's right. They talk about it—"

"But we gonna *do* something about it. No doubt. No doubt."

Denny extended his fist for a bump, then started up the car. He backed out the long way to get a good look at the ladies from behind.

"Speaking of tacos," he said, and Mitch laughed. "Where you want to eat? We've got paper to burn today."

"Taco Bell, man," Mitch said without even having to think.

Denny pulled hard on the gearshift to get it into drive and took off. "Why am I not surprised?"

Chapter 3

THE LEAD STORY in my life these days was Bree—Brianna Stone, known as the Rock at Metro Police. And, yes, she was all of that—solid, profound, lovely. She'd become a part of my life to the point where I couldn't imagine it without her anymore. Things hadn't been this sane and balanced for me in years.

Of course, it didn't hurt that Homicide at Metro was so quiet lately. As a cop, you can't help but wonder when that next ton of bricks is going to fall, but in the meantime, Bree and I had an unheard-of two-hour lunch that Thursday afternoon. Usually the only way we see each other during the day is if we're working the same murder case.

We sat in the back at Ben's Chili Bowl, under all the signed celeb photos. Ben's isn't exactly the world capital of romance, but it is an institution in Washington. The half-smokes alone are worth the trip.

"So you know what they're calling us around the office these days?" Bree said, halfway through a coffee milk shake. "Breelex."

"Breelex? Like Brad and Angelina? That's *awful*."

She laughed; she couldn't even keep a straight face at that. "I'm telling you, cops have no imagination."

"Hmm." I put a hand lightly on her leg under the table. "With exceptions, of course."

"Of course."

Any more than that would have to wait, and not just because the bathrooms at Ben's Chili Bowl were definitely not an option. We did in fact have somewhere important we had to be that day.

After lunch, we strolled hand in hand up U Street to Sharita Williams's jewelry store. Sharita was an old friend from high school, and she also happened to do outstanding work on antique pieces.

A dozen tiny bells tinkled over our heads as we breezed in the door.

"Well, don't you two look in love." Sharita smiled from behind the counter.

"That's 'cause we are, Sharita," I said. "And I highly recommend it."

"Just find me a good man, Alex. I'm in."

She knew why we were there, and she removed a small black velvet box from under the case. "It came out beautifully," she said. "I love this piece."

The ring used to belong to my grandmother, Nana Mama, she of the impossibly small hands. We'd had it resized for Bree. It was a platinum deco setting with three diamonds across, which struck me as perfect—one for each of the kids. Maybe it's corny, but it was like that ring represented everything Bree and I were committing to. This was a package deal after all, and I felt like the luckiest man in the world.

"Comfortable?" Sharita asked when Bree slipped it on. Neither one could take her eyes off the ring, and I couldn't take my eyes off Bree.

"Yeah, it's comfortable," she said, squeezing my hand. "It's the most beautiful thing I've ever seen."

Chapter 4

I PUT IN a late-afternoon appearance at the Daly Building. This was as good a time as any to catch up on the flood of paperwork that never seemed to stop flowing across my desk.

But when I got to the Major Case Squad room, Chief Perkins was just coming out into the hall with somebody I didn't recognize.

"Alex," he said. "Good. You'll save me another trip. Walk with us?"

Something was obviously up, and it wasn't good. When the chief wants a meeting, you go to him, not the other way around. I did a one-eighty, and we headed back over to the elevators.

"Alex, meet Jim Heekin. Jim's the new AD at the Directorate of Intelligence over at the Bureau."

We shook hands. Heekin said, "I've heard a lot about you, Detective Cross. The FBI's loss was MPD's gain when you came back over here."

"Uh-oh," I said. "Flattery's never a good sign."

We all laughed, but it was also true. A lot of new managers at the Bureau like to shake things up when they start, just to let people know they're there. The question was, what did Heekin's new job have to do with me?

Once we were settled in Perkins's big office, Heekin got a lot more specific.

"Can I assume you're familiar with our FIGs?" he asked me.

"Field Intelligence Groups," I said. "I've never worked with them directly, but sure." The FIGs had been created to develop and share intelligence "products" with the law enforcement communities in their respective jurisdictions. On paper, it seemed like a good idea, but some critics saw it as part of the Bureau's general passing of the buck on domestic criminal investigation after 9/11.

Heekin went on, "As you probably know, the DC group interfaces with all police departments in our area, including MPD. Also NSA, ATF, Secret Service—you name it. We've got monthly conference calls and then face time on an as-needed basis, depending on where the action is."

It was starting to seem like a sales pitch, and I already felt pretty sure I knew what he was selling.

"Generally, police chiefs represent their departments with the FIGs," he continued with his steady, well-paced speech, "but we'd like you to take over that position for MPD."

I looked at Perkins, and he shrugged. "What can I say, Alex? I'm just too damn busy."

"Don't let him fool you," Heekin said. "I spoke with the chief here, and with Director Burns at the Bureau before that. Your name was the *only one* that came up in either meeting."

"Thank you," I said. "That's very nice, but I'm good where I am."

"Yes, exactly. Major Case Squad's a perfect fit for this position. If anything, it's going to make your job easier."

This wasn't an offer, I realized, so much as an assignment. When I'd rejoined the force, Perkins had given me just about everything I'd asked for. Now I owed him one, and we both knew it, and *he* knew that I liked to play fair.

"No title change," I said. "I'm an investigator first, not some kind of administrator."

Perkins grinned across his desk. He also looked relieved. "Fine with me. Keeps you in the same pay grade."

"And my cases take priority over anything else I might have to do?"

"I don't think that's going to be a problem," Heekin said, already standing up to go. He shook my hand again at the door. "Congratulations, Detective. You're moving up in the world."

Yeah, I thought. *Whether I want to or not.*

Chapter 5

DENNY LED THE WAY, and Mitch followed like the man-child in that old Steinbeck book *Of Mice and Men*. "Right up here, bud. Let's keep it moving."

The tenth floor was also the top floor. Sheets of plastic hung over sections of two-by-four wall frame, with nothing but raw plywood underfoot. A stack of pallets by the Eighteenth Street windows made a good roosting spot.

Denny unrolled the plastic tarp and spread it on the floor. They dropped their packs. He put a hand on Mitch's back and pointed to where they'd just come up.

"Primary exit," he said, then turned ninety degrees to face another door. "Alternate exit." Mitch nodded once each time. "And if we get separated?"

"Wipe down the weapon, dump it, and meet you back at the car."

"That's my man."

They'd been over it maybe fifty times, beginning to end. Drilling was the key. Mitch had all kinds of raw talent, but Denny did the thinking for both of them.

"Any questions?" Denny asked. "This is the time to ask them. Later on, it won't matter worth a damn."

"Nah," Mitch said. His voice had gone flat and distant, the way it always did when he was concentrating on something else. He'd already set the M110, fitted with a sound suppressor, on its bipod and was zeroing it out, calibrating the scope.

Denny assembled his own M21 and slung it flat against his back. If everything went according to plan, he'd never have to use it, but it made sense to have a backup. The Walther was also holstered on his thigh.

He used a compass-set diamond blade to cut a perfect two-inch circle in the window, then pulled the section away with a small suction cup. The streetlights outside sent up a glare that made the window act like a mirror from below.

While Mitch got into position, Denny cleaned another small spot just up and to the left, where he could practically look over Mitch's shoulder and down the rifle barrel. Even their difference in height worked well.

He took his sighting scope out of its case. From here, they had a clear line to the entrance of Taberna del Alabardero. With the scope's 100x magnification, Denny could practically see the pores on the faces of the people coming and going from the hot-shit restaurant.

"Here, piggy, piggy, piggy," he whispered. "Hey, Mitch, you know when a pig knows he's had enough to eat?"

"Nope."

"When he's stuffed."

"Good one," Mitch said, in the same dead voice as before. He was in his stance now—a slightly freaky looking, ass out, elbows cocked kind of thing, but it worked for him. Once he hit the position, he would not move or look away until it was over.

Denny made his final check. He eyeballed the steam coming from a vent across the way—how it traveled straight up. The air temperature was approximately sixty degrees. Everything was a go.

All they needed now was a target, and that would be arriving real soon.

"You ready to let this genie out of the bottle, Mitchie?" he asked.

"Who's Jeannie, Denny?"

He chuckled low. Mitch was a beautiful piece of work, he really was. "Just the girl of your dreams, man. The girl of your *wildest* goddamned dreams."

Chapter 6

AT AROUND 7:35, a black Lincoln Navigator pulled up in front of Taberna del Alabardero, a hotsy DC eatery for the stars.

Two men got out of the back on either side and another emerged from the front, while the driver stayed in the car. All three wore dark suits, with barely distinguishable ties.

Banker's tie, thought Denny. *Wouldn't wear one to my own funeral.*

"The two from the backseat. You got it covered?"

"I got it, Denny."

Everything was dialed in. The scope's bullet drop compensator would account for the two biggest drags on any bullet—wind, if there was any, and gravity. From this angle, the barrel might be pointing high, but the crosshairs would put Mitch's eye right where it needed to be.

Denny watched the targets through his own scope. This

was the best seat in the house. *Second best anyway.* "Shooter ready?"

"Ready."

"Send it."

Mitch slowly exhaled, then pulled off two shots in the same number of seconds.

Vapor trails showed in the air. Both men went down—one on the sidewalk and the other flat up against the front door of the restaurant. It was kind of visually spectacular, actually—two perfect head shots to the bases of two skulls.

People were already freaking out in the street. The third man literally dove back into the car, while everyone else ran or ducked and covered their heads.

They didn't need to worry. The mission was over. Mitch had already begun to break down—the man was as fast as a speedway mechanic.

Denny unslung the M21, pulled off the magazine, and started packing. Forty seconds later, they were both on the stairs, double-timing it down to street level.

"Hey, Mitch, you weren't planning on running for elected office, were you?"

Mitch laughed. "Maybe president someday."

"You did perfect up there. You should be proud."

"I am proud, Denny. That's two dead crumbums nobody's got to worry about no more."

"Two dead piggies in the street!"

Mitch squealed, a pretty good imitation of swine, actually, and Denny joined in until their voices echoed up the empty stairwell. Both of them were drunk on how well it had gone. *What a rush!*

"And you know who the hero of the story is, right, Mitchie?" he asked.

"Nobody but us, man."

"Damn straight. We did it ourselves. A couple of real live American heroes!"

Chapter 7

THE SCENE OUTSIDE Taberna del Alabardero was a total zoo when we got there. This was no ordinary hit or rubout. I knew that much without even getting out of the car. The radio had been blaring about a long-distance hit, from a gunman that *nobody had seen*, firing shots that *nobody had heard*.

And then there were the victims. Congressman Victor Vinton was dead, along with Craig Pilkey, a well-known banking lobbyist who had recently dragged both of them into the headlines. These homicides were a scandal wrapped in another scandal. So much for quiet times in Homicide.

Both dead men were the subject of a federal inquiry regarding influence-peddling on behalf of the financial services industry. There were allegations about backroom deals and campaign contributions and all the wrong people getting rich—or richer—while middle-class citizens had continued to lose their homes in record numbers. It wasn't hard to imagine someone wanting Vinton and Pilkey dead. A lot of people probably did.

Still, motivation wasn't the first question on my mind right now. It was method. Why the long gun, and how did someone pull this off so effortlessly on a crowded city street?

Both bodies were covered on the sidewalk when my buddy John Sampson and I reached the awning in front of the restaurant. Capitol Police were already there, with FBI on the way. "High profile" means "high pressure" in DC, and you could all but cut with a knife the mounting tension inside that yellow perimeter tape.

We found another of our own, Mark Grieco from Third District, and he briefed us. Given all the noise in the street, we had to shout just to hear one another.

"How many witnesses do we have?" Sampson asked.

"At least a dozen," Grieco told us. "We've got them all corralled inside, each one more freaked out than the last. No visual on the shooter, though."

"What about the shots?" I asked in Grieco's ear. "We know where they came from?"

He pointed over my shoulder, up Eighteenth Street. "Way over there—if you can believe it. They're securing the building now."

On the north corner of K Street, a couple of blocks away, there was a building under some kind of renovation. Every floor was dark except for the top one, where I could just make out people moving around.

"You've got to be kidding me," I said. "How far is that?"

"Two hundred fifty yards—maybe more," Grieco guessed. The three of us started jogging in that direction.

"You said these were head shots?" I asked as we went. "That's right?"

"Yeah," Grieco answered grimly. "Dead on, pardon my pun. Someone knew what the hell he was doing. Hope he's not still around somewhere, watching us."

"Someone with the right equipment, too," I said. "Considering the distance." With a suppressor, the shooter could have gone completely unnoticed.

I heard Sampson say under his breath, "Damn, I hate this thing already."

I looked back over my shoulder. From this level, I couldn't even see the restaurant anymore—except for the red-and-blue lights flashing off the buildings around it.

This whole MO—the distance of the shot, the impossible angle, the murders themselves (not one perfect hit, but two in a crowded environment)—was completely audacious. I think we were meant to be impressed—in a strictly professional capacity, I was a little stunned.

But I also had a sinking dread in the pit of my stomach. That ton of bricks I'd been wondering about—it had just fallen.

Chapter 8

BACK AT HOME, I high-stepped over the second and third porch steps, avoiding the squeak with my long legs. It was just after one thirty in the morning, but the kitchen still smelled like chocolate chip cookies when I came in. They were for Jannie, who had some kind of school function. I gave myself half credit for knowing she had a function but points off for not knowing what it was.

I stole one cookie—delicious, with a hint of cinnamon in the chocolate—and took off my shoes before I snuck upstairs.

In the hall, I could see Ali's light was still on, and when I looked in, Bree was sleeping next to the bed. He'd been running a slight fever before, and she had dragged in the ancient leather armchair, aka laundry stand, from our room.

A library copy of *The Mouse and the Motorcycle* was open across her lap.

Ali's forehead was cool, but he'd kicked off the blankets

in the night. His bear, named Truck, was upside down on the floor. I tucked both of them back in.

When I tried to take the book from Bree, her hand tightened around it.

"And they all lived happily ever after," I whispered in her ear.

She smiled but didn't wake up, as if I'd worked my way into a dream of hers. That was a nice place to be, so I slipped my hands under her knees and arms and carried her back to bed with me.

It was tempting to help her out of her pajama bottoms and T-shirt, and everything else while I was at it, but she looked so beautiful and peaceful like that, I didn't have the heart to change a thing. Instead, I lay down and just watched her sleep for a while. Very nice.

Inevitably, though, my thoughts returned to the case, to what I'd just seen.

It was impossible not to think about those dark days in 2002, the last time we'd witnessed anything like this. The word "sniper" still strikes a bad chord with a lot of people in Washington, myself included. At the same time, there were some scary differences here, considering the skill of this shooter. It all felt more calculated to me, too. And then, thank God, I was asleep. Counting bodies instead of sheep, though.

Chapter 9

NANA MAMA ALREADY had the *Washington Post* spread out on the kitchen table when I came down at 5:30. The case was right there on page one, above the fold: "Sniper Murder Downtown Leaves Two Dead."

She double-tapped the headline with one bony finger, as if I might miss it.

"I'm not saying anyone, no matter how greedy, deserves to die," she told me straight-out. "This is absolutely awful. But those two men were no angels, Alex. People are going to take a certain satisfaction from this, and *you're* going to have to deal with that."

"And good morning to you, too."

I leaned down to kiss her cheek and instinctively put a hand on the mug of tea in front of her. A cold mug means she's been up for a long time, and this one was cool to the touch. I don't like to nag, but I do try to make sure she gets enough rest, particularly since her heart attack. Nana appears to be going strong, but she's still ninety plus.

I poured some coffee into a travel mug and sat down for a quick look at the paper. I always want to know what a killer might be reading about himself. The story was opinionated, and wrong in a few important places. I never pay attention when supposedly smart people write idiotic things—here was another example of news that needed to be ignored.

"It's just a big shell game anyway," Nana went on, warming to her subject. "Someone gets caught with a hand in the cookie jar, and we all pretend as though the ones we hear about are the only ones doing anything wrong. You think that congressman was the first and last to ever take a bribe here in Washington?"

I ruffled the paper open to the continuation on page twenty. "An optimistic mind is a terrible thing to waste, Nana."

"Don't be fresh with me so early in the day," she said. "Besides, I'm still an optimist, just one who happens to have her eyes wide open."

"And were they open all night, too?" I said a little hamhandedly. Asking about Nana's health is like trying to slip vegetables into the kids' mac and cheese. You have to be sneaky, or you don't get anywhere, and usually you don't get anywhere anyway.

Sure enough, she raised her voice to make it clear that I'd been heard and would be ignored.

"Here's another nugget of wisdom for you. Why is it when we hear about people getting killed in this city, they're always poor and black, or rich and white? Why is that, Alex?"

"Unfortunately, that's a longer conversation than I have time for this morning," I said, and pushed my chair back.

She trailed a hand after me. "Where are you going this early? Let me make you some eggs—and where are you taking that paper?"

"I want to do some digging at the office before my first interview," I told her. "And why don't you stick to the entertainment section for a while?"

"Oh, because there's no racism in Hollywood—is that it? Open your eyes."

I laughed, kissed her good-bye, and stole one more chocolate chip cookie off the table all at the same time.

"That's my girl. Have a good day, Nana. Love you!"

"Don't be condescending, Alex. Love you, too."

Chapter 10

BY MIDMORNING, I was facing down Sid Dammler, one of two senior partners at the L Street lobbying firm of Dammler-Mickelson. Craig Pilkey had been one of their biggest rainmakers, as they're called in the biz, pulling down eleven million in fees the previous year. One way or another, these people were going to miss him.

So far, the firm's official comment was that they "had no knowledge" of any wrongdoing among their staff. In the Washington playbook, that's usually code for covering one's behind without actually getting backed into a legal corner.

Not that I was prejudiced against Dammler to begin with. That came after forty minutes of waiting in reception, and then another twenty of monosyllabic noncommittal answers from him, with an expression on his face like he'd rather be getting a root canal about now—or maybe like he *was* getting a root canal about now.

This much, I'd already pulled together on my own: Before joining the staff at D-M, Craig Pilkey, originally from Topeka, Kansas, had spent three two-year terms in Congress, where he'd earned a reputation as the banking industry's mouthpiece on the Hill. His unofficial nickname had been the "Re-Deregulator," and he'd sponsored or cosponsored no fewer than fifteen separate bills aimed at extending the scope of lenders' rights.

According to D-M's website, Pilkey's specialty was helping financial service companies "navigate the federal government." His biggest client by far at the time of his death was a coalition of twelve midsize banks around the country, representing more than seventy billion in total assets. These same companies were the ones whose campaign contributions to the other dead man, Congressman Vinton, had triggered the federal inquiry just under way.

"Why are you telling me all this about Craig and Dammler-Mickelson?" Sid Dammler wanted to know. So far, he hadn't indicated if any of it was news to him or not.

"Because, with all due respect, I have to imagine that some number of people out there are going to be happy about Craig Pilkey's death," I said.

Dammler looked deeply offended. "That's a disgusting thing to say."

"Who might have wanted to kill him? Any idea at all? I know there were threats."

"*Nobody*. For God's sake!"

"I find that hard to believe," I said. "You're not helping us find his murderer."

Dammler got to his feet. The red on his face and neck

stood out against the tight white collar of his shirt. "This meeting's over," he said.

"Sit down," I told him. *"Please."*

I waited until he was back in his seat.

"I understand that you don't want to give more airtime to your critics than they've already had," I went on. "You're a PR firm, I get it. But I'm not a reporter for the *Post,* Sid. I need to know who Craig Pilkey's enemies were—and don't tell me he didn't have any."

Dammler leaned way back with his hands behind his head. He looked as if he were waiting to be cuffed.

"I guess you might start with some of the national homeowners associations," he said finally. "They weren't exactly fans of Craig's." He sighed and looked at his watch. "There's also the entire consumer lobby, the nut-job bloggers, the anonymous hate mailers. Take your pick. Talk to Ralph Nader while you're at it."

I ignored the sarcasm. "Is any of this information tracked in one place?"

"To the extent that it concerns our clients, sure. But you're going to need a warrant before I even think about putting you in the same room with any of that. It's private, it's confidential."

"I thought you might feel that way," I said, and laid two sets of paperwork out on the desk between us. "One for files—one for e-mail. I'd like to start with Pilkey's office. You can lead the way, or I'll find it myself."

Chapter 11

Dear Fuckstick,

I HOPE YOU'RE satisfied with yourself. Maybe someday you'll lose YOUR fucking job and YOUR house, and then you'll have some MOTHERFUCKING CLUE what you're putting innocent people through out here in the REAL world.

A lot, but not all, of the letters were pretty much like that. I'll tell you what—when people get really mad, they *curse!*

The writers were angry, disappointed, threatening, heartbroken, crazy. It ran the gamut. My warrant was good until ten p.m., but I could have spent the whole night reading hate mail in Pilkey's office.

After a while, I got tired of the slow walk-bys from the staff, so I closed the door and kept sorting.

The mail was from all over the country but especially

from Pilkey's home state of Kansas. There were stories about homelessness, lost life savings, families who couldn't stay together—all types of people who had suffered in the financial downturn and placed a whole lot of the blame on K Street and Washington.

The blog entries, at least the ones that D-M tracked, were more radicalized, tending toward the political instead of the personal. One group, the Center for Public Accountability, seemed to lead the charge. They—or, for all I knew, some guy in a basement somewhere—had a regular column called "Fight the Power." The latest entry was titled "Robbin' the Hood: Steal from the Poor and Give to the Rich."

> Using free-market principles as their Teflon cover, the members of the Boys & Girls Club of Washington, which is to say the banking lobbyists and our very own elected officials, have crafted one blank check after another for their corporate cronies. Yes, the very people who brought this country's economy to its knees are still being treated like royalty on Capitol Hill, and guess who's picking up the tab? These are your tax dollars I'm talking about, your money. In my book, that's called stealing, and it's all happening right before our eyes.
>
> Click here to get home addresses and phone numbers for some of DC's most outrageous robber barons. Give them a call during dinner some night and let them know how you feel. Better yet, wait till they're not there, then break in and help yourself to some of their hard-earned cash. See how they like it.

In some ways, the most unexpected thing in Pilkey's office was the collection he kept of his own press about the scandal. One recent article was still in an unmarked folder on his desk. It was a *New York Times* op-ed.

Both Pilkey and Vinton are the subject of what will no doubt become yet another long, drawn-out investigation, proving nothing, punishing no one, and accomplishing negative gain when it comes to protecting the people who matter the most—the average joes of the world, just struggling to make ends meet.

So, no surprise, Pilkey had more than his share of haters. This was almost the opposite of no leads. Everything I'd read was just the tip of the iceberg. I flagged anything that mentioned specific threats, but the information was mounting, and the list of suspects was going to be impossibly long.

One thing was clear to me already: we were going to need a bigger team.

Chapter 12

DENNY HATED THE SHELTER on Thirteenth Street with a passion that bordered on homicide, and particularly tonight. Lining up on the sidewalk for a bed sucked big-time, especially while the rest of the city went apeshit over their two perfect sniper hits on Eighteenth Street. What a rush! And what a waste of a good night when he and Mitch should have been celebrating.

Of course, it also made more sense than ever to be seen going about their business right now. So that's what they were doing.

Mitch stuck close as always, shaking his head and jacking his knee up and down the way he did when he got stoked. It made him look just like any of the other basket cases who called this place home, which was fine, so long as the big man kept his mouth shut.

"Don't talk to no one," Denny reminded him as they filed

like an army of zombies into the dorm. "Just keep your head down and get some sleep."

"I won't say nothing, Denny, but I'll tell you what. I'd sure rather be sucking down a little Jim Beam about now."

"Party starts tomorrow, Mitchie. Promise."

Denny put Mitch on the bottom bunk for a change and took the top for himself so he could keep an eye on things from the bird's nest.

Sure enough, not long after lights-out, Mitch was back up. *Now what?*

"Where you going, man?" he whispered.

"Gotta piss. I'll be right back."

Denny wasn't feeling paranoid exactly—just extra cautious. He sat up and waited a minute, then followed Mitch just to make sure.

It was quiet in the hall. The place used to be a school, and these lockers were originally built to hold little kids' lunches and book bags and whatnot. Now grown men used them to hold on to everything they owned in the world.

And what a fucked-up world it was! No doubt about that.

When Denny got to the bathroom, he found all the showers running with no one in them. Bad sign. This wasn't good at all.

He came around the corner to where the sinks were and saw that two big guys had Mitch pushed up against a wall. He recognized them right away—Tyrone Peters and Cosmo "the Coz" Lantman. Exactly the type of scumbags who kept decent people sleeping on the street rather than risking a bed in one of these shelters. Mitch's pockets were turned out, and there were still a few quarters on the tile floor around his feet.

"What seems to be the problem here?" Denny said.

"No problem." Tyrone didn't even turn around to look at him. "Now get the fuck out!"

"Yeah, I don't think so."

Cosmo eyeballed him now and hunkered on over. His hands looked empty, but he was obviously palming something.

"You want in? All right, you're in." He put a thumb and forefinger around Denny's throat and held up a sickle-shaped blade until it was just under his nose. "Let's see what you got to contribute—"

Denny's hand clamped down on the asshole's wrist in a flash and twisted it almost three-sixty, until Cosmo had to double over to keep the arm from snapping in two. From there, it was nothing to stab the Coz with his own blade, three times fast into the ass, and even that was just a warning. The liver would have been just as easy to hit. Already, Cosmo was down and bleeding all over the floor.

Meanwhile, Mitch had gone ballistic. He got his arms around the much bigger Tyrone's waist and pile-drove him straight into the opposite wall. Tyrone got off two fast jabs—Mitch's nose exploded with blood—but the asshole left his own jaw wide open. Mitch saw this and drove the heel of his hand straight up into it, until Tyrone went spinning. Just for good measure, Denny grabbed him on the fly and whipped him around once so his face caught some sink on the way down. A few teeth got left behind, and also a thick red smear on the dirty porcelain.

They retrieved Mitch's cash and took whatever else Tyrone and Cosmo had on them. Then Denny pulled the thugs back into a couple of stalls.

"Punks don't know who they're messing with!" Mitch crowed in the hall. His eyes were practically shining, even with blood running down over his lips and onto his shirt.

"Yeah, well, let's keep it that way," Denny said. He'd wanted them to be seen at the shelter tonight, but at this point they'd more than accomplished their mission. "You know what? Grab your stuff. Let's get you that bottle of Jim Beam."

Chapter 13

LIKE A LOT of the law enforcement brotherhood, FBI Case Agent Steven Malinowski was divorced. He lived alone—except when his two daughters visited, every other weekend and one month out of the summer—in a decent-on-the-outside, kind-of-pathetic-on-the-inside little ranch in Hyattsville, Maryland.

Accordingly, there wasn't much to come home to, and he didn't pull into his driveway until just after eleven thirty that night. His gait, when he got out of his Range Rover, had at least a few beers in it, a shot or two as well, but he wasn't drunk. More like out-with-the-boys tipsy.

"Hey, Malinowski."

The agent's whole body jerked, and he reached for the holster under his jacket.

"Don't shoot. It's me." Kyle stepped around the corner of

the garage and into the light of the streetlamp just long enough to give a glimpse of his face. "It's Max Siegel, Steve."

Malinowski squinted hard at him in the dark. "Siegel? What in Christ's . . . ?" He let the flap of his jacket fall back again. "You almost gave me a damn heart attack. What the hell are you doing here? What time is it anyway?"

"Can we talk inside?" Kyle asked. It would have been three years since Malinowski and Siegel had spoken; the voice had to be good but not perfect. "I'll go around back, okay? Let me in."

Malinowski looked up and down the street. "Yeah, yeah. Of course." By the time he let Siegel in through the sliding-glass door to the kitchen, he'd turned off the lights in front and pulled all the shades. There was just the hood light on over the stove.

He dropped his weapon into a kitchen drawer and pulled two longnecks out of the fridge. He offered one to Max.

"Talk to me, Siegel. What's going on? What are you doing here at this hour?"

Kyle refused the beer. He didn't want to touch anything he didn't have to.

"The op's completely blown," he said. "I don't know how, but they found me out. I had no choice but to come in."

"You look like shit, by the way. Those bruises around your eyes—"

"Should have seen me a week ago. A couple of Arturo Buenez's boys worked me over pretty good." Kyle patted the army-green duffel on his back. Inside was the liquid stun gun and water pack, wrapped in a thick blanket. "This was everything I managed to get out with."

"Why didn't you signal?" Malinowski asked, and that was the one thing Kyle had never been able to figure out—how Max Siegel was to have made contact with his handler in an emergency.

"I was lucky to get out at all," he said. "I've been lying low in Florida until I could get up here. Fort Myers, Vero Beach, Jacksonville."

Maybe it was the beer, but Malinowski didn't seem to notice that Kyle hadn't actually answered the question he'd been asked. How could he? He didn't know the answer.

"So, who else should I be talking to?" Kyle asked.

The agent shook his head. "Nobody."

"Not DEA? Anyone in DC?"

"There's no one, Siegel. You were out there on your own." He looked up suddenly. "Why don't you know that?"

"Give me a break, man. I'm all messed up. Look at me." Kyle took a step closer to where Malinowski was leaning back against the range. "Seriously, really look at me. What do you see?"

Malinowski smiled sympathetically. "You definitely need some rest, Max. It's good you're here."

The guy didn't have a clue, did he? This was just too much fun to stop.

"I've seen Kyle Craig, Steve."

"What? Hang on—*the* Kyle Craig?"

Kyle spread his arms and smiled. "*The* Kyle Craig. In the flesh."

"I don't understand. How the hell does that figure in . . . ?"

It was like watching numbers add up across Malinowski's face. And just when he seemed to come up with the right answer, Kyle made his move. His Beretta was out and pressing into Malinowski's chin before the guy even saw it coming.

"Amazing what they can do with plastic surgery these days," he said.

Malinowski's half-finished beer clunked to the floor. "What are you talking about? That's . . . impossible!"

"I'm 99.99 percent sure that it's not," Kyle told him. "Unless I'm imagining all this. Consider it in an honor, Steve. You're the first and last to know what I look like now. Are you honored?" Malinowski didn't move, so he pushed the Beretta a little deeper into his face. *"Are you?"*

Now he nodded.

"Say it, please."

"I'm . . . honored."

"Good. Now here's what's going to happen. We'll be moving to the back of the house, and you'll be getting inside that filthy bathtub you never clean." Kyle patted the duffel on his back again. "Then I'm going to unpack, and you and I are going to talk some more. I need to know some things about Max Siegel."

Chapter 14

HE WAITED TWO MORE DAYS, spent a few nights around DC, got himself laid at the Princess Hotel. Then Kyle brought Max Siegel in from out of the cold once and for all.

It was an unbelievable thrill, driving Siegel's newly leased BMW past the familiar guard booth and down into the Hoover Building parking garage. Every security measure in the world, and here they were, waving Mr. Most Wanted himself right into FBI headquarters.

Sweet.

Siegel's ID got Kyle right up to the fifth floor. They met with him in one of the Strategic Information Operations Center (SIOC) conference rooms overlooking Pennsylvania Avenue—two reps from the Gang and Criminal Enterprise Section, one from the Directorate of Intelligence, and two assistant directors from the main and field offices in DC.

AD Patty Li seemed to be in charge of the meeting. "I

know this is a stressful time, Agent Siegel, but there's something you need to know. Your original handler, Steven Malinowski, died two days ago."

Kyle kept up his professional composure, with just the right amount of emotion. "Oh my God. What happened to Steve?"

"Apparently he dropped dead of a heart attack in the shower at his home."

"This is unbelievable. I was at his house yesterday. I knocked on his door." He stopped and ran a hand over his million-dollar face—the master performer in action.

"You were right to contact us directly," Li said. "Once you've made your report and received a full debriefing, I'm putting you on administrative leave—"

"No." Kyle sat up and looked Li straight in the eye. "Excuse me, but that's the last thing I need right now. I'm ready to go back to work."

"You need to acclimate. Sleep in, go to a game, whatever. You've been someone else for years, Max. That takes a toll."

The whole thing was like great food, great sex, and driving 120 with the headlights off all at the same time. Best of all, these Friendly But Ignorant pinheads were eating it up like free doughnuts.

"With all due respect," he told everyone in the room, "I'd like my record to speak for itself. Give me a fitness-for-duty eval, if that's what you need to do. Just don't sideline me. I want to work. Trust me, it's what I need."

There were some open glances around the table. One of the drug-squad guys shrugged and closed the personnel file in front of him. This was Li's call.

"Just for the sake of argument," she said, "what did you have in mind?"

"I believe I'm up for SSA," he told her, which was true. "That's what I want."

"Supervisory special agent? I see you haven't lost any of your ambition."

"I'd also like to stay right here in Washington, ultimately in the field office. I think that's where I can do the most damage," he said—just a touch of self-deprecation to keep them on the line.

There would be no promises today, but Kyle could tell he'd pretty much cinched it. And the field-office placement, while not strictly necessary, was a nice bit of gravy.

That facility was over in Judiciary Square, maybe a stone's throw from the Daly Building. He and Alex could practically string up a couple of tin cans between their offices and play catch-up. How much fun would that be?

Now it was just a matter of time until they met again.

Chapter 15

I OFFERED UP a couple of Washington Nationals tickets to the Fingerprint Examination Section for a fast turnaround with the sniper hits. They got me some results that morning.

A single print had been found on an otherwise freshly cleaned area of glass where the shots had been taken. And, as it turned out, it was a match for two other prints found on-site—one on a stair rail between the building's eighth and ninth floors, and another on the crash bar of a ground-level steel door that had almost certainly been the shooter's exit point.

That was all the good news, or at least the interesting news. The bad part was that our print didn't match any of the tens of millions of samples in the IAFIS database. Our presumed killer had no criminal record to help point the way to his arrest.

So I widened my net. Recently I'd been to Africa and back,

chasing down a mass murderer who called himself the Tiger. As part of the fallout from that case, I'd struck up a pretty good rapport with a guy named Carl Freelander. He was Army CID, embedded with the FBI in Lagos, Nigeria, as part of a Joint Terrorism Task Force. I was hoping Carl could help me cut a few corners with the investigation.

It was late afternoon in Lagos when I caught Carl on his cell.

"Carl, it's Alex Cross calling from Washington. How about if I ask you my favor first, and we do the chitchat later?"

"Sounds good, Alex, minus the chitchat, if you don't mind. What can I do for you?" This was one of the reasons I liked Carl; he worked the way I did.

"I've got a print on a homicide, two kill shots from two hundred sixty-two yards. The guy obviously had some training, not to mention good equipment, and I'm wondering if maybe there's a military connection."

"Let me guess, Alex. You want a red phone into the civil database."

"Something like that," I said.

"Yeah, okay. I can run it by CJIS," he said. "Shouldn't take too long."

CJIS stands for Criminal Justice Information Services, a part of the FBI that's based in Clarksburg, West Virginia. This was one of those loopy situations—calling halfway around the world to access something so close to home, but it wouldn't be the first time.

Less than two hours later, Carl was back with some discouraging news.

"Your boy's not U.S. military, Alex. Not FBI or Secret

Service either. And I hope you don't mind, but I ran it through ABIS at Defense while I was at it. He's never been detained by U.S. forces, and he's not a foreign national who's ever had access to one of our bases. I don't know if that helps or not."

"It gets rid of some of the obvious possibilities anyway. Thanks, Carl. Next time you're in DC—"

"Drinks and all that, sure thing. I look forward to it. Take care, Alex."

My next call was to Sampson, to share the news, such as it was.

"Don't worry, sugar, we're just getting started," he told me. "Maybe this print didn't even come from our guy. That crime scene was crawling with our people the other night—and you can bet not everyone was wearing gloves."

"Yeah," I said, but a different possibility had already wormed its way to the front of my mind. "John, what if it is the shooter's print, and he *wanted* us to find it? Maybe it gets him off, knowing we're going to waste our time chasing it down—"

"Oh man, no. No, no, no." Sampson knew just where I was headed.

"And maybe that gives him exactly the confidence he's looking for—when it comes time to do it all over again."

Chapter 16

I WAS THERE for Bree outside of Penn Branch when she got off that afternoon. I couldn't wait to see her, and when she finally came out of the building, it brought a big smile to my face.

"This is a nice surprise," she said, and gave me a kiss. We'd stopped trying to draw a line around that stuff at work anymore. "To what do I owe the pleasure? This is a *treat*."

"No questions," I said, and opened the car door for her. "I want to show you something."

I'd been planning this for a while now, and even though work was starting to pile up again, I was too stubborn to give up on my scheme. I drove us along North Capitol Street, over to Michigan, and then to the edge of the Catholic University campus, where I parked.

"Um, Alex?" Bree looked out the windshield—and almost

straight *up*. "When we talked about a small wedding, I think I should have been a little more specific."

The Basilica of the National Shrine of the Immaculate Conception is one of the ten biggest churches in the world and, for my money, the most beautiful in Washington, maybe in the whole country.

"Not to worry," I told her. "We're just passing through. Come on."

"Okay, Alex. I guess."

The Romanesque-Byzantine architecture inside those walls is almost overwhelming, but it's unbelievably peaceful in there, too. The soaring arches make you feel tiny, while the million little gold mosaic tiles in the artwork fill every corner with a kind of amber light I've never seen anywhere else.

I took Bree's hand and walked her up one of the side aisles, through the transept, and into the wide area at the back. It's enclosed from behind with a row of arched stained-glass windows, and open to the whole length of the cathedral at the front.

"Bree, can I see your ring?" I asked her.

"My ring?"

She smiled, a little puzzled, but gave it to me anyway. Then I got down on one knee, and I took her hand again.

"Is this a proposal?" she asked me. "Because I've got a little news for you, sweetie. I'm already there."

"In front of God, then," I said, and took a breath because I realized suddenly I was a little nervous.

"Bree, I didn't need you before we met. I thought I was doing okay—I *was* doing okay. But now... here you are, and

I have to think that's for a reason." I hadn't rehearsed any speech, and it felt like I was stumbling over my words, not to mention the lump in my throat. "You make me believe, Bree. I don't know if I can explain what that means for someone like me, but I hope you'll let me spend the rest of my life trying. Brianna Leigh Stone, will you marry me?"

She was still smiling, but I could see her fighting back tears now. Even here, Bree was trying to stay tough.

"You know you're a little crazy, right?" she said. "You know that?"

"If lovin' you is wrong," I whisper-crooned to her, *"I don't want to be right."*

"Okay, okay, anything but the singing," she said, and we both laughed like a couple of kids cutting up in the library. But it was laughter through tears, for both of us.

Bree knelt down with me, put her hand gently over mine, and slid the engagement ring back onto her finger. When she kissed me lightly on the lips, I felt the warmth, and a quiver, all the way down my spine.

"Alexander Joseph Cross, as many times as you want to ask me, the answer is *yes*. Always has been, always will be."

Chapter 17

ROMANTIC FOOL THAT I AM, I wasn't done yet. From Immaculate Conception, I drove us back downtown, where we checked into the Park Hyatt for the night. I had told Nana we wouldn't be home.

After the bellman left us to our suite, Bree looked around and asked, "Alex, how much is this costing?"

I had a chilled bottle of Prosecco waiting, and handed her a glass. "Well, I'm not sure we can still swing college for Damon after this, but the view's great, isn't it?"

Then I sat down at the baby grand—absolutely the reason I'd chosen this place—and started to play. I stuck to old standard love songs, things like "Night and Day" and "Someone to Watch Over Me," each one with a little message for Bree. And, by request, I mostly stayed away from the singing.

She sat next to me on the piano bench, listening and

sipping the wine. "What did I do to deserve all this?" she asked finally.

"Oh, that part's still coming up," I said. "Something about taking off all your clothes. Slowly. Piece by piece."

First, though, we had dinner sent up from Blue Duck Tavern and shared everything—orange and arugula salad, fresh ahi tuna, soft-shell crabs, and a warm-centered chocolate cake for two.

I opened a bottle of Cristal with dessert, and we finished it in the big limestone soaking tub afterward.

"I feel like we're already on our honeymoon. First a church, and now this," she said.

"Consider it a preview," I told her, running a bar of lavender soap up and down her back, then her long legs. "Just a little taste of the future."

"Mmm, I like the future." She put her mouth on my shoulder and bit down softly when I abandoned the soap and started using my hands.

Eventually, we spilled right out of the tub and onto the floor. I made a makeshift bearskin rug out of two fluffy hotel robes, and we spent the next few hours trying to get enough of each other.

The first time I brought Bree to climax, her head tilted and her mouth opened soundlessly, while she held on to the small of my back with that amazing strength of hers.

"Closer, Alex. Oh God, closer. Closer!"

It was like nothing could come between us, literally or figuratively. I felt a million miles away from anything but her, and I never wanted that night to end.

But of course it would—*and all too soon.*

Chapter 18

THE HOTEL PHONE RANG at almost exactly twelve o'clock. I'd realize later that it hadn't been a coincidence. Midnight is also the start of a new day, and the caller meant that, literally.

"Alex Cross," I answered.

"All this, and romance, too? Tell me, Detective Cross, how do you manage it?"

Kyle Craig's voice registered like ice water—and just as fast as that, everything changed.

"Kyle," I said for Bree's benefit. "How long have you been in Washington?"

She was already sitting up, but as soon as she heard the name, she grabbed her cell out of the nightstand and took it into the bathroom.

"What makes you think I'm in Washington?" Kyle asked me. "You know I've got eyes and ears everywhere. I don't have to be there, to be there."

"True," I said, trying hard to keep my voice calm. "But I'm one of your favorite subjects."

He laughed softly. "I'd like to say you're flattering yourself, but I can't. So tell me about the family. How's Nana Mama doing? The kids?"

They weren't questions. They were threats, and we both knew it. Families were Kyle's thing, maybe because his own had been so messed up. In fact, he'd killed both of his parents, on separate occasions. It was everything I could do not to rise to the bait, but I held back my temper.

"Kyle, why are you calling? You never do anything without a good reason."

"I haven't seen Damon around," he went on. "He must still be up at Cushing Academy, yes? That's due west of Worcester, correct? But Ali! Now there is the definition of a growing boy."

I gripped the edge of the mattress with my free hand. Having my kids in Kyle Craig's thoughts was almost more than I could take.

But if there was one thing I knew, it was that idle threats and warnings only added fuel to his fire. He'd always been insanely competitive with me, and I mean that literally. It had been nearly impossible to bring him down the first time.

How in the hell was I going to do it again?

"Kyle," I said as evenly as I could manage, "I'm not going to have this conversation if I don't know where it's going. So if you have something to tell me—"

"Ashes to ashes, and dust to dust," he said. "It's no big secret, Alex."

"What's that supposed to mean?"

"You asked where this is going. Ashes to ashes, and dust to dust—the same place everything goes. Of course, some of us get there faster than others, isn't that right? Your first wife, for example, but I can't take credit for that one."

And then he got his wish—I snapped, lost it.

"Listen to me, you piece of shit! Stay away from us. I swear to God, if you ever—"

"If I *what?*" he fired back just as forcefully. "Hurt your ridiculous family? Take away your precious fiancée?" His tone had changed on a dime to pure rage. "How *dare* you talk to me about what's been taken away. What you get to *keep!* Just how many lives have *you* taken, Alex? How many families have you shattered with that nine millimeter of yours? You don't even know the meaning of loss—not yet, *you fucking hypocrite!*"

I'd never heard him go on like this before. In fact, Kyle rarely even cursed. Not the Kyle I'd known.

Was he devolving in some way? Or was this just another one of his carefully timed acts?

"Do you want to know the real difference between us, Alex?" he went on.

"I already know the difference," I said. "I'm still sane and you're not."

"The difference is, I'm alive because none of you people have been able to bring me down, and you're alive because I haven't decided to kill you yet. *Please* tell me that obvious fact hasn't escaped you."

"I'm not going to kill you, Kyle." The words were just spilling out of me now. "I'm going to make sure you rot to death, slowly, back in that cell in Colorado where you came from. You're going back."

"Oh, that reminds me," he said—and then abruptly hung up. It was pure Kyle, just one more way of saying he'd started this thing and he was going to finish it, his way. Control was like oxygen to him.

Suddenly, Bree was right there, with her arms around me. "I spoke to Nana," she said. "Everything's fine, but she knows we're coming home. And I've got a squad car headed over there right now."

I got up and started dressing as fast as I could. My body was shaking with anger, and not just at Kyle.

"I messed up, Bree," I said. "Bad. I can't let him get to me like that. I can't! It's only going to make things worse."

If that was possible.

Chapter 19

GODDAMN HIM! For everything.

Kyle had just accomplished exactly what he wanted, which was to inject himself into my life. He had my number, in more ways than one. Now I had no choice but to respond.

An MPD cruiser was in front of the house when we got there, with another uniformed officer in the back by the garage. Sampson was there, too; I'm not even sure who called him, but I was glad he came.

"All cool, sugar, we're good here," he said as we came in. He and Nana were hanging out in the kitchen. She'd even managed a ham sandwich and chips for him by then.

"This isn't over," I said. It was a struggle to keep my voice down while the kids slept upstairs. "We have to talk about moving the family."

"Oh, is that so?" Nana said, and the temperature in the room dropped about twenty degrees.

"Nana—"

"Alex, no. Not again. You do what you need to with the children. I, for one, meant it the last time when I said it would *be* the last time. I'm not moving out of this house, and that's my final word on the subject."

Before I could even respond, she decided she wasn't done after all.

"And another thing. If this Kyle Craig is as good as you say he is, then it doesn't matter where you put the children. What matters, Detective Cross, is that you protect them where they are." Her voice was shaking, but her finger was steady as she pointed it right at my face. "Defend your home, Alex. Make it happen! You're supposed to be good at your job."

She smacked the table twice with the flat of her hand and leaned back again. My move.

First, I took a breath and counted to ten. Then I asked Bree to start the APB process right away. "Get it out on WALES, all jurisdictions, and then NCIC at the Bureau as soon as we can." For that, we'd need a warrant number, and Sampson got on the stick to track it down.

I put in my own call to the FBI field office in Denver. Technically, Kyle was their case, since he'd escaped from prison in Colorado.

Over the phone, an Agent Tremblay told me that they had nothing new to report but that he'd be in touch with all mid-Atlantic field offices right away. This was a priority case for them, too, and not just because of the damage Kyle had done to the Bureau's reputation the first time around. I had a feeling I'd be hearing from Jim Heekin at the Directorate in Washington first thing in the morning.

Meanwhile, I made another call—and woke up my good buddy and sometimes sparring mate Rakeem Powell.

Rakeem had been with the force for fifteen years, and a detective with the 103 for eight. Then, in the same six-month period, he'd gotten married and shot, in that order, and ended up taking early retirement.

No one ever thought Rakeem would leave the department, but then again, no one thought he'd ever settle down either. Now he had his own close-security firm in Silver Spring, and I was about to become a client.

By seven that morning, we had a whole system in place. The kids were covered to and from school by me and Bree, with Sampson as backup. Rakeem's firm would provide overnight security, front and back, with daytime coverage as needed. They'd also spend the first day working up an assessment of penetrable areas of the house and try to have them wired up before the kids got home.

Nana tried to put her foot down about FBI agents in the yard, but I came out on top of that one. As instructed by her, I was doing whatever I needed to do to make things happen. She and I were barely speaking at this point, and no one was happy about any of it, but this was our reality now.

Life under siege. Kyle Craig was back in our lives.

Chapter 20

AND THEN LIFE does go on, ready or not.

Once I got the kids to school, I made it over to St. Anthony's in time for my second appointment of the morning, after missing the first. I'd been doing pro bono counseling for the hospital ever since I shut my private practice. These were high-need folks who couldn't afford even basic mental-health care, so I was glad to do my part. It also helped keep me sharp and on my toes.

Bronson "Pop-Pop" James pimp-walked into my dank little office with the same too-cool-for-school attitude as always. I'd met him when he was eleven; now he was a little older, and more confident in his cynical assessment of the world than ever.

Two of his friends had died since I'd started seeing him, and most of his heroes—street thugs barely older than he was—were already dead, too.

Sometimes I felt as if I were the only one in the world who cared about Bronson, which is not to say he was easy to work with, because he wasn't.

He sat on the vinyl couch across from me, with his jaw pointed at the ceiling, looking at something up there, or probably just ignoring me.

"Anything new since the last time?" I asked.

"Nothin' I can talk about," he said. "Man, why you always bringin' that Starbucks in here?"

I looked at the cup of Tall in my hand. "Why? Do you like coffee?"

"Nah, never touch the stuff. It's nasty. I like them Frappuccino shits they sell, though."

I could see him angling now, like maybe I'd pick him up a treat next time. Get him all sugared up. It was one of those rare flashes where the actual kid showed through the armor he seemed to wear day and night.

"Bronson, when you said it's nothing you can talk about, does that mean there's something going on?"

"You *deaf*? I said, *Nothin'. I can. Talk about!*"

His leg jerked out, and he punctuated his words with kicks at the little table between us.

Bronson was the type of boy people write psych papers about all the time—the debatably untreatable kind. As far as I'd been able to tell, he had no empathy for other people whatsoever. It's a basic building block of what could become antisocial personality disorder—Kyle had it, too, in fact—and it made acting out his violent impulses very easy to do. Put another way, it made it very hard for him not to act on them.

But I also knew Bronson's little secret. Inside that street-ready shell of his and behind the mental-health issues was a scared little kid who didn't understand why he felt the way he did most of the time. Pop-Pop had been bouncing around the system since he was a baby, and I thought he deserved a better shake than life had ever given him. That was why I came to see him twice a week.

I tried again. "Bronson, you know these talks of ours are private, right?"

" 'Less I'm a danger to myself," he recited. "Or someone else." The second point seemed to make him smile. I think he liked the power this conversation gave him.

"*Are* you a danger to someone else?" I asked. My main concern was gangs. He hadn't shown any tats or noticeable injuries—no burns, bruises, or anything else that looked like an initiation to me. But I also knew that his new foster home was near Valley Avenue, where the Ninth Street and Yuma crews ran, pretty much right on top of each other.

"There's nothin' happenin'," he said with conviction. "Just talkin'."

"And which crew are you 'just talking' with these days? Ninth Street? Yuma?"

He was starting to lose patience now and trying to stare me down. I let the silence hang, to see if he might answer. Instead, he jumped up and pushed the table aside to get in my face. The change in him was almost instantaneous.

"Don't be grittin' on me in here, man. Get your fuckin' eyes off me!"

Then he took a swing.

It was as if he didn't even know how small he was. I had

to block him and sit him back down by the shoulders. Even then, he tried for me again.

I pushed him onto the couch a second time. “No way, Bronson. Don’t even think about that with me.” I absolutely hated getting physical with him, given his history, but he’d crossed the line. In fact, it didn’t seem to matter to Bronson where the line was. That’s what scared me the most.

This boy was headed over a cliff, and I wasn’t sure I could do anything to stop him.

Chapter 21

"COME ON, BRONSON," I said, and stood up. "Let's blow this joint."

"Where we goin'?" he wanted to know. "Juvie Hall? I didn't hit you, man."

"No, we're not going to Juvie," I said. "Not even close. Let's go."

I looked at my watch. We still had about thirty minutes left in the session. Bronson followed me into the hall, probably more out of curiosity than anything else. Usually when we left the room together, I escorted him out to his social worker.

When we got outside and I clicked open the doors to my car, he stopped short again.

"You a perv, Cross? You takin' me somewhere private or something?"

"Yeah, I'm a perv, Pop-Pop," I said. "Just get in the car."

He shrugged and got in. I noticed him running his hand over the leather seat, and his eyes checking out the stereo, but he kept any compliments, or any digs, to himself.

"So what's the big secret, then?" he said as I pulled out into traffic. "Where the hell we goin'?"

"No secret," I said. "There's a Starbucks not far from here. I'm going to buy you one of those Frappuccinos."

Bronson turned to look out his window, but I caught a little flash of a grin before he did. It wasn't much, but at least for a few minutes that day, he just might have thought we were on the same side.

"Venti," he said.

"Yeah, Venti."

Chapter 22

THE IMBECILES WERE still in charge of the Bureau, or so it seemed. As far as Kyle Craig could tell, no one had even blinked when the freshly debriefed and newly reactivated Agent Siegel got himself assigned to the sniper case in DC. Siegel's earlier stint in Medellín, Colombia, during their "murder capital of the world" days, was a matter of record, and an impressive calling card at that. They were lucky to have him on this one.

Luckier than they knew—two agents for the price of one! He sat at his new desk in the field office, staring down at the photo ID he'd been issued that very morning. Max Siegel's mug stared back. He still got a rise just looking at it—still half expected to see the old Kyle whenever he passed by a mirror.

"Must be strange."

Kyle looked up to see one of the other agents standing

over the cubicle wall. It was Agent What'shisname, the one everyone called Scooter, of all absurd things—Scooter, with the eager eyes and constant snacking on sugared carbs.

Kyle slid the ID back into his pocket. "Strange?"

"Returning to fieldwork, I mean. After all that time."

"Miami *was* fieldwork," Kyle said, salting his speech with a dash of Siegel's *New Yawk* attitude and patois.

"I hear you. Didn't mean to imply anything," What'shisname said. Kyle just stared and let the awkwardness hang like a sheet of glass between them. "All right, well...you need anything before I head out?"

"From you?" Kyle said.

"Well, yeah."

"No thanks, Scooter. I'm all set."

Max Siegel was going to be antisocial. Kyle had decided that before he'd arrived. Let the other agents coo over baby pictures and share microwave popcorn in the break room. The wider the berth they gave him around here, the more he could get done, and the more secure his masquerade.

That's why he liked after hours so much. He'd already spent most of the previous night right there at the office, sucking up everything there was to know about the Eighteenth Street shooting. Tonight, he focused on crime-scene photos and anything to do with the shooter's methods. His profile was shaping up nicely.

Certain words kept coming to mind as he worked. "Clean." "Detached." "Professional." There had been no specific calling card from this killer, and none of the "come and get me" gamesmanship you so often saw with these things. It was almost sterile—homicide from 262 yards, which was an absolute yawn from Kyle's perspective, even if the shock and awe of it, to borrow a phrase from the newspapers, were rather elegantly rendered.

He worked for several hours, even lost track of time, until a ringing phone somewhere broke the silence in the office. Kyle didn't think too much about it, but then his own line went off a minute later.

"Agent Siegel," he answered, with a smile in his voice, though not on his face.

"This is Jamieson, over in Communications. We just got a homicide report from MPD. Looks like there's been another sniper attack. Up in the Woodley Park area this time."

Kyle didn't hesitate. He stood up and shrugged on his jacket. "Where am I going?" he said. "Exactly where?"

A few minutes later, he was pulling out of the parking garage and driving on Mass Avenue at around sixty. The sooner he got up there, the sooner he could head off Metro Police, who were no doubt fouling up his crime scene at that very moment.

And more important—*Ladies and Gentlemen, start your engines*—this was the moment he'd been waiting for. With any luck, it was time for Alex Cross and Max Siegel to meet.

Chapter 23

I WAS AT HOME when I got the call about the latest sniper murder near Woodley Park.

"Detective Cross? It's Sergeant Ed Fleischman from Two D. We've got a nasty homicide up here, very possible sniper fire."

"Who's the deceased?" I asked.

"Mel Dlouhy, sir. That's why I called you. He fits right into the mold on your case."

Dlouhy was currently out on bail but still at the center of what looked to be one of the biggest insider tax scandals in U.S. history. The allegations were that he'd used his position in the District's IRS office to funnel tens of millions in taxpayer dollars to himself, his family, and his friends, usually through nonprofit children's charities that didn't actually exist.

Another sniper incident, and another bad guy right out of the headlines—we had a pattern.

The case had just jumped to a new level, too. I was determined we'd get this right from the very start. If it had to be a circus, I could at least try to make sure it was *my* circus.

"Where are you?" I asked the sergeant.

"Thirty-second, just off of Cleveland Avenue, sir. You know the area?"

"I do."

Second District was the only one in the city with *zero homicides* in the last calendar year. So much for that statistic. I could already feel the neighborhood panic going up.

"Did the fire board get there?"

"Yes, sir. The victim's confirmed dead."

"And the house is clear?" I asked.

"We ran a protective sweep, and Mrs. Dlouhy's with us now. I can ask for consent to search if you want."

"No. If anyone's inside, I want them out. Call DC Mobile Crime. They can start photographing, but nobody touches anything until I get there," I told Sergeant Fleischman. "Do you have any idea where the shots came from yet?"

"Either the backyard, or the neighbor's place behind that. Nobody's home over there," Fleischman told me.

"Okay. Set up a command post on the street—not in the yard, Sergeant. I want officers at the front and back doors, and another at the neighbor's house. Anyone wants to get into either place, *they go through you first*—and then the answer is *no*. Not until I'm on-site. This is an MPD crime scene, and I'm ranking Homicide. You're going to see FBI, ATF, maybe the chief, too. He lives a lot closer than I do. Tell him to call me in the car if he wants."

"Anything else, Detective?" Fleischman sounded just a

little overwhelmed. Not that I blamed him. Most 2D officers aren't used to this kind of thing.

"Yeah, talk to your first responders. I don't want any jaw jacking with the press or the neighbors—*no one.* As far as your guys are concerned, they haven't seen a thing, they don't know a thing. Just keep the whole place locked down tight until I'm there."

"I'll try," he said.

"No, Sergeant. You'll just do it. Trust me—we have to keep this thing locked down tight."

Chapter 24

UNFORTUNATELY THE PRESS was going berserk when I got there. Dozens of cameras were jockeying for an angle on Mel and Nina Dlouhy's white stone house, either out front at the barriers that Sergeant Ed Fleischman had established, or over on Thirty-first, where a separate detail had been dispatched just to keep people from coming in through the back, which they certainly would do.

Most of the looky-loos on the street, if they weren't press, were probably wandering up from Cleveland Avenue. The neighbors seemed to have stayed home. I could see silhouettes in the windows up and down the block as I drove in. I signed up with crime-scene attendance and immediately ordered a canvassing detail to start knocking on doors.

Sampson met me at the scene, straight from a faculty thing at Georgetown, where his wife, Billie, taught nursing. "Can't say I'm glad this happened," he told me, "but, shit, how much wine and cheese can a man eat in one lifetime?"

We started in the living room, where the Dlouhys had reportedly been watching an episode of *The Closer.* The TV was still on, ironically with a live news shot of the house now. "That's creepy," said Sampson. "The press like to talk about invasion of privacy—except when they're doing the invading."

Mrs. Dlouhy's initial statement was that she'd heard a tinkle of glass, looked over at the broken window, and only then noticed her husband's head slumped over with his eyes wide open in the recliner next to hers. I could still hear her crying in the kitchen with one of our counselors, and my heart went out to her some. What a nightmare.

Mel Dlouhy was still sitting in his chair. The single bullet wound in his temple looked relatively clean, with a small blue-black halo around the entry. Sampson pointed to it with the tip of a pen.

"Let's say he gets shot here," he said, and raised the pen about six inches to where Dlouhy's head would have been positioned. "And it comes in"—he drew the pen in an arc until it was pointing at the broken glass—"over there."

"That's a downward angle," I said. The bullet had pierced one of the top panes in a six-over-one window that looked out to the backyard. Without any discussion, we both walked around to the dining room and outside through a pair of French doors.

A brick patio in the back gave way to a long, narrow yard. Two floodlights on the side of the house lit about half the space, but it didn't look like there were any outbuildings or trees big enough to support someone's weight.

Beyond that, the rear neighbor's three-story Tudor was backlit by the streetlamp on Thirty-first. Two huge oaks dominated that yard, mostly obscured in the shadow of the house.

"You said nobody was home over there?" Sampson asked. "That right?"

"Out of town, in fact," I said. "Someone knew exactly what he was doing. Maybe showing off. Shooter's got a reputation to live up to after that first hit."

"Assuming this is he."

"It's he," I said.

"Excuse me, Detective?" Sergeant Ed Fleischman was suddenly standing there. I looked down at his hands, to make sure he was gloved.

"What are you doing back here, Sergeant? There's plenty for you to do out front."

"Two things, sir. We've had a couple of neighbors reporting strange vehicles."

"Vehicles, plural?"

Fleischman nodded. "For whatever it's worth. One old Buick with New York plates parked up the street off and on for several days." He checked the pad in his hand. "And a large, dark-colored SUV, maybe a Suburban, definitely beat up. It was out on the street for a few hours late last night."

This wasn't the kind of neighborhood where old cars looked at home, at least not outside of service hours. We'd have to follow up on both the vehicles right away.

"What was the other thing?" I asked.

"FBI's here."

"Tell them to send ERT around to the neighbor's yard," I told the sergeant.

"Not 'them,' sir. It's an agent. He asked for you specifically."

Peering back inside, I could see a tall white guy in a generic Bureau suit. He was leaning over, with his blue-gloved hands on his knees, staring at the hole in Mel Dlouhy's head.

"Hey!" I called through the broken window. "Why do you need to be in there?"

He either didn't hear me or didn't want to.

"What's his name?" I asked Fleischman.

"Siegel, sir."

"Hey, Siegel!" I shouted this time, and then I started inside. "Don't touch anything in there!"

Chapter 25

WHEN ALEX CAME INTO THE ROOM, Kyle stood up and looked right into his eyes. *Dead man walking,* Kyle thought, and smiled as he extended a hand.

"Max Siegel, Washington field office. How're you doing? Not so good, I imagine."

Cross shook Kyle's hand begrudgingly, but it was still an electric moment, like the tip-off of an NBA game. *Here we go, here we go, here we go, now!*

"What are you doing in here?" Cross wanted to know.

"I'm just hitting the ground on this one," Kyle told him.

"No shit. I mean, what specifically do you need on this body?"

It was magnificent—Cross had no idea who he was looking at! The face was flawless, of course. If there was any danger here, it was with Alex's ears, not his eyes. This was where the weeks of audio surveillance on Max Siegel in Miami would really start to pay off.

But first he did exactly what Cross wouldn't expect. He turned his back on him and knelt down to look at the entry wound again.

A blue-and-black residue covered the skin around the opening. Some of the man's hair had been sucked inside with the bullet as it broke through the skull. So efficient. So impersonal. He was beginning to like this killer.

"Ballistics," he said finally, and stood up again. "My money's on 7.62 by 51 NATO match grade, but not jacketed. And some kind of military training on this shooter."

"You've read the file," Alex said, not offering any compliment, just noticing. "Yeah, we could definitely use some ballistics support from the Bureau to confirm, but let's get the ME in here before anything else. In the meantime, I need you to step out."

Cross couldn't have been easier to read. Right now, he was hoping a little bluster would tamp down this aggressive new FBI agent, who was no doubt just another overreaching Bureau asshole with an inflated sense of entitlement—kind of like Alex himself had been when he was an agent.

"Listen," said Kyle, "I'm not going to stress about who gets credit for what on this one. I mean, the U.S. attorney's going to step in and get all front and center no matter who brings it home, am I right?"

"Siegel, I don't have time for this right now. I—"

"But make no mistake." Kyle let the last of Siegel's buddy-buddy smile fade away. "We've got two incidents and three homicides, all inside the District. That's a federal crime. So you can work with us if you like, or you can get the fuck out of the way."

He showed Cross his sweet little encrypted Sigillu, fresh off the line. "One call, and I can make this whole crime scene my own private country club. It's up to you, Detective. What do you want to do?"

Chapter 26

IT TOOK ABOUT ten seconds for me to figure out what Max Siegel was all about, and I wasn't going to have any of it.

"Listen, Siegel, I'm not going to pretend I can keep you off this case any more than you can do the same to me," I told him. "But let *me* make one thing very clear here. This is an MPD crime scene. I'm ranking Homicide, and if you want to take that up with the chief, he's right outside. Meanwhile, if I have to tell you how quickly a room like this can cool, then you shouldn't be here to begin with."

No doubt, there would be a full task force after tonight, and I'd probably find myself working with this Bureau jerkoff as we moved forward. But right now was not the best time for pissing contests. By him—or by me.

Sampson came in from the yard, looking at me as if to say, *Who is this guy?* I made the necessary introductions.

"Agent Siegel and I were just comparing theories," I said,

trying to lighten things up a little and put us back on track. "He's got a military take on this, too."

Right away, Siegel started talking again. "Holding forth" was more like it.

"Military snipers go after high-value targets—officers, not enlisted men," he said. "The way I see it, that's what these victims are. Not the bank president but the congressman and the lobbyist who keep him juiced. And not the taxpayer who's been ripping off Uncle Sam but the other way around."

"A killer for the common man," Sampson said.

"With the very best training in the world." Siegel reached out until he was almost touching the black hole centered one inch above Mel Dlouhy's left ear. "That kind of accuracy doesn't lie."

I listened without saying too much. This guy wanted to lecture, not collaborate, but he was also pretty good at what he did. If there were things he could see here that I couldn't, then I needed to bite my tongue long enough to find out what they were.

It was just what Nana Mama's old refrigerator magnet had been telling me to do for as long as I could remember: *You find yourself with a lemon—make lemonade.*

Chapter 27

THE STREET OUTSIDE the Dlouhy house was filling up slowly and steadily—a thing of beauty. Denny and Mitch hung around the edge of the crowd, not coming too close but close enough to take it in. Given the shitty night they'd had at the shelter after the first hit, Denny figured Mitch could use a little positive exposure.

Either Mel Dlouhy's body was still inside or they'd snuck the fuck out the back. Cops in jackets and ties kept walking past the living room windows, and you could see that there were brilliant floodlights on behind the house.

Mitch didn't say much, but Denny could tell he was pumped. The scope of this whole thing was really starting to settle over the big guy. Nah, big *kid* was more like it.

"Excuse me, Officer. Did they catch the guy?" Denny asked one of the cops around the perimeter—and now he was just showing off for Mitch.

"You'll have to check the paper or TV, sir," the cop told him. "Honestly, I don't know."

Denny turned halfway around and spoke low. "You hear that? *Sir.* Must be a good neighborhood." Mitch looked off to the side and scratched at his jaw to keep from cracking up too much.

The cop was just about to get on the radio when Denny spoke up again. "Sorry, but I don't suppose you've got a spare ciggie on you?" He held up a blue Bic lighter. People always like to see the homeless guy with his own match, and sure enough the porker reached into his cruiser for a pack of Camel Lights.

"One's fine," Denny said, making sure Mitch was visible over his shoulder. "We can share."

The cop took two out of the pack. "What unit were you with?"

Denny looked down at his faded camo jacket. "Third Brigade Combat Team, Fourth Infantry Division, best unit overseas."

"Second best," Mitch said. "I was New Jersey Army National Guard, out of Balad."

In fact, Mitch had never known a uniform, but Denny had drilled him enough that he could fake it a little. People loved vets. It always worked to their advantage.

Denny took the ciggies from the piggy with a friendly nod and handed one over to Mitch. "Word on the street is that this guy might be one of us, the way he's been shooting," he said.

The cop shrugged in the direction of the sloped front yard.

"Word don't trickle down that hill too quick. You should ask a reporter. I'm just on crowd control."

"All right, well..." Denny lit his own cigarette, blew smoke, and smiled. "We'll get out of your hair now. God bless you, Officer, and thank you for what you're doing."

Chapter 28

THE FRIDAY AFTER the Dlouhy shooting was one of those breezy spring days, the kind where you can feel summer coming on the wind, even though it was still jacket weather.

Kyle buttoned his blazer as he turned onto Mississippi Avenue and walked north, blending in with the local color, so to speak. His wig, makeup, and contacts were all perfectly effective, even if they were comically rudimentary. Ever since the surgery on his face, anything less was simply beneath him—if not also a necessary evil.

Likewise, this run-down neighborhood was not a place he'd choose to spend a lovely spring afternoon. It was the kind of locale that kept white liberal guilt alive and well in America, just never enough that anyone actually did something about it.

All of which was neither Kyle's problem nor his concern right now.

He ambled up the street slowly, making a point of arriving outside the Southeast Community Center just before four thirty. Word was that they were giving out Wizards tickets today, along with the latest "Just Say No" inculcation for the kiddies. Even some of the roughest boys had shown up, and a stream of them came running out through the double glass doors just as Kyle approached the squat redbrick building.

One boy in particular caught his eye. He bypassed the front steps and jumped off a low wall, then stopped to drop the wrapper off a 3 Musketeers bar before continuing up the street.

Kyle followed, close enough to register on the boy's radar but far enough back that they'd be well out of earshot before anything happened.

A block and a half later, the boy stopped short and turned around quickly. He was still chewing the candy bar, and he spoke around it.

"Man, whatha fuck you comin' up on me like that?"

He was child-young, but there was nothing resembling fear in those brown doe eyes of his. The sneer on his face was a carbon copy of every other wannabe gangster who trawled these miserable streets for a living.

The boy lifted the hem on his too-long white undershirt and showed a black leather-wrapped hilt of a knife that probably went halfway down his skinny leg. "You got somethin' to say, *punk?*" he asked.

Kyle smiled approvingly. "It's Bronson, right? Or do you prefer Pop-Pop?"

"Who wants to know?" His instincts were good—and he

was just stupid enough. Bronson pulled the knife out a little farther, to show off some steel.

Kyle angled himself away from the street and opened his own jacket. Inside was a compact Beretta pistol, holstered at his side. He took it out and held it by the barrel, with the grip toward the boy.

Little Bronson's pupils dilated—not with fear but with sudden interest.

"I've got a nice job for you, little man, if you're up to it. You want to earn five hundred dollars?"

Book Two

FOXES IN THE HENHOUSE

Chapter 29

BALLISTICS WERE IN.

This was the report everyone had been waiting for, and I scheduled it to coincide with that day's Field Intelligence Group conference call. On the line, we had the whole team from MPD, as well as people from FBI, ATF, Capitol Police—just about everyone was dialed into this case by now.

Reporting in, we had Cailin Jerger, from the Forensic Analysis Branch at the FBI lab in Quantico, and Alison Steedman, who was with their Firearms-Toolmarks Unit.

After a few quick introductions, I handed the call over to them.

"Based on fragments in all three victims' skulls, I can tell you conclusively that the same weapon was used every time," Jerger told the group. I'd gotten most of this in the morning, but it was news to almost everyone else on the call. "A 7.62 caliber can trace back to dozens of weapons, but given the nature and distance of these shots, we believe we're looking at a high-grade sniper system. That brings it down to seven possibilities."

"And it gets better from there," Agent Steedman joined in. "Four of those seven are bolt-action rifles. By all accounts, the first two victims, Vinton and Pilkey, went down within two seconds of each other. That's too fast for bolt-action, which leaves three semiautomatic possibilities—the M21, the M25, and the newer M110, which is state of the art. We can't rule any of those out, but these shots were all taken at night into variable lighting conditions, and the M110 comes with a thermal optical site, standard."

"All of which is to say that your shooter is likely to be very well equipped," Jerger said.

"How hard is it to put your hands on an M110?" I recognized Jim Heekin's voice from the Directorate of Intelligence.

"They're made in only one place," Steedman told us. "Knight's Armament Company in Titusville, Florida."

I'd already been tracking this, so I spoke up here.

"So far, all of Knight's stock is accounted for," I said. "But once these systems hit the field, mostly in Iraq and Afghanistan, they can and do go missing. Souvenirs from the war, that kind of thing. So they're pretty much impossible to trace."

"Detective Cross, this is Captain Oliverez at Capitol Police. Didn't your report say the fingerprints you found on Eighteenth Street were *nonmilitary*?"

"Yes," I said. "But we're not ready to rule out a military connection, in terms of how the weapon might have been procured and how it's been used. In fact, that brings up another point." I'd been sitting on this one for half a day, but really it made no sense not to share it with the group now.

"Let me stress something here," I said. "I want to keep this out of the press until we have some kind of proof either way. I know it's like herding cats—there's a lot of us on this call—but I'm counting on your discretion across the board here."

"Whatever happens in Vegas...," someone joked, and there were a few soft laughs.

"The point is this," I said. "All of these systems we're talking about are crew-served weapons. The military model is one shooter and one spotter in the field." I could hear people on the line mumbling to one another in their various conference rooms. "So you can see where I'm going here. It could be shades of two thousand two all over again. We're probably not looking for a single shooter anymore. Most likely, we're looking for a two-man team."

Chapter 30

AS SAMPSON AND I came out of the conference room, we found Joyce Catalone from our Communications Office standing outside the door.

"I was just going to pull you out," she said. "I'm glad I didn't have to."

I looked at my watch—four forty-five. That meant at least three dozen reporters were downstairs, waiting to grill me for their five and six o'clock news cycles. Damn it—it was time to feed the beast.

Joyce and Sampson walked down with me. We took the stairs so she could run through a few things for me to consider on the way.

"Keisha Samuels from the *Post* wants to do a profile for the Sunday magazine."

"No," I told her. "I like Keisha, she's smart and she's fair, but it's too early for that kind of in-depth piece."

"And I've got CNN and MSNBC both ready to give this thing thirty minutes in prime time, if you're ready to sit down."

"Joyce, I'm not doing any special coverage until we have something we want to get out there. I wish to hell that we did."

"No prob," she said, "but don't come crying to me when you *want* some coverage and they've moved on to something else." Joyce was an old hand in the department and the unofficial mother hen of Investigative Services.

"I never cry," I said.

"Except when I get you on the ropes," Sampson said, and threw a punch my way.

"That's your breath—not your punches," I told him.

We'd reached the ground floor, and Joyce stopped with her hand on the door. "Excuse me, Beavis? Butt-Head? We ready to focus, here?" She was also excellent at her job and great to have as backup at these daily press briefings, which could get kind of hectic.

Did I say "kind of"? A buzzing swarm of reporters came at us the second we hit the front steps of the Daly Building.

"Alex! What can you tell us about Woodley Park?"

"Detective Cross, over here!"

"Is there truth to the rumors—"

"*People!*" Joyce shouted over the group. Her volume was the stuff of legend around the office. "Let the man make his statement first! *Please.*"

I quickly ran down the facts of the last twenty-four hours and said what I could about the Bureau's ballistics report without going into too much detail. After that, it was back to the free-for-all.

Channel 4 got in first. I recognized the microphone but not the reporter, who looked about twelve years old to me. "Alex, do you have any message for the sniper? Anything you want him to know?"

For the first time, something like quiet broke out on the steps. Everybody wanted to hear my answer to that one.

"We'd welcome contact of any kind from whoever is responsible for these shootings," I said into the cameras. "You know where to find us."

It wasn't a great sound bite, and it wasn't badass or anything else that some people out there might have wanted me to say. But within the investigation, we were all in agreement: there would be no goading, no lines in the sand, and no public characterizing of the killer—or killers—until we knew more about who we were dealing with, here.

"Next question. James!" Joyce called out, just to keep things focused and moving along.

It was James Dowd, one of the national NBC correspondents. He had a thick pad of notes in his hand, which he worked off of as he spoke.

"Detective Cross, is there any truth to the rumors about a blue Buick Skylark with New York plates—or a dark-colored, rusted-out Suburban—near the scene in Woodley Park? And can you tell us if either of those vehicles has been traced back to the killer?"

I was pissed and taken off guard all at once. The problem was, Dowd was good.

The truth was, I had an old friend—Jerome Thurman from First District—quietly following up on both of those leads from the night of the Dlouhy murder. So far, all we had was a mile-long list of matching vehicles from the DMV, and no proof that any of them were connected in any way to the shootings.

But more than that, we had a strong desire to keep this information under wraps. Obviously someone had spoken to the press, which was ironic given my lecture about discretion on the FIG call just a few minutes ago.

I gave the only answer I could. "I have no comment on that at this time." It was like dangling a steak in front of a pack of wild dogs. The whole mass of them pressed in even closer.

"People!" Joyce tried again. "One at a time. You know how this works!"

It was a losing battle, though. I threw out at least four more "no comments" and stonewalled until someone finally changed the subject. But the damage was already done. If either of those vehicles did in fact belong to the snipers, they now had full warning, and we'd just lost an important advantage.

It was our first major leak of the investigation, but something told me it wasn't going to be our last.

Chapter 31

LISA GIAMETTI LOOKED at her watch for maybe the tenth time. She was going to wait five more minutes and then take off. It was just amazing, the way some people didn't think twice about wasting your time in this business.

Four and a half minutes into the five she'd allowed, a dark-blue BMW pulled up and double-parked in front of the house. *Better late than never anyway. Nice car.*

She checked her teeth in the rearview mirror, ran a hand through her short auburn hair, and got out to meet the client.

"Mr. Siegel?"

"Max," he said. "Sorry to keep you waiting. I'm not used to the city traffic."

His handshake was warm, and he was just tall, dark, and hot enough to forgive easily. Considering all the eye contact, she figured he liked what he saw as well. Interesting guy, and well worth the wait.

"Come on in," she told him. "I think you'll like this place. I know I do."

She held the door open for him to go first. The place was a half-decent row house on Second in Northeast, a little overpriced for the current rental market but a good fit for the right tenant. "Are you new to Washington?"

"I used to live here, and now I'm back," he said. "I don't really know anybody in the city anymore."

He was doing the code thing—new in town, alone, etc. No ring on the finger either. Lisa Giametti was not an easy mark, but she knew a hungry man when she saw one, and if something happened to happen here, well, it wouldn't be the first time.

She closed the door and locked it behind them.

"It's a great block," she went on. "You've got the back of the Supreme Court Building right across the street. Not exactly a lot of loud parties over there. And then a nice little yard in the back with off-street parking."

They came through to the kitchen, where the garage was visible outside. "I don't have to tell you how handy that can be around here."

"No," he said, looking somewhere south of her eyes. "That's a very nice pendant you're wearing. You have good taste—in apartments and jewelry."

This guy didn't waste any time, did he?

"And how about the basement?" he asked next.

"Excuse me?" she said.

"I'd like to see the basement. There is one, isn't there?"

Normally the client might have asked about the upstairs at this point. Maybe even the bedroom, if she was reading this guy correctly. But whatever. The customer was always right, especially when he looked like this one did.

She left her briefcase on the kitchen counter, opened the basement door, and led him down the old wooden stairs.

"You can see it's nice and dry. The wiring's been redone, and the washer and dryer are only a couple of years old."

He walked around, nodding approvingly. "I could get a lot of work done down here. Plenty of privacy, too."

Suddenly, he took a step toward her, and she backed into the washing machine.

If there had been any doubt about where this was headed, it was gone now. Lisa tossed her hair. "Do you want to see the upstairs?"

"Of course I do—just not quite yet. You mind, Lisa?"

"No, I guess not."

When she went to kiss him, he reached between her legs at the same moment, right up her skirt. It was a little presumptuous—and a little hot, too.

"It's been a while," he told her apologetically.

"I can tell," she said, and pulled him closer.

Then, before they ever got to the paperwork still waiting on the kitchen counter upstairs, Lisa Giametti got the fuck of her life, right there on the two-year-old Maytag washer. It was hot, and dirty, and quite wonderful.

And the 12 percent commission was very nice, too.

Chapter 32

THE FEDS DIDN'T KNOW SHIT. Metro Police didn't know shit either. All anyone knew was that Washington was becoming one very hot and scary place to live.

Denny ate up the headlines—page A01 every morning, lead story every night at five, six, and eleven. He and Mitch sold their papers in the afternoon, then caught the evening news at Best Buy or, if they had a few extra bucks, at one of the watering holes that didn't mind a couple of dusty guys like them sitting at the bar.

It was always the same story: unknown assailant, phantom fingerprint, and very high-grade weaponry. A few channels were throwing around rumors about a Buick Skylark with New York plates, and a supposedly dark-blue or black rusted-out Suburban—which would have worried Denny a lot more if his own Suburban wasn't white. Even eyewitnesses were going south these days, just like everything else in the republic.

For Mitch's part, he liked the hoopla well enough, but as the days slipped by, he seemed to get a little more sluggish, a little less engaged. There was no doubt about it in Denny's mind: these "missions" were the thing that kept Mitch focused. Nothing else did it for the big guy.

So on the seventh day of no action, Denny told Mitch it was time to go again.

They were driving on Connecticut, away from Dupont Circle in rush-hour traffic, which was perfect, as it turned out. The longer it took to crawl past the Mayflower Hotel, the more they could scope it out on the first pass.

"That the place?" Mitch asked, looking up from the passenger seat.

"We'll do a full recon tonight," Denny said. "Tomorrow night, we go."

"What kind of crumbum we bringing down this time, Denny?"

"You ever heard of Agro-Corel?"

"Nope."

"You ever eat corn? Or potatoes? Or drink bottled water? They were into everything, man, a whole vertically integrated conglomerate, and our boy sat right at the top of the pyramid."

"What'd he do?"

Mitch kept picking Taco Bell crumbs out of his lap and eating them, but Denny knew he was listening, too, even if some of it went over his head.

"Man lied to his company. Lied to the Feds, too. He sent the whole place down the shitter and took some hundred-million-dollar parachute, while everyone else took the shaft—no pensions, no jobs, nothing. You know what that's like, don't you, Mitchie? Doing everything you should, and still getting the short end while the Man just keeps getting fatter?"

"Why ain't the Man in jail, Denny?"

He shrugged. "How much does a judge cost?"

Mitch stared out the windshield, not saying anything. A light changed, and the traffic surged forward again.

Finally, he said, "I'll put a bullet in his brain stem, Denny."

Chapter 33

THE NEXT NIGHT, they did things a little differently, trying to shake up the routine. Denny dropped Mitch off with both packs in an alley behind the Moore Building, then parked a good four blocks away and walked back. Afterward he'd pull the car around again.

Mitch was waiting inside the building. Neither one of them spoke while climbing the twelve flights of stairs. The packs were sixty pounds each. It wasn't a picnic anyway.

On the roof, they could hear traffic noises from down on Connecticut but could see nothing until they got right up to the edge.

The whole facade of their building was built up, so all anyone could see from the street was a twenty-foot-high triangle of brickwork instead of the usual flat roofline. The spot was like a bird blind, with a perfect view of the Mayflower Hotel across the street—still one of the most famous hotels in DC.

Denny scoped things out while Mitch got himself set up for the turkey shoot.

The target, Skip Downey, had some very regular habits. He liked one suite in particular, which made Denny's job a hell of a lot easier than it might have been.

Right now, the curtains were open, which meant Mr. Downey hadn't checked in yet.

Twenty minutes later, though, Downey and his "friend" were waiting around for the bellman to take his twenty-dollar tip and skedaddle out of the suite.

Downey had an embarrassing reddish-blond comb-over to go with his million-dollar bank account. And apparently he liked the Mensa type. His companion today had her hair up in a bun, with heavy horn-rimmed glasses and a little business suit that was way too short for any real librarian to wear.

"Bow-chicka-wow-wow," Denny sang—a little porn theme for the occasion. "Two windows down and four over—you got it?"

"I'm there," Mitch said. He was eyeing over his own scope and flipped off the safety as he watched. "Nice-looking piece of ass, Denny. Shame to mess her up, you know?"

"That's why you're just going for the shoulder, Mitchie. Just enough to put her down on the ground. Mr. D. first, and then the girl."

"Mr. D. first, and then the girl," he repeated, and settled into his final stance.

Downey poured a couple of scotches on rocks. He drained his own and then walked straight over to the suite's living room window.

"Shooter ready?" Denny asked.

"Ready," Mitch said.

The man of the moment reached up to close the heavy coffee-colored drapes, his arms spread in a wide V.

"Send it!"

Chapter 34

AT TEN THIRTY that night, I was standing on the roof of the Moore Building, looking across to the hotel suite where Skip Downey had just joined a small but growing fraternity of those recently deceased by sniper fire.

This latest made three incidents—the magic number. Our guys were now serial killers in the public eye.

Connecticut Avenue down below was a forest of mobile broadcast towers, and I knew from experience that the blogosphere was about to officially catch on fire with this thing.

"Can you see me?" I said into my radio.

I had Sampson on the wireless, from inside the hotel room. He was standing right where Skip Downey had gone down.

"Wave your arm or something," he said. "There you are. But, yeah—that's pretty good cover."

Someone behind me cleared his throat.

I wheeled around and saw Max Siegel standing there. *Great. Just who I didn't want to see.*

"Sorry," he said. "Didn't mean to scare you."

"No problem," I said. Unless you counted the fact that he was up here at all.

"What have we got?" He came over to get the same view I had, and looked out across Connecticut. "How far a shot is that? Fifty yards?"

"Less," I said.

"So they're obviously not trying to top themselves. At least, not in terms of distance."

I noticed he said "they" and wondered if he'd been on that FIG conference call—or if he'd come up with it on his own.

"The MO's the same otherwise," I said. "The shots came from a standing position. Caliber seems like a match. And then there's the target profile, of course."

"Bad guy out of the headlines," he said.

"That's it," I said. "Plenty of people got screwed over by this Downey guy. The whole thing has vigilante justice written all over it."

"You want to know what I think?" Siegel asked—of course, it wasn't really a question. "I think you're oversimplifying. These guys aren't hunting, not in the traditional sense. And there's nothing personal in the work at all. It's completely detached."

"Not completely," I said. "That print they left at the first scene had to have been deliberate."

"Even if it was," Siegel said, "that doesn't mean the whole thing was their idea."

Already I was getting tired of the jawing. "Where are you going with this?"

"Isn't it kind of obvious?" he said. "These guys are guns for hire. They're working for someone. Maybe there's an agenda—but it belongs to whoever's footing the bill. That's who wants all these bad boys dead."

He had laid out his opinion as fact, not to be questioned—as usual. But, still, the theory wasn't completely off the wall. I owed it to myself to consider it, and I definitely would. Score one for Max Siegel.

"I'm a little surprised," I told him honestly. "I'm used to the Bureau sticking to harder evidence and staying away from supposition."

"Yeah, well, I'm full of surprises," he said, and put an unwelcome hand on my shoulder. "You've got to widen your mind, Detective, if you don't mind my saying so."

I minded very much, but I was determined to do the one thing Siegel seemed incapable of—taking the high road.

Chapter 35

I LEFT THE MAYFLOWER crime scene soon after that, glad for an excuse to get away from Siegel.

Our second victim that night, Rebecca Littleton, was at George Washington University Hospital with a single gunshot wound to the shoulder. Word from the emergency room was that it had been a penetrating trauma, as opposed to a perforating one. That meant the bullet still had to come out. If I hurried, I could catch her before surgery.

When I got there, they had Littleton on a gurney in one of the blue-curtained ER cubicles. The truss over her shoulder was stained dark with Betadine, and whatever the IV meds were doing for her physical pain, they sure weren't helping her mental state—she still looked ghost white and scared as hell.

"Rebecca? I'm Detective Cross from Metro Police," I said. "I need to talk to you."

"Am I, like, being charged with anything?" I don't think

she was much more than eighteen or nineteen. Barely legal. Her voice was tiny, and it quavered when she spoke.

"No," I assured her. "Nothing like that. I just need to ask you some questions. I'll try to make this easy, and fast."

The truth was, even if someone wanted to pursue the solicitation angle, there were no witnesses to it—with the possible exception of the man who had shot her.

"Did you see anything tonight that might give you an idea of who did this? Anyone outside the window? Or even just something out of place in the hotel room?"

"I don't think so, but... I don't remember very much. Mr. Downey started to close the curtains, and then I was just... on the floor. I don't even know what happened after that. Or right before."

In fact, she'd been the one to drag a phone off a side table and call for help. The incident would probably come back to her in pieces, but I didn't push it for now.

"Was this the first time you'd met up with Mr. Downey?" I asked.

"No. He was kind of a regular."

"Always at the Mayflower?"

She nodded. "He liked that suite. We always went to the same room."

A nurse in pink scrubs came into the cubicle. "Rebecca, hon? They're ready for you upstairs, okay?"

The curtain around us slid open, and several other people were there now. One of the residents started unlocking the wheels on her gurney.

"Just one more question," I said. "How long were you in the room tonight before this happened?"

Rebecca closed her eyes and thought for a second. "Five minutes, maybe? We just got there. Detective... *I'm in college. My parents...*"

"You won't be charged with anything, but your name will probably get out. You should call your parents, Rebecca."

I walked with her as she was rolled out into the hall and toward the elevators. There didn't seem to be any family or friends around, and it broke my heart a little that she had to go through this alone.

"Listen," I said. "I've been where you are. I've had a bullet in my shoulder, and I know how scary this is. You're going to be fine, Rebecca."

"Okay," she said, but I don't think she believed me. She still looked terrified.

"I'll check on you later," I said, just before the elevator doors slid shut between us.

Chapter 36

I HOOFED it back to the car and started scribbling notes against the steering wheel, trying to capture all the different threads running through my head.

Rebecca said she and Downey had been in the room for only a short time. That meant the snipers were set up and ready for them. The killers knew exactly when and where they needed to be, just like they knew when Vinton and Pilkey would be outside the restaurant, and just like they knew Mel Dlouhy's neighbors were out of town when they came by to murder him.

Whoever was behind this had a firm handle on the victims' habits, the movements of the people around them, and even the most private details of their otherwise public lives. It struck me that this kind of intelligence gathering took time, manpower, and know-how, and quite possibly money.

I thought about what Siegel had said to me on the roof of

the Moore Building tonight. *These guys are guns for hire.* I hadn't ruled it out then, and I was a step closer to ruling it in now. I just didn't like thinking that Siegel had beaten me to it. Usually I'm not like that, but he just rubbed me the wrong way.

There was obviously some kind of specific and disciplined agenda behind these killings. If a shooter as skilled as this one had wanted Rebecca taken out, she would have been dead for sure. But she didn't fit the profile; her only crime had been to land in the wrong place at the wrong time. Not so for the others. By the apparent rules of this game, Rebecca didn't deserve to die, but Skip Downey and the other Washington "bad guys" did.

So whose game was it? Who was writing the rules? And where was it all heading?

I still couldn't dismiss the possibility that our gunmen were operating on their own. But I also was just paranoid enough by now—or maybe experienced enough—that a list of scarier alternatives was taking shape in my mind.

Could this somehow be government backed? Some domestic agency? An international one?

Or was the Mob behind it somehow? The military? Maybe even just a very well-connected individual, with deep pockets and a serious ax to grind?

In any case, the most important questions were still left hanging: Who did they have their eye on next? And how the hell were we supposed to protect every high-profile scumbag in Washington? It just couldn't be done.

Unless we got very, very lucky, someone else was going to die before this was over. And it was most likely somebody who many people wouldn't mind seeing dead. That was the beauty of this terrifying game.

Chapter 37

THE NEXT DAY was a benchmark for Nana and me. Things had been chilly between us since I'd brought in the security at the house, but when I came down and found her cooking breakfast for Rakeem and his guys, I knew we were at least partway over the hump.

"Oh, Alex, you're here. Good. Take these plates outside," she said as if breakfast delivery were something I did every day. "Scoot, while it's hot!"

When I came back, my own plate was waiting for me—scrambled eggs with linguica, wheat toast, orange juice, and a steaming cup of Nana's chicory coffee in my old favorite *#1 Dad* mug with the dent where Ali had thrown it against the wall.

Her own breakfasts were a lot more heart-healthy these days—grapefruit sections, toast with unsalted butter, tea, and then one half of one sausage link, because as Nana liked to say, there was a fine line between eating smart to live longer and boring oneself to death.

"Alex, I want to call a truce," she said, finally settling down across from me.

"Here's to that," I said, and raised my juice glass. "I accept your terms, whatever they are."

"Because there's something else I need to talk to you about."

I had to laugh. "That was just about the shortest cease-fire I've ever seen. What is this, the Middle East?"

"Oh, relax. It's about Bree."

As far as I knew, Bree was right up there with sliced bread, Barack Obama, and handwritten letters in Nana's book. How bad could this be?

"You know, after all this, you'd be a silly fool to let that girl slip through your fingers," she started in.

"Absolutely," I said, "and if I may, I'd like to draw the court's attention to the very nice diamond ring on Ms. Stone's left hand."

Nana waved my logic away with her fork. "Rings come off just as easily as they go on. I hope you don't mind my saying so, but you've got something of a track record with women, and not in a good way."

Ouch. Still, I couldn't deny it. For whatever reasons, I'd never been able to find real stability in a relationship since my first wife, Maria, had been murdered so many years earlier.

At least, not until now with Bree.

"If it makes you feel any better," I said, "I took Bree up to Immaculate Conception and asked her to marry me all over again, right there in front of God and creation."

"And what did she say?" Nana deadpanned.

"She's going to have to get back to me on that. But seriously, Nana, where is this coming from? Have I given you some reason to doubt us?"

She was up to her half sausage now, and she held up a finger for me to wait while she lovingly, almost reverently, devoured the cylinder. Then, as if she were starting a whole new conversation, she looked up again and said, "You know I'm going to be ninety this year?"

It came out with a smile—I *think* she was going to be around ninety-two—but the words stopped me cold anyway.

"Nana, is there something you're not telling me?"

"No, no," she said. "I'm right as rain. Couldn't be better. Just thinking ahead, that's all. No one lasts forever. At least, not that I know about."

"Well, think a little *less* ahead, okay? And, by the way, you're not car parts. You're one hundred percent irreplaceable."

"Of course I am!" She reached over to put her hand on top of mine. "And *you* are a strong, capable, and wonderful father. But you can't do this alone, Alex. Not the way you run the other half of your life."

"Maybe so, but it's not why I'm marrying Bree," I told her. "And it's not a good enough reason to either."

"Well, I can think of worse. Just don't blow it, mister," she said, and sat back again with a wink to let me know she was joking.

Half joking anyway.

Chapter 38

I SHOWED UP at St. Anthony's that morning feeling pretty good about the way the day had started. My conversation with Nana was a little hard, but productive, I thought. It felt as if we were on the same team again. Maybe it was a sign that things were looking up in general.

Then again—maybe not.

Bronson James's social worker, Lorraine Solie, was waiting for me in the hall when I got there. As soon as I saw how red and puffy her eyes were, my stomach dropped.

"Lorraine? What's happened?"

She started to explain, and then she just broke down in tears. Lorraine was tall and very thin, but I'd seen her hold her own with some very rough characters. This could mean only that the worst kind of thing had happened.

I ushered her into the office, and we sat down on the vinyl couch where Bronson usually perched for our sessions.

I finally had to ask, "Lorraine, is he dead?"

"No," she said, wiping her eyes. "But he's been shot, Alex. He's in the hospital with a bullet in his head, and they don't think he's going to wake up."

I was stunned. I shouldn't have been, but I was. This was exactly the kind of thing I'd always tried *not* to think of as an inevitability for Bronson. It was also why I had tried my best not to care too much about the boy, and had failed.

"What happened?" I asked. "Tell me everything. Please."

Slowly, Lorraine choked out the rest of the story. He had apparently made a robbery attempt on a liquor store in Congress Heights—a place called Cross Country Liquors, she said. The name—Cross—was enough of a coincidence that I noticed, but I didn't make too much of it. My mind was on Bronson, and little else.

This was the boy's first actual armed-robbery attempt, as far as either of us knew. He'd brought a handgun into the store, but the owner had one, too—no surprise. Congress Heights was one of MPD's designated hot spots for violent crimes. Part of the problem was that the locals had gotten fed up and started fighting back—in the street, at home, and in their places of business.

There had been an argument. Bronson fired first and missed. The man returned fire and struck Bronson in the back of the head. Pop-Pop was lucky just to be alive, if that's what you could call it.

"Where is he, Lorraine? I have to go see him."

"He's at Howard, but I don't know where Medicaid's going to land him. The whole foster system's in a state of flux, as you know. It's a mess."

"What about the gun? Do we have any idea where he got it?"

"Take your pick," she said bitterly. "Alex, he never even had a chance."

It was true, in more ways than one. If I had to guess, I'd say this was a gang initiation, and whoever sent him in there knew exactly what his chances were. That's how it worked. If he could pull it off, they'd want him in their crew, and if he couldn't, then he was no use to them anyway.

Damn it, I hated this city sometimes. Or maybe I just loved Washington too much and couldn't stand what it had become.

Chapter 39

DENNY STOOD AT THE EDGE of Georgetown Waterfront Park, scoping the scene, while Mitch shifted from foot to foot, finishing off a Big Gulp Mountain Dew.

"What are we doing here, Denny? I mean, I like it fine and all."

"All part of the big picture, bud. Keep an eye out for anyone surfing the Net."

This whole stretch, from the Key Bridge down to Thompson Boat Center, was hopping with tourists, locals, and students, all taking advantage of the spring weather before the real humidity set in. Some inevitable number of them were bent over their laptop computers, and some number of those, no doubt, had satellite Internet connections.

Mitch and Denny would kill two birds while they were here: split up to sell their papers while they looked for a good mark.

After about half an hour, some goofball frat boys Denny had his eye on got up from their stuff to play a little Ultimate on the lawn. He sat down in the grass nearby and motioned to Mitch, who took up a position on the fence by the river.

Once the game had moved about as far from Denny as it was going to get, he gave Mitch the next signal—a scratch on the top of his head—and Mitch went into his crazy dance.

He screamed at the top of his lungs. He flapped his arms. He grabbed on to the fence and shook it back and forth like a crazy man in a cage. And for at least thirty seconds, every eye in the immediate area was on him.

Denny worked fast. He slipped one of the frat boys' laptops—a sweet little MacBook Air—into his stack of papers, stood up, and hurried away. A second later, he was walking a straight line out of the park.

As he passed under the Whitehurst Freeway, he could still hear Mitch going at it, way longer than he needed to. No harm done there—they'd have a good laugh about it later, at least the big guy would. Jeez, he loved to laugh.

The Suburban was parked halfway up the hill, on a side street near the Chesapeake and Ohio Canal. Denny climbed in, fired up the computer, and got right to work.

Ten minutes later, he was back out of the car, with only one thing on his mind.

He walked around the block to a rickety wooden staircase that led down to the old canal, twenty-five feet below street level. The crushed-gravel towpath that ran alongside it was popular with joggers, but it didn't take more than half a cigarette before he got a few moments' privacy.

He leaned down and gently slipped the laptop into the

brackish water, where it quickly sank to the bottom, probably never to be seen again. It was almost too easy.

Mission accomplished, Denny thought, and smiled to himself as he started back up the stairs to go find that wild man, Mitch.

Chapter 40

THE *TRUE PRESS* OFFICE was hectic this afternoon, but no more than any other deadline day. Final copy was due to the printers by seven, nothing was proofed yet, and the clock was running down.

Colleen Brophy scrubbed at her eyes, trying to focus on her lead article. She'd been editor for two years now and still loved the job, but the pressure was constant. If they didn't get the paper out on time, eighty homeless vendors would have nothing to sell, and that's when people started choosing between things like breakfast, lunch, and dinner.

So when Brent Forster, one of the college interns, interrupted her train of thought for the umpteenth time that day, it was everything Colleen could do not to bite his head off and eat it whole.

"Hey, Coll? You want to take a look at this? It's real interesting. Coll?"

"Unless something's on fire, just deal with it," she snapped at College Boy.

"Then let's say something's on fire," he said.

She had to swivel only halfway around to take a look over his shoulder—one of the very few advantages of working in a teeny-tiny office.

An e-mail was up on his screen. The sender was a jayson .wexler@georgetown.edu, and the subject line was "Foxes in the Henhouse."

"I don't have time for spam, Brent. Not now, not ever. What is this?"

The young intern rolled his chair out of her way. "Just read it, Coll."

Chapter 41

to the people of dc—

theres foxes in the henhouse. they come at night when no ones looking and take what dont belong to them. then they get fat on what they took while too many others go hungry and get sick and sometimes even die.

theres only one way to deal with foxes. you dont negoshiate and you dont try to understand them. you wait until they come around where your hiding and then you put a bullet in their brain. studies show that dead foxes are 100 percent less likely to rip you off, ha-ha.

vinton pilkey dlouhy downey are all just a start. theres plenty more foxes where they came from. they are in our government, our media, our schools, churches, armed services, on wall street, you name it. and their ruining this country. can anyone really say their not?

to all the foxes out there, hear this. we are coming for you. we will hunt you down and kill you before you can do any more damage than you already done. change your ways now or pay the price.

god bless the united states of america!

signed, a patriot

Colleen pushed back fast from the computer. "'A patriot'? Is this for real?"

"Funny you should ask," College Boy said, and pulled up a second e-mail. "Well, not funny, really, but—check it out."

p.s. to the true press—you can tell the dc police this is no joke. we have left a fingerprint on the lion statue in the law enforcement memorial, near d street. it will match what they found before.

Colleen swiveled back around to her own desk.

"Do you want me to call the police?" College Boy asked.

"No, I'll do it. You call the printers. Tell them we're going to be a day or two late, and I'm going to want to run twenty thousand copies this time, plus another thousand of last week's issue to tide us over."

"Twenty thousand?"

"That's right. And if any of the vendors ask, tell them it'll be worth the wait," she said. For the first time that day, Colleen was smiling. "They're all going to be eating a little better this week."

Chapter 42

AS SOON AS we got word on the *True Press* e-mails, I called in an old contact at the Bureau's Cyber Unit, Anjali Patel. She and I had worked together before on the DCAK case, and I knew she could hold her own under pressure.

A short while later, Anjali and I showed up at the paper's office, a single donated room at a church on E Street.

"You can't stop us from printing this!"

That was the first thing Colleen Brophy said when we introduced ourselves. Ms. Brophy, the paper's editor, just kept hammering away on her keyboard while we stood there, with three other staff members jammed into the tiny space between us.

"Who was the first person to open those e-mails?" I asked the room.

"That'd be me." A scruffy college-aged kid raised his hand.

His T-shirt said PEACE, JUSTICE, AND BEER. "I'm Brent Forster," he added.

"Brent, meet Agent Patel. She's your new best friend," I said. "She's going to take a look at your computer. *Right now.*" I'd worked with Patel enough to know she could hold down this end on her own.

"And, Ms. Brophy?" I said, holding the door open to the hall. "Could we talk outside, please?"

She got up then, begrudgingly enough, and took a pack of smokes off her desk. I followed her down to the end of the hall, where she opened a window and lit up.

"If we can make this quick, I've really got a full plate today," she said.

"No doubt," I told her. "But now that you have your scoop, I'm going to need some cooperation on this. This is a murder case."

"Of course," she said, as if she hadn't made us feel about as welcome as an outbreak of herpes so far. A lot of homeless people—and by extension their advocates—tend to see the police as more obstacle than ally. I got that but thought, *Tough.*

"There's not much to tell," she offered. "We got the e-mails a few hours ago. Assuming they're not from this Wexler kid, I have no idea who sent them."

"Understood," I said, "but whoever it was, they just did your paper a huge favor, wouldn't you say? I wonder if there might be some connection you can help us with?"

"They've also got a pretty good point to make, wouldn't *you* say?"

She reminded me of my FBI friend Ned Mahoney, with the rapid-fire speech and hyperactive hands. I'd never seen anyone smoke so fast either. Not Ned—Brophy.

"I hope you're not going to turn these guys into some kind of heroes," I told her.

"Give me a little credit," she said. "I've got a master's from Columbia Journalism. Besides, they don't need us to turn them into anything. They're already famous, and they're already heroes—with anyone who has the guts to admit it."

My pulse took a step up. "I'm surprised to hear you talk this way. Four people are dead. These punks aren't any heroes."

"Do you know how many people die of exposure on the streets every year?" she said. "Or because they can't afford prescription meds, much less a trip to the doctor? These victims of yours could have made a lot of other people's lives better instead of worse, Detective, but they didn't. They looked out for themselves, period. I'm no fan of vigilante justice, but I do like poetry—and this is just a little bit poetic, don't you think?"

She may have been defensive, but she definitely wasn't stupid. This case could easily turn into a PR nightmare, for exactly the reasons she was describing. Still, I wasn't here to debate. I had my own agenda.

"I'm going to need a list of all your vendors, advertisers, donors, and staff," I told her.

"That's not going to happen," she said right away.

"I'm afraid so. We can wait for the U.S. attorney to process the affidavit, and then for the judge to sign off on a subpoena, and the officer to get it over here. Or I can be out of your hair in about five minutes. Didn't you say something about having a full plate?"

She gave me a glare as she twisted the last of her cigarette ash out the window and pocketed the butt. "It's not like most of these people have regular addresses," she said. "You're never going to find them all."

I shrugged. "All the more reason I have to get started right away."

Chapter 43

I STEPPED OUTSIDE of the churchyard about fifteen minutes later and saw a whole throng of press parked up and down the block.

Then I saw Max Siegel. His back anyway.

He was talking to a dozen or more reporters, blocking the sidewalk and running his mouth.

"Our Cyber Unit's tracking every possible channel," he was saying as I came up closer, "but we're inclined to believe what this appears to be, which is a case of a stolen laptop."

"Excuse me, Agent Siegel?" He and everyone else turned, until I had a face full of microphones and cameras. "Could I have a word, please?"

Siegel grinned from ear to ear. "Of course," he said. "Excuse me, everyone."

I walked back into the churchyard and waited for him to follow. It was at least a little more private.

"What is it, Cross?" he said, coming over.

I turned my back to the press and kept my voice down. "You need to be more careful about who you're talking to."

"Meaning what, exactly?" he said. "I don't follow."

"Meaning, I know Washington better than you do, and I know half of those people out on the curb. Stu Collins? He wants to be the next Woodward *and* Bernstein, and he's got everything but the talent to do it. He *will* misquote you. And Shelly What'shername, with the big red mike? Slams the Bureau every chance she gets. We've had one leak we can't afford already. I don't want to run the risk of another, do you?"

He looked at me as if I'd been speaking Swahili. And then I realized something else.

"Oh Jesus. Please tell me you're not the one who talked to the press about those vehicles in Woodley Park." I stared at him. "Tell me I'm wrong, Siegel."

"You're wrong," he said right away. He took a step toward me then and lowered his voice. "Don't accuse me of things you don't know anything about, Detective. I'm warning you—"

"Shut the hell up!" I shouted at him as much for the "warning" as the fact that he'd stepped up on me. I'd had enough of his crap for one day.

Still, I was instantly sorry I'd yelled. The whole press corps was watching us from the sidewalk. I took a breath and tried again.

"Listen, Max—"

"Give me a little credit, *Alex,*" he said, and stepped back to put some room between us. "I'm not exactly wet behind the ears. Now, I'll bear in mind what you said, but you've got to let me do my job, just like I let you do yours."

He even smiled and put his hand out, as if he were trying to diffuse the situation and not manipulate it. With everyone watching, I went ahead and shook, but my first impressions of Siegel hadn't changed a bit. This was an agent with a giant ego for a blind spot, and unfortunately there was only so much I could do to rein him in.

"Just be careful," I said.

"I'm always careful," he said. "Careful's my middle name."

Chapter 44

"YOU SEE THAT GUY over there, Mitchie? The tall brother talking to the suit?"

"Guy looks like Muhammad Ali?"

"That's the cop, Alex Cross. And I think the other one's FBI. Just a couple of piggies from different farms."

"They don't look too happy to me," Mitch said.

"That's 'cause they're looking for something they're never going to find. We're in the big top now, buddy. Just you and me. There's nothing gonna touch us anymore."

Mitch cracked up, too excited to contain himself.

"When's the next hit, Denny?"

"You're looking at it. We got to spread the good word, get folks on our side. And then—bam! We'll surprise them again when the time's right. That's what this whole e-mail thing's all about—getting the word out."

Mitch nodded like he understood, but he didn't try to

hide his disappointment either. That wasn't the kind of mission he meant.

"Don't worry," Denny told him. "We'll have you back in the saddle before you know it. Meantime—come on. This is gonna be great, trust me."

The printers' truck was just pulling up to the church's side entrance. Word had gotten around that the new issue—the *big* issue—was going to take another few days, so they'd printed up some of last week's paper to tide people over. Anyone who helped unload the truck got thirty extra copies to sell for free. That meant sixty bucks between the two of them, and sixty could go a hell of a long way if you wanted it to.

As they headed over to the truck, a voice exploded out from the churchyard.

"Shut the hell up!" It was Alex Cross.

"Huh-oh," Denny said. "Sounds like trouble in paradise."

"You mean *piggy-dise?*" Mitch said, and this time, Denny was the one cracking up.

Chapter 45

THEY SET UP shop at a construction zone near Logan Circle, and by nightfall, their pockets were bulging with singles and loose change, and their stack of newspapers was gone.

The extra cash got them a couple of nice cheesesteaks, a fifth of Jim Beam, a pack of ciggies for each, a pair of loose joints from a guy they knew in Farragut Square, and, best of all, a flop for the night at a cheap motel on Rhode Island Avenue.

Denny brought the old boom box up from the car. It didn't have any batteries, but they could plug it in here and have some tuneage for their little celebration.

It was sweet, just to lie back on a real mattress for a change, copping a buzz, with no worries about lights-out or who might be stealing your shit in the middle of the night.

When some old Lynyrd Skynyrd came on the radio, Denny perked up his ears. It had been a long time; Mitch probably didn't even know this one.

"*'Cause I'm as free as a bird, now...*"

"You hear that, Mitchie? Listen to the lyrics. That's the shit right there."

"What is, Denny?"

"Freedom, man. The difference between us and them crooks we been taking down.

"You think people like that are free? Nohow, no way. They don't wipe their damn noses without checking with some committee on dumbass details first. That ain't freedom. That's a fuckin' anchor around their necks."

"And a target on their asses!" Mitch started giggling like a little kid. He was definitely feeling the weed. His eyes looked like a couple of pink marbles, and he'd downed the lion's share of the Beam, too.

"Here you go, man. Drink up," Denny said, and handed over the bottle again. Then he lay back and just listened to Lynyrd Skynyrd for a while, counting cracks in the ceiling until Mitch started to snore.

"Yo, Mitchie?" he said.

There was no response. Denny got up and prodded him on the shoulder.

"You out cold, buddy? Looks like it. Sounds like it."

Mitch just rolled halfway over and kept sawing wood, a little louder now.

"All right, then. Denny's got a little errand to run. You sleep tight, man."

He stepped into his black engineer boots and picked up the room key, and a second later he was gone.

Chapter 46

DENNY HURRIEDLY WALKED DOWN Eleventh Street and over on M to Thomas Circle. It felt good to get out on his own, without Mitch on his back for a change. The kid could be a lot of fun, but he was a real piece of luggage, too.

Just past the Washington Plaza Hotel, on the relative quiet of Vermont Avenue, a black Lincoln Town Car was parked under a flowering crab apple.

Denny walked up the opposite side of the street and crossed over at N, then came back down. When he reached the car, he opened the back door and got in.

"You're late. Where have you been?"

His contact was always the same guy, with the same stiff attitude. He went by Zachary, whatever his real name might have been. It didn't matter. To Denny—whose name was *not* Denny—this asshole was nothing more than a well-paid mule in a Brioni suit.

"These things don't run on a fixed schedule," Denny said. "You need to get that through your head."

Zachary ignored the tone. He was like Spock, this guy, the way he never showed emotion. "Any issues?" he asked. "Anything I need to know about?"

"None," Denny said. "I don't see any reason not to proceed to the next phase."

"What about your shooter?"

"Mitch? You tell me, partner. You're the ones who vetted him."

"How is he in the *field,* Denny?" Zachary pressed.

"Exactly the ringer I thought he'd be. As far as he's concerned, this is the *Mitch and Denny Show,* nothing else. I've got him completely under control."

"Yes, well, all the same, we'd like to take some further precautions."

He gave Denny two folded sheets from his inside breast pocket. Each one had a simple map printed on it, with a handwritten name and address beneath, and a single color photograph paper-clipped to the front.

"Hang on," Denny said once he'd seen them. "We never discussed anything like this."

"We never set any parameters at all," Zachary said. "Isn't that the whole point? I hope you're not going to start quibbling *now.*"

"That's not what I said," Denny replied. "I just don't like surprises, that's all."

Zachary's laugh was less than convincing. "Oh, come on, *'Denny.'* You're the king of surprises, aren't you? You've got all of Washington on tenterhooks."

Zachary reached over the front seat and took a canvas pouch from the driver, then laid it on the padded armrest between them. This was a pay-as-you-go contract, and Denny's price, as always, had been nonnegotiable.

Inside the pouch were six unnumbered ten-ounce gold ingots, each with a minimum millesimal fineness of 999. Nothing was more portable, and the fact that the gold was hard to come by only helped Denny weed out the wrong kind of client.

Denny took a few minutes to memorize the next assignment. Then he handed the sheets back to Zachary and picked up the pouch. Once he'd wrapped the goods in an old Safeway bag from his jacket pocket, he opened the car door to go.

"One other thing," Zachary told him as he started to get out. "It's a little close in here. You might think about a shower next time."

Denny closed the door behind him and walked away, back into the night.

I clean up just fine, he said to himself, *but you'll always be a lackey asshole.*

Chapter 47

THE DOORBELL RANG in the middle of our dinner the next day. Usually it was the phone, and was almost always one of Jannie's girlfriends. And she wondered why I didn't want to get her a cell phone.

"I'll get it!" she chirped, and jumped right up from the table.

"Five dollars says it's Terry Ann," I said.

Bree put her money down on the table. "I'm going with Alexis."

Whoever it was had obviously been cleared by Rakeem.

But almost right away, Jannie was back. Her face looked totally blank, almost shell-shocked.

And then Christine Johnson walked into my kitchen.

"Mommy!" Ali knocked over his chair getting out of it. Then he ran over to be scooped up in his mother's arms.

"Look at you! Look at you!"

Christine hugged him tight and smiled at the rest of us

over his shoulder—that brilliant smile I remembered so well, the one that said all was right with the world, even when it wasn't even close to that.

"My God," she said as her eyes went around the table. "You all look like you've seen a ghost!"

In a way, that's how I felt. A few years ago, at Christine's request, we'd signed a stipulation reversing legal custody of Ali to me. She saw him at her home in Seattle for thirty days every summer and fifteen days during the school year. My only condition had been that we stick to the agreement, for everyone's sake. So far, that's what we'd done... *until tonight anyway.*

"I can't believe this boy!" She set Ali down and looked him over again. Her eyes were glassy with tears. "How did you get so much bigger since the last time I saw you?"

"I don't know!" Ali squealed, and looked over at us.

I smiled for his sake. "Look who it is, bud! Can you believe it?" I stared at Christine. "What a surprise."

"Guilty," she said, still smiling. "Hello, Regina."

"Christine." Nana's voice was tight and controlled. It sounded like a slow boil to me.

"And you must be Bree. I'm so glad to finally meet you. I'm Christine."

Bree was fantastic, no surprise. She got right up, walked over to Christine, and gave her a hug. "You've got an amazing son," she said. Typical Bree—she can always find a way to speak the truth in any situation, even one as uncomfortable as this.

"Mommy, you want to see my room?" Ali was already tugging on her hand, leading her toward the hall and stairs.

"I sure do," she said, and looked back at me—for *permission,* I think. In fact, everyone was staring at me now.

"How about we all three go?" I said, and got up to follow them out of the kitchen.

At the bottom of the stairs, Christine stopped and turned to me. Ali ran up ahead of us.

"I know what you're thinking," she said.

"Do you?"

"Honestly, it's nothing more than it seems, Alex. Just a surprise visit. I've got a conference in DC this week—and I couldn't stay away from Ali."

I didn't know whether to believe her or not. Christine had shown herself to be a very changeable person over the years, including the way she fought for custody so hard and then gave it up just as quickly.

"You could have called first," I said. "You *should* have called, Christine."

Ali practically screamed from the top of the stairs, he was so excited. *"Come on, you guys!"*

"Here we come, little man!" I called to him. As we started up, I spoke low to Christine. "This is going to be a onetime thing. Nothing more than that. Okay?"

"Absolutely," she said, and reached back to give my arm a squeeze. "Cross my heart and hope to die."

Chapter 48

THE NEXT DAY was jam-packed for me, and I honestly didn't give Christine much thought as my morning and most of my afternoon slipped away.

I saw both Bronson and Rebecca at their respective hospitals, performed some follow-up interviews in Woodley Park, did a consultation with the DA's office on a separate case, and, finally, took some much-needed desk time to try and chip away at my stack of overdue reports.

Then, around three, I was picking up a late sandwich at the Firehook near the Daly Building—and I got a call from Ali's school.

"Dr. Cross? It's Mindy Templeton at Sojourner Truth." Mindy was a school secretary and had been there for years, including during Christine's tenure as principal.

"I feel a little awkward about this, but Christine Johnson's here to pick up Alexander, and she's not on his caregiver list. I just wanted to get your permission before we let him go."

"What?"

I didn't mean to raise my voice so loud, but suddenly everyone in the coffee shop was turning to look at me. A second later, I was out on the sidewalk, still talking on my cell. "Mindy, the answer is no. Christine may not take Ali, do you understand?"

"Yes, of course."

"I don't mean to alarm you," I said more evenly. "If you could just please ask Christine to wait, I'll be there as soon as I can. Maybe fifteen minutes. I'm on my way right now."

When I hung up, I was already running for the parking garage, my mind completely unsettled. What the hell was Christine thinking?

Had she been planning this all along?

And, for that matter, what *was* she planning?

As far as I was concerned, I couldn't get to the school fast enough.

Chapter 49

"I'M HIS MOTHER, for God's sake! I wasn't doing anything wrong! I'm not one of your stalkers."

Christine was defensive from the minute I got there. We had it out in the hall while Ali waited in the school office.

"Christine, there are rules about this kind of thing—rules you used to abide by. You can't just show up and expect to—"

"What are you saying?" she snapped. "Brianna Stone, this woman I hardly even know, can pick my son up from school and I *can't*? Half the teachers here still know who I am!"

"You're not listening," I said. I couldn't tell if she was trying to squirm out of this or if she truly believed she was in the right. "What exactly were you planning to do with him anyway?"

"Oh, don't look at me like that," she said dismissively. "I was going to call."

"But you didn't. Again."

"When I got him out of school, I mean. We were going to go for ice cream, and he would have been home for dinner. Now he's all confused and upset. It didn't have to be this way, Alex."

It was like listening to an out-of-tune piano. Everything just seemed a little off. Even her clothes. She was dressed to the nines today, in a fitted white linen suit, sling-back heels, and full makeup. In fact, she looked absolutely gorgeous. But who was she trying to impress?

I took a deep breath and tried again to get through to her.

"What happened to your conference?" I said.

For the first time, Christine looked away from me. She stared over at one of the bulletin boards in the hall. It was covered in crayon drawings of cars, planes, trains, and boats, with the word TRANSPORTATION in construction paper letters across the top.

"Did you see Ali's?" she said, pointing at his sailboat. *Of course I had seen it.*

"Christine, look at me. Did you even have a conference?"

She crossed her arms and blinked several times as she met my eyes again.

"Well, what if I didn't? Is it such a crime that I missed my son? That I thought he might want to see his mommy and daddy in the same room, just for once? God, Alex, what's happened to you?"

It seemed as if there were an answer for everything here, except my questions. The only part I really trusted was that she loved and missed Ali. But that wasn't enough.

"Okay, here's what's going to happen," I said. "We're going

to go get some ice cream. You can say your good-byes after that, and then you'll see him again in July, like always. Anything else, and we're going back to mediation. That's a promise, Christine. Please don't test me on this."

To my surprise, she smiled. "Make it dinner. Just the three of us, and then I'll get on my plane to Seattle like a good little girl. How's that?"

"I can't," I said.

Her mouth tightened into a hard, straight line again. "Can't? Or won't?"

The answer was *both,* but before I could say anything else, the office door opened and there was Ali. He looked so all alone, and scared.

"When can we go?" he wanted to know.

Christine scooped him up just as she had the night before. To her credit, there was none of the thunderstorm in her eyes that I'd seen a second ago.

"Guess what, honey? We're going to go out for some ice cream. You, me, and Daddy, right now. What do you think of that?"

"Can I get two scoops?" he asked right away.

I couldn't help laughing—for real. "Always the broker, aren't you, little man?" I said. "Yeah, two scoops. Why not?"

As we left the school, Ali took each of us by the hand, one on either side, and it was smiles all around. But it still wasn't lost on me that Christine hadn't committed to a thing.

Chapter 50

BY THE TIME I finally got to the Hoover Building for my five thirty meeting, it was quarter after six. I signed in and took the elevator.

The Information Sharing and Analysis Center where Agent Patel worked could have been anywhere in corporate America, with its ugly tan-and-mauve cubicle maze, low ceiling tiles, and fluorescent box lights. The only tip-off was the endless computers, at least one internal and two outside machines at every desk. The real sci-fi-looking stuff—the enormous servers and surveillance banks—was elsewhere on the floor, behind closed doors.

Patel jumped when I knocked on the half wall of her work space.

"Alex! Jesus! You scared me."

"Sorry," I said. "And sorry I'm so late. I don't suppose

Agent Siegel's still around?" I wasn't keen to end my day with him, but in the name of collaboration, here I was.

"He got tired of waiting," she said. "We're supposed to meet him in the SIOC conference room."

She called his extension and left a message that we were on our way, but when we got there—surprise, surprise—no Siegel. We waited a few more minutes and then started our meeting without him. Fine with me.

Chapter 51

PATEL QUICKLY BROUGHT me up to speed on the *True Press* e-mails. Actually, there wasn't that much to tell, at least not at this point in her investigation.

"Based on the header, the IP address, and what I got from the registry over at Georgetown, Jayson Wexler's account was open and active at the time both messages were sent," she told me.

"Which is not to say that Wexler sent them himself," I said.

"Not at all. Just that they either originated from or somehow passed through his account."

"Passed through?"

"It's possible someone used an anonymous remailer from a remote location, but really they'd have no reason to. A stolen laptop that never turns up is a perfect dead end, forensically speaking. You're better off looking for any witnesses to the theft itself."

"We canvassed up, down, and sideways where Wexler claims the computer was taken," I told her. "Didn't get anywhere. And the closest surveillance cameras are DDOT's, over on K Street. There's nothing from the park at all. No one saw a thing—which is a little odd."

Patel sat back, twiddling a pen between her fingers. "So should I keep going? Because there's more bad news."

I ran my hand over my mouth and jaw, an old tic of mine. "You're just full of sunshine today, aren't you?"

"Technically, this is Siegel's piece, so you can't hold it against me," she said. I liked working with Patel. She seemed to keep her sense of humor no matter what, and the humor was dark and deep.

"Go ahead," I said. "I can take whatever you're dishing out here."

"It's about this 'Patriot' moniker they used in one of the e-mails. Ever since *True Press* ran the story, the name seems to have stuck, in a really scary way. We've got people at both ends of the spectrum foaming at the mouth, from the radical antiglobalization types all the way over to the hard-right survivalists. The Bureau's already working up contingencies around the possibility of tribute killings."

She ran a simple open-source search on her laptop. Less than a minute later, I was looking through pages of results—websites, blogs, vlogs, chat rooms, mainstream commentary, fringe press—all of it giving credence to the supposed "patriotism" behind these sniper murders.

I'd certainly seen this kind of thing before. Kyle Craig alone had legions of fans, or disciples, as he liked to call them. But Patel was right. This had the potential to be something else again—a whole grassroots movement of people who saw nothing less than America at stake, and nothing short of wholesale violence as the only solution with a chance of working.

"Best way to stir the crazy pot?" she said over my shoulder. "Wrap your dogma in an American flag and wait to see who bites. Like I said—*scary*."

Chapter 52

AROUND SEVEN THIRTY, Patel and I finally got up to go. As we did, though, she turned away from the door and toward me. The sudden look in her eyes was all but unmistakable—and it was scary in a whole other way.

"Have you ever had homemade chana masala?" she asked.

Still, I didn't want to be too presumptuous. "Homemade? Never."

"Because I'm a pretty good cook, despite appearances." She gestured at her nondescript gray slacks and white blouse. "I think everyone here assumes I'm just some wonk who goes home to her seven cats and a Lean Cuisine every night."

"I doubt that," I said. Patel had always struck me as a classic diamond in the rough. She was the kind of woman who arrived at the office Christmas party all done up and dropped every jaw in the room.

"So, my car's in the shop," she went on. "I was thinking if

you could save me the cab fare home, I'd pay you back with dinner." Then she *really* threw me. Patel reached over and put her hand on top of mine. "Maybe even dessert," she said. "What do you think?"

"I think you're full of surprises," I said, and we both laughed, a little nervously. "Listen, Anjali—"

"Oh God." Her hand fell away. "It's never good when they start with your name."

"I'm in a relationship. We're getting married."

She nodded and started gathering up her stuff. "You know what they say about all the good men, right? *Taken or gay*. In fact, that's going to be the title of my memoir. Think it will sell?"

This time we laughed for real. It cut right through the tension, which I think was nice for both of us.

"I appreciate the invitation," I said, and meant it. If this were some other time in my life, I definitely would have been eating chana masala that night. Maybe dessert, too. "And I can still give you that ride if you want."

"Don't worry about it." She tucked her laptop under her arm and held the conference room door for me. "If I'm not cooking, I'm going to stick around here and get some more work done. Meanwhile, if you wouldn't mind forgetting we ever had this conversation—"

"What conversation?" I gave her my best wide-eyed innocent face on the way out. "I can't remember a thing."

Chapter 53

AFTER SOME REHEATED supper that night, and long after the kids had gone to bed, I got a call from Christine.

The second her name came up on the caller ID, I felt torn in a big way. I couldn't just ignore her, but the last thing I wanted right now was more talk. The only reason I picked up in the end was to keep her from possibly coming over to the house again.

"What is it, Christine?"

Right away, I could hear she was crying. "It was wrong, what you did today, Alex. You didn't have to push me away like that."

I was already walking from the bedroom up to my office, and waited until I'd closed the door behind me to go on.

"I kind of did," I said. "You showed up out of the blue and, even worse, you lied. More than once."

"I only lied because I thought our son deserved to see his family together!"

It was as if we'd started fighting in record time, which was saying something for us. The whole thing made me feel exhausted. It brought back the terribleness I'd felt during the court case over Ali.

"Ali sees his family together every day," I said. "Just not his mother."

She sobbed again. "How can you say a thing like that?"

"I'm not trying to hurt you, Christine. I'm just telling it like it is." My patience, meanwhile, was hanging at the other end of a very thin thread. Christine had brought this on herself with her terrible inconsistency as a mother.

"Well, don't worry, because you got your wish. I'm at the airport."

"My *wish* is that we could all be happy with the choices we've made," I said.

"Just as long as you're happy first, isn't that right, Alex? Isn't that how it's always been?"

And then my thread snapped.

"*Do you remember leaving me?*" I said. "Do you remember how I begged you to stay in Washington? Do you remember leaving Ali? Damn it, does any of that even register with you anymore?"

"Don't you curse at me!" she shouted back, but I wasn't finished.

"So now what? You think just by showing up here, you can change everything that's happened since then? It doesn't work that way, Christine, and I wouldn't change it if I could!"

"No." Her voice was constricted now. Tight as a drum. "Apparently not."

Then she hung up on me. I was stunned but also a little

relieved. Maybe this was some kind of test, to see if I'd call back, but I wasn't even remotely tempted. I sat on the office couch, staring at the ceiling and trying to collect myself again.

It was almost shocking, to think how much I'd loved Christine, once. Back then, there was nothing I wanted more than for all of us to be a family forever. Now, it felt like someone else's history.

And I just wanted Christine out of my life.

Chapter 54

IT WAS JUST short of midnight when Agent Anjali Patel stepped out to the curb on E Street in front of the Hoover Building, craning her neck, searching for a cab. As soon as he saw her, Max Siegel pulled around the corner and lowered the passenger-side window.

"Someone call for a taxi?"

She gave him a nice view of cleavage as she bent down to see who it was. "Max? What are you doing here? It's late."

"Sorry about earlier," he said. "Had to run out unexpectedly. I just came back for my car, but maybe I could give you a ride and you can fill me in."

Her glance up the street said everything. Not a cab in sight, not much traffic at all.

Max Siegel's coworkers seemed to prefer him at a distance, which was exactly according to plan. Distance afforded him the privacy he needed and could always be broached if and when he wanted it to be. Like right now.

"Come on," he said. "I won't bite. I won't even talk about Cross behind his back. Promise."

"Um...sure," she said with a practiced smile, and got in.

Her perfume was lemony, he noticed. Or maybe it was her shampoo. Nice anyway. Feminine. She gave him an address in Shaw.

Then she proceeded to chatter on about the case, making sure to fill up any spaces that might have otherwise been left open to the awkwardness of small talk between them.

Siegel drove fast, goosing the yellow lights where he could. He hadn't been with a woman since the real estate agent, and damned if he wasn't getting a little hard just thinking about her.

When he turned onto her block, he mashed the gas pedal once more and then coasted to a stop in front of a dark storefront just past her yellow-brick townhome.

"Hey, that was it," she said, looking back. "You missed my place."

Chapter 55

KYLE LOOKED BACK, too. The block was still clear of any traffic or pedestrians.

"Oops. Sorry. My fault."

"All right, well..." Her fingers were already on the door handle. "Thanks for the ride."

"That's it?" he said.

"Pardon? I don't think I follow."

"See, this is supposed to be the part where you offer to cook dinner for me," he said.

Her face fell. She squinted at him in the dark, probably not ready to believe this was anything more than a weird coincidence. "I'm not much of a cook, Max."

"Oh, I don't know about that," he said. "Ever seen one of these before?" He reached into his breast pocket and took out a small black box, no bigger than a lighter. "It's one of those

GSM ultraminiature transmitters. You can stick them practically anywhere."

Patel gave the thing a cursory glance. "Yeah?" she said. Her discomfort, and her attempt to hide it, were absolutely delicious.

"Let's just say I made the meeting between you and Cross after all."

Again, her energy shifted. Now she was pissed off and a little embarrassed—too much to be scared anymore.

"You bugged our meeting? Jesus, Max, why the hell would you do something like that?"

"That's your first good question," he said. "How much time do you have for an answer?" But before she could say a word, he put a hand to her lips. "Wait, I'll tell you myself. You have no time at all."

The ice pick, his old favorite, was up and through her larynx before Patel could even scream. Still, her jaw dropped silently open with the effort.

He was on her now, his mouth covering hers, his hand over her nose—a literal kiss of death, but just an ordinary kiss between two lovers in a car to anyone who might have glanced out his window. Her strength, her desire to live, were nothing compared to his. Even the blood loss was minimal—Patel had been too polite to ask about the plastic seat covers in the car.

Or the raincoat Max Siegel was wearing on this dry night.

Once she'd stopped moving altogether, his excitement only grew. He would have loved to climb into the backseat with her while her lips were still warm and her belly still so soft to the touch. He wanted to be inside her right now. Hell, he owned her.

But it would have been a foolish risk, and an unnecessary one at that. He had decided hours ago that tonight was going to be an exception to the usual rules. He'd earned it after all, and this game was his to change. In fact, there were a lot of changes just around the corner.

But first, Anjali Patel was coming home with him—for a sleepover.

Book Three

MULTIPLICITY

Chapter 56

SAMPSON KNEW I was usually awake by five, or even earlier, but it wouldn't have made a difference today. I could tell he was already at work from the street sounds in the background and the tension in his voice.

"I need a favor, Alex. Maybe a big one."

Instinctively, I started eating my eggs a little faster while Nana gave me the hairy eyeball. Very early and very late calls in our house are never a good thing.

"Go ahead," I said. "I'm listening. Nana is watching me listen. I can't tell if her evil eye is for you, me, or both of us."

"Oh, it's for both of you," Nana said in a low voice that could have been mistaken for a growl.

"We've got a homicide in Franklin Square. A John Doe. It looks a lot like that freaky one I had before, over in Washington Circle?"

My fork stopped in midair. "*With the numbers?*"

"That's the one. Any chance I can get you over here for a consult before things heat up too much?"

"I'm on my way."

John and I never keep track of who owes how many favors to who. Our unwritten rule is, if you need me, I'm there. *But make sure you need me.*

A few minutes later, I was knotting my tie on the way down the back stairs toward the garage. It was practically still dark out, but light enough to show a mass of slate-gray nothingness overhead—cloudy with a chance of a shit storm.

Based on what I remembered of Sampson's earlier case, this was exactly the kind of thing MPD could not afford to be investigating right now.

Months ago, a young homeless man had been found beaten to death, with a series of numbers carved carefully across his forehead. It probably would have hit every headline inside the Beltway—*if the poor man hadn't been a street junkie.* Even at the department, the case hadn't generated much heat, which wasn't exactly fair, but you could drive yourself crazy over "fair" in this capital city of ours.

Now it had happened again. This was a whole new ball game. With the sniper case raging, MPD brass were going to have a hair trigger on anything even remotely sensitive. They'd want to flip this thing up to Major Case Squad before the morning was out.

I figured that was why John called. If the case got transferred to my unit, I could say I was already consulting on it, ask to take the lead, and then put Sampson back in charge. Just our version of creative accounting, and God knows it wouldn't have been the first time.

Chapter 57

THE NUMBERS KILLER—Jesus God—not now.

When I got to Franklin Square, the entrances were already cordoned off. Additional units were parked on the longer K and I Street sides of the rectangular park, although the action seemed to be just off of Thirteenth, where Sampson was right now waving me over.

"Sugar," he said when I came up close to him, "you're a lifesaver. I know the timing sucks."

"Let's go take a look."

Two crime-scene techs in blue Windbreakers were working inside the tape line, along with a medical examiner whom I easily recognized from behind.

Porter Henning's unofficial nickname is "Portly," and, widthwise, he makes "Man Mountain" Sampson look practically dainty. I've never been sure how Porter squeezes into some of those tighter crime scenes, but he's also one of the most insightful MEs I've worked with.

"Alex Cross. Gracing us with your presence," he said as I walked up.

"Blame this guy." I thumbed at Sampson but then stopped short when I saw the victim.

People say the extreme stuff is my specialty, which it kind of is, but there is no getting used to human mutilation. The victim had been left faceup in a clump of bushes. The multiple layers of dirty clothes marked him as homeless, maybe even someone who slept right there in the park. And while there were signs of a severe beating, it was the numbers carved into his forehead that made the biggest impression. As in the previous murder, it was almost too bizarre.

2^30402457-1

"Are those the same numbers as the last time?" I asked.

"Similar," Sampson told me, "but no, not the same."

"And we don't know who the victim is?"

John shook his head. "I've got guys asking around, but most of the bench crashers made themselves scarce as soon as we showed up. It's not exactly a trust fest around here, you know?"

I knew, I knew. This was part of what made homeless deaths so hard to trace.

"There's also the shelter just a few blocks up on Thirteenth Street," John went on. "I'm going to head up there after this, see if anyone knows anything about this man."

The scene itself was hard to interpret. There were fresh footprints in the dirt, flat soles as opposed to boots or sneakers. Also, some kind of grooved tracks, maybe a shopping cart, but that could have been completely unrelated. Homeless folks rolled through here all day, every day. All night, too.

"What else?" I asked. "Porter? You find out anything yet?"

"Yeah. Found out I'm not getting any younger. Other than that, I'd say cause of death is tension pneumothorax, although the first strikes were probably here, here, and here."

He pointed at the crushed side of the dead man's head, where a pink ooze had filled his ear. "Basal skull fracture, jawbone, zygomatic arch, the whole frickin' works. If there's any silver lining, the poor guy was probably out cold when it happened. There's track marks all over him."

"All just like the last time," Sampson said. "Has to be the same perp."

"What about the cutting on the forehead?" It was the cleanest knife work I'd ever seen. The digits were easily readable, the cuts shallow and precise. "Any initial thoughts about the cuts, Porter?"

"This is nothing," he said. "Check out the real masterpiece."

He reached down and rolled the young man onto his side, then lifted up the back of his shirt.

$$\zeta(s) = \sum_{n=1}^{\infty} \frac{1}{n^s}$$

"You've got to be kidding."

The math equation covered the whole area from his waistband to his shoulder blades. I'd never seen anything like it. Not in this context anyway. Sampson motioned the scene photographer over to get a shot.

"This is new," John said. "The last numbers were just on

the face. Makes me wonder if our guy's been practicing. Maybe other bodies we haven't found."

"Well, he definitely wanted you to see this one," Porter told us. "That's the other thing. There's not near enough blood here for the amount of blunt force trauma. Someone pounded this kid, then brought him here, and *then* did the fancy knife work."

"Doo-doo, doo-doo." The photographer let out a snatch of *The Twilight Zone* theme before Sampson stared him down. "Sorry, man, but...damn, I'm glad I don't have your jobs today."

Him and everyone else.

"So the question is, why bring him here?" Sampson said. "What's he trying to say to us? To whoever?"

Porter shrugged. "Anyone speak math?"

"I know a prof at Howard," I said. "Sara Wilson. You remember her?" John nodded, still staring down at those numbers. "I'll give her a call if you want me to. Maybe we can head up there this afternoon."

"I'd appreciate it, that'd be good."

So much for my quick consult. I had no time for this, but God help me, now that I'd seen the damage this perp was capable of, I wanted a piece of him.

Chapter 58

I'D KNOWN SARA WILSON for more than twenty years. She and my first wife, Maria, were freshman roommates at Georgetown and remained good friends until Maria's death. Now it was just Christmas cards and the occasional chance meeting between us, but Sara hugged me hello when she saw me and still remembered Sampson by name—first and last.

Her tiny cell of an office was in the unimaginatively named Academic Support Building B on the Howard campus. It was crammed with bookshelves to the ceiling, a big sloppy desk just like mine, and a huge whiteboard covered in mathspeak, in different colors of dry-erase marker.

Sampson took the windowsill, and I sat down in the lone guest chair.

"I know you've got exams coming up," I said. "Thanks for seeing us."

"I'm happy to help, Alex. If I *can* help?" She tipped a pair of rimless specs off her forehead and looked down at the page I'd just handed her. It had transcripts of the numbers and equations that were found on the victims. We also had crime-scene photos with us, but there was no reason to share the gory details if we didn't have to.

As soon as she looked at the page, Sara pointed at the more complicated of the figures.

"This is Riemann's zeta function," she said. It was the one we'd seen that morning on John Doe's back. "It's theoretical mathematics. Does this really have something to do with one of your cases?"

Sampson nodded. "Without going into too much detail, we're wondering why this might be on someone's mind. Maybe obsessively."

"It's on a lot of people's minds, including mine," she said. "Zeta's the core of Riemann's hypothesis, which is arguably the biggest unsolved problem in mathematics today. In the year two thousand, the Clay Institute offered a million dollars to anyone who could prove it."

"Sorry, prove what?" I said. "You're talking to a couple of high school algebra cutups here."

Sara sat up straighter, getting into it now. "Basically, it's about describing the frequency and distribution of all prime numbers to infinity, which is why it's so difficult. The hypothesis has been checked against the first one and a half billion instances, but then you have to ask yourself—what's one and a half billion compared to infinity?"

"Exactly what I was about to ask myself," Sampson said, straight-faced.

Sara laughed. She looked almost exactly the same as she

did back when we were all pooling our pocket change for pitchers of beer. The same quick smile, the same long hair flowing down her back.

"How about the other two sets of numbers?" I asked. These were the ones that had been carved into the victims' foreheads.

Sara glanced down for a second, then turned to her laptop and googled them from memory.

"Yeah, right here. I thought so. Mersenne forty-two and forty-three. Two of the biggest known prime numbers to date."

I scribbled some of this down while she spoke, not even sure what I was writing. "Okay, next question," I said. "So what?"

"So what?"

"Let's say Riemann's hypothesis gets proved. What happens then? Why does anyone care?"

Sara weighed the questions before she answered. "There's two things, I suppose. Certainly, there are some practical applications. Encryption could be revolutionized with something like this. Writing and breaking code would be a whole new game, so whoever you're chasing might have that in mind."

"And number two?" I asked.

She shrugged. "The whole because-it's-there aspect. It's a theoretical Mount Everest—the difference being that people have actually been to the top of Everest. Nobody's ever done this before. Riemann himself had a nervous breakdown, and that guy John Nash from *A Beautiful Mind*? He was obsessed with it."

Sara leaned forward in her chair and held up the page of numbers so we could see them. "Let's put it this way," she said. "If you're looking for something that could really drive a mathematician crazy, this is as good a place to start as any. *Are you, Alex?* Looking for a crazy mathematician?"

Chapter 59

MITCH AND DENNY left DC in the old white Suburban before the sun had even come up that morning, with Denny at the wheel as always. He'd handed Mitch some easily digestible bullshit the day before, all about reconnecting with his people now that he was a "real man," and Mitch had gobbled it up, even taken it to heart.

In truth, the less Mitch knew about the reason for this little road trip, the better.

It was about five hours to Johnsonburg, PA, or, as Denny thought of it when they got there, *Johnsonburg, PU.* The paper mills here put up the same sour stench as the ones he'd grown up around, on the Androscoggin. It was an unexpected little reminder of his own white-trash roots, the ones he'd ripped out of the ground twenty years ago. He'd been around the world more than once since then, and this small town was as close to going home again as he ever cared to get.

"What if she don't want to talk to me, Denny?" Mitch asked for about the eighty-fifth time that morning. The closer they got, the faster his knee jacked up and down, and he clutched at the stuffed yellow monkey on his lap like he wanted to strangle the damn thing. It already had a tear in its fur where Mitch had pulled off the security tag at a Target in Altoona, right before he'd stuck it under his jacket.

"Just try to relax, Mitchie. If she don't want you here, it's her loss. You're an American hero, man. Don't ever forget that. You are a bona fide hero."

They came to a stop outside a bleak little brick duplex on a block of bleak little brick duplexes. The front lawn looked like the place where old toys went to die, and there was a rusty blue Escort heaped in the driveway.

"Seems pretty nice," Denny said with a frown. "Let's go see if someone's home."

Chapter 60

SOMEONE SURE WAS. You could hear the music coming right through the front door, some kind of Beyoncé shit or something like that. It took a couple of rounds of knocking before the volume finally went down.

A second later, the door opened.

Alicia Taylor was prettier than her surveillance photo, by far. Denny wondered for a second how Mitch had ever bagged her in the first place, but then Alicia saw who it was on her stoop, and her face got ugly and nasty real quick. She stayed behind the screen door.

"What the hell are you doing here?" she said by way of hello.

"Hey, Alicia." Mitch's voice was husky with fear. He seemed a little flustered, and he held up the stuffed monkey. "I, uh... brought a present."

Behind Alicia, a little waist-high girl was giving them

wide eyes from under her braided and beaded bangs. She smiled when she saw the toy, but those lights went out as soon as her mother spoke again.

"Destiny, go to your room."

"Who is that, Momma?"

"No questions, baby. Just do as I say. *Right now.* Go ahead."

Once the girl had disappeared back into the duplex, Denny figured it was time to insert himself into the mix. "How you doing?" he said, all friendly-like. "I'm Mitch's buddy and expert driver, but you can call me Denny."

Her eyes flitted his way just long enough to throw a few poison darts. "Mister, I don't have to call you shit," she said, and then turned back to Mitch. "And I asked you what the hell you're doing here. I don't want you around here. Neither does Destiny."

"Go ahead, man," Denny said, and nudged him in the shoulder.

Mitch pulled a small envelope out of his pocket. "It ain't much, but here." Inside was a twenty, two fives, and fifty rumpled singles. He tried to hand it to her right through the broken screen, but she shoved it back at him.

"Oh, *hell no!* You think that little envelope gon' make you a daddy?" Her voice dropped. "You're just an old mistake, Mitch, that's all. Far as Destiny's concerned, her daddy is dead, and that's how we gon' keep it. Now, are you two getting off my property—or am I calling the police?"

Mitch's round face looked about as long as it could get.

"At least take this," he said.

He opened the screen door, and when she stepped back fast, he dropped the stuffed monkey on the floor at her feet. It was pathetic to watch. Besides, Denny had seen all he needed to.

"Alrighty, then," he said, "we got a long drive back to Cleveland, so we'll just be on our way to O-hi-o. Sorry to bother you, ma'am. I guess this little visit wasn't such a good idea after all."

"You think?" she said, and slammed the door in both their faces.

On the way down the walk, Mitch looked like he wanted to cry.

"It sucks, Denny. She'd be proud if she knew what we were doing. I wanted to tell her so bad—"

"But you didn't." Denny threw an arm around his shoulder and spoke close. "You stuck to the mission, Mitchie, and that's what counts. Now come on—let's hit ourselves a Taco Bell on the way out of town."

While he walked around to the driver's side of the car, Denny reached inside his jacket and flipped the safety on the Walther nine millimeter holstered there. As it turned out, Mitch was more of a hero than he'd ever get to know. He'd just saved his own daughter's life.

Alicia may have been fairly cunty, but she was clueless; and there was no way in hell Denny was going to shoot a five-year-old girl who didn't even know who Mitch was. The whole point of the assignment was threat assessment, and there was no threat here.

If the man back in DC didn't like it, he could find himself another contractor.

Chapter 61

ACTUALLY, IT HAD BEEN kind of a fun day—relaxing and surprising, especially Mitch's pretty ex-wife. It was just after dark when they reached Arlington that night. Mitch had spent most of the trip watching the side of the road, sighing and tossing around like someone who couldn't sleep.

But now, as they came up on the Roosevelt Bridge, he sat bolt upright, looking straight ahead through the windshield.

"What the hell is that, Denny?"

Cars were backed up on the highway in either direction. There were cruisers with lights flashing on both sides, and uniformed officers out on the road. It wasn't just a traffic jam, and it didn't look like an accident either.

"Traffic checkpoint," Denny said, realizing what it was.

The city had been instituting them for a few years now, but only in the really violent neighborhoods. He'd never seen anything like this before.

"Something big must have happened. Like, really big."

"I don't like this, Denny." Mitch's knee started bouncing. "Ain't they been looking for a Suburban since we made that hit in Woodley Park?"

"Yeah, but a dark-blue or black one. Besides, they're stopping everyone, see? Hell, I wish we had some papers to sell in this traffic," Denny said, as upbeat as he could make it. "Might earn back some of that gas money we spent today."

Mitch wasn't buying it. He stayed all hunched down and tense as they crawled along toward the head of the line.

Then, out of the blue, Mitch said, "Where *did* we get the gas money, Denny? And that envelope for Alicia? I don't get how we're paying for this."

Denny gritted his teeth. The one thing Mitch could usually be counted on for was a distinct lack of probing questions.

"You know what happened to that curious cat, don't you, Mitchie? D-E-D, dead," he said. "You just focus on the big stuff and let me handle the rest. Including this."

They were coming up on the checkpoint now, and an NBA-size officer motioned them forward.

"License and registration, please."

Denny reached into the glove compartment and handed them over without a blink. Here's where it paid to work for the right people. "Denny Humboldt" had a record as clean as a show cat's ass—even that parking ticket would be history by now.

"What's going on, Officer?" he asked. "It looks big."

The cop answered with a question, while his eyes played over the piles of junk in the backseat. "Where are you two coming from?"

"Johnsonburg, PA," Denny said. "Nowhere you ever want to go, by the way. The place is a hole."

"How long have you been gone?"

"Just since this morning. Day trip. So I guess you can't tell me anything, huh?"

"That's right." The officer handed him back his items and motioned them on. "Move along, please."

As they pulled away, Mitch pried his hands off his knee and heaved a big sigh. "That was too damn close," he said. "That sonofabitch knew something."

"Not at all, Mitchie," Denny told him. "Not at all. He's like everybody else—none of 'em have a clue, not a clue."

It didn't take them long to find some coverage on the radio. Word was coming in fast that the DC Patriot sniper had struck again. An unnamed police officer had been gunned down from a distance, right there on the DC side of the Potomac.

Sure enough, as they crossed the Roosevelt Bridge into the city, they could see a whole mass of law enforcement parked along Rock Creek Parkway off to the left. Denny hooted out loud. "Check out the piggy convention! Looks like Christmas came early this year."

"What are you talking about, Denny?" Mitch still looked a little glazed from the checkpoint stop.

"The dead cop, man. Aren't you listening?" Denny said. "It's all going down exactly like we hoped. We just bagged ourselves a goddamn copycat!"

Chapter 62

NELSON TAMBOUR HAD BEEN shot just before dusk, on a grassy strip of no-man's-land between Rock Creek Parkway and the river. The highway was already shut down by the time I got there, all the way from K Street to the Kennedy Center. I parked as close as I could and walked the rest of the way in.

Tambour had been a detective with NSID, the Narcotics and Special Investigations Division. I didn't know him personally, but that didn't make this incident any less of a nightmare. MPD had just lost one of its own, and horribly so. Detective Tambour had been found with his skull blown half open—a large-caliber bullet had passed right through his head.

It was dark now, but several klieg lights had the scene lit up like the inside of a football stadium. Two tents had been erected off to the side, one as a command center, and another for evidence collection out of sight of the pesky news choppers circling overhead.

We also had Harbor Patrol on the water, keeping pleasure craft at a good distance from the shore. And command staff were everywhere.

When I saw Chief Perkins, he motioned me right over. He was huddled off to the side with the assistant chiefs from NSID and Investigative Services, as well as with a woman I didn't recognize.

"Alex, this is Penny Ziegler from IAD," he said, and the knot in my stomach tightened right up. *What is Internal Affairs doing down here?*

"Something I should know about?" I said.

"There is," Ziegler told me. Her face was just as creased with tension as ours were. Murdered cops tend to make everyone wiggy.

"Detective Tambour's been on no-contact status for the last month," she said. "We were going to be filing criminal charges against him later this week."

"What charges?" I said.

She looked to Perkins for a nod before she went on. "Over the last two years, Tambour oversaw an undercover operation at three of the big housing projects in Anacostia. He's been skimming half of everything they've seized, mostly PCP, coke, and Ecstasy. He was reselling it through a network of street dealers in Maryland and Virginia."

"He may have been on a drop right here," Perkins added with a shake of his head. "They found a key of coke in his trunk."

Four words flashed through my mind: *Foxes in the henhouse.*

Suddenly Tambour was a lot more in line with the snipers' victim profile than he'd been a minute ago.

At the same time, though, he was an unknown to the general public. He hadn't been in the headlines like the others, at least not yet, and that was a difference.

An important one? I couldn't be sure, but I also couldn't shake the feeling that maybe something was off here.

"I want to impose radio silence on anything to do with the investigation," I told Perkins. "Whoever made this hit obviously has some kind of inside line."

"Agreed," he said. "And, Alex?" Perkins put a hand on my arm as I turned to go. His eyes looked strained. Maybe even a little desperate. "Work the hell out of this," he told me. "This is close to getting out of control."

If this hit wasn't by our sniper team, it already was out of control.

Chapter 63

FBI PERSONNEL STARTED showing up right after I did. That was definitely a double-edged sword for me. Their Evidence Response Teams bring some of the best toys in the business—but it also meant Max Siegel wouldn't be far behind.

In fact, we bumped heads over Nelson Tambour's body.

"That's a hell of an exit wound," Siegel said, coming into my airspace with his usual sensitivity. "I heard the guy was dirty. Is it true? I'll find out anyway."

I ignored the question and answered the one he should have been asking. "It was definitely long-range," I said. "There's no stippling at all. And, given the body position, the shots probably had to come from over there."

Directly across from us, maybe 250 yards offshore, we could see flashlight beams crisscrossing the underbrush on Roosevelt Island. We had two teams over there, scouring for shells, suspicious footprints, anything.

"You said shots, *plural?*" Siegel asked.

"That's right." I pointed at the slope behind the spot where Tambour had gone down. Four yellow flags were stuck into the ground, one for each of the slugs that had been recovered so far.

"Three misses and one hit," I said with a sigh. "I'm not sure we're looking at the same gunmen here."

Siegel peered back and forth between the river and Tambour's body several times. "Maybe they were firing from a boat of some kind. There's a decent chop out there today. Could explain the multiple shots, the misses."

"There's no cover on the open water," I said, "and all kinds of risk for an eyewitness. Besides, it's always been one shot, one kill with these guys. They don't miss."

"The sniper's motto," Siegel said. "What about it?"

"I think it's a point of pride for them. If nothing else, the work's been immaculate. Up until now."

"So it's more likely that we have another wackjob with a high-powered sniper rifle running around out there?"

I could just hear the disdain rising in his voice. *Here we go again.*

"Isn't that exactly the contingency your office has been working on?" I said. "That's what Patel told me—at the meeting you blew off."

"I see." Siegel rocked back on his heels. "So are you working up any theories of your own these days—or just going by what you overhear at the office?"

My guess was that he felt threatened by me, and it helped him if he could goad me into some kind of unprofessional behavior. I'd already put a toe in, but I pulled back now and focused on the ground around Tambour's body instead.

When it became clear I wasn't going to respond, he tried again from a different angle.

"You know, it's possible these guys are just that good," he said casually. "Terrorism One Oh One, right? Best way to stay ahead of the police is to keep everything unpredictable. That's a valid perspective on this, right?"

"I'm not ruling anything out," I said without turning around.

"That's good," he said. "It's good that you learn from your mistakes. I mean, isn't that what tripped you up with Kyle Craig?"

Now I did look up.

"He basically just outthought you, right? Just kept changing up his game? I mean—that's what he's still doing, isn't it? Even today?" Siegel shrugged. "Or am I getting that wrong, too?"

"You know what, Max? Just—*stop talking*." I stood up to face him now, getting closer than I needed to be. I wasn't trying to "manage" Siegel anymore. I just needed to say what I was going to say.

"Whatever issues these are that you need to work through, I can recommend some professionals. But in the meantime, if you haven't noticed, we lost an officer here today. Show a little respect."

I guess I'd given him the rise he was looking for. Siegel took a step back, but still kept that obnoxious grin on his face. It was as if he always had some kind of private joke going on.

"Fair enough," he said, and motioned over his shoulder. "I'll just be over here if you need me."

"I won't need you," I said, and went right back to work.

Chapter 64

BY NINE O'CLOCK, I'd had an emergency phone call with the Bureau Directorate and the Field Intelligence Group; a briefing with the mayor's office; and a separate report-in with my own team from MPD, who were all on the scene by now.

The important question at this point was whether we were dealing with the Patriot snipers or someone else. Ballistics was the fastest way to prove a connection, if there was one, and Cailin Jerger from the FBI lab in Quantico was brought out by chopper for a consult.

It was an amazing sight, watching the black Bell helicopter come in for a landing right there on the deserted parkway.

I ran out to greet the chopper and walk Jerger back in.

She was in jeans and a hooded Quantico sweatshirt; they probably pulled her right out of her living room. You'd never guess to look at this small, unassuming woman that she knew more about firearms examination than anyone in a three-state radius.

When I showed her where Tambour had gone down, and the spread on the four shots, she looked back at me with a knowing glance. I didn't respond at all, not a word. I wanted Jerger to draw her own, unfettered conclusions.

At the evidence tent, the whole world was waiting for us. Outside, there was a crowd of cops and agents, including most of Tambour's unit from NSID. Inside, we found Chief Perkins, Jim Heekin from the Directorate, Max Siegel, various assistant chiefs from MPD and assistant SACs from the Bureau, and a few reps from ATF. Jerger looked around at the sea of expectant faces and then dove right in as if she and I were the only ones there.

Each of the four slugs was bagged separately on a long folding table. Three of them were in relatively good shape; the fourth was badly mangled, for obvious reasons.

"Well, they're definitely rifle shot," Jerger said right away. "But these weren't fired from an M110 like the previous incidents."

She took a pair of tongs off the table and plucked one of the good slugs from its bag. Then she used a magnifier from her pocket to look at the base.

"Yeah, I thought so, .388," she said. "And see this 'L' stamped here? That tells me it's an original Lapua Magnum. They were developed specifically for long-range sniping."

"Can you get any kind of weapon report off of these?" I asked her.

She shrugged one shoulder. "Depends. I'll look for rifling

patterns back at the lab, but I have to tell you ahead of time—these puppies have some pretty tough jackets on them. Striations are going to be minimal."

"How about first impressions?" I asked. "We're really in a jam here."

Jerger took a deep breath. I don't think she liked speculating. Her job was all about precision.

"Well, outside of equipment failure, I don't know what the motivation would be for coming off an M110 and using something else."

She held up another evidence bag and looked at it. "I mean, don't get me wrong. This is damn fine ammo, but in terms of long-range shooting, the 110's a Rolls-Royce, and everything else is just... well, everything else."

"So you think this was a different gunman?" Chief Perkins asked, probably leading her more than he should.

"I'm saying it would be kind of strange if it wasn't, that's all. I *don't know* the shooter's motivations. As for the weapon itself, I can tell you that some possibilities are more likely than others."

"Such as?" I asked.

She rattled them right off. "M24, Remington 700, TRG-42, PGM 338. Those are some of the most common applications, militarily anyway." Then she looked right at me, with a grim kind of smile on her face. "There's also the Bor. Ever heard of it?"

"Should I have?" I said.

"Not necessarily," she said, and continued to stare at me. "Just that it would be a really weird coincidence. The .338 variant on that one's called an Alex Rifle."

Chapter 65

KYLE CRAIG WORE a ridiculous grin on his face—on Max Siegel's face—all the way home to Second Street. He couldn't help himself. In his entire career and all of its incarnations, he'd never had such a good time as tonight.

Big kudos went to Agent Jerger for picking up on the Alex Rifle reference, and so quickly!

Maybe the Bureau still had a few sharp knives in the drawer after all. These arcane little clues of his had become something of a hallmark, but to actually be there when one of them was discovered? A unique thrill, to say the least. A total blast.

But also just a prelude. This little drama down by the river was the "one" in a one-two punch that nobody was going to see coming—and no one would feel more than Alex when it landed.

Brace yourself, my friend. It's on the way!

Kyle checked his watch as he closed the front door behind him. It was only twelve thirty, and the sun didn't come up for hours. There was still plenty of time for what he had to get done.

Chapter 66

FIRST THINGS FIRST, he unlocked the basement door and let himself down the narrow stairs to the cinder-block-walled workshop underneath the house. It wasn't exactly his father's old walnut-paneled den, with the twelve-foot fireplace and rolling ladders, but it did the trick and would work just as well. A big bulkhead door at the back had allowed him to bring down a new chest freezer the other day, and he went to it now.

Agent Patel was sleeping peacefully inside. She still looked basically like herself, but she'd grown quite stiff, which seemed fitting. The girl had been pretty much the same way when she was alive.

"Ready for a change of scenery, my dear?"

He lifted her out and laid her on a sheet of four-millimeter painter's plastic to loosen up while he went about his other business. It reminded him of his not so dear but very much departed mother, Miriam—the way she used to leave a frozen tray of pork chops or a flank steak on the counter in the morning so it would be ready to cook up for dinner that night. He couldn't say the old girl never taught him anything useful.

Next, he tackled the walls. Dozens of new photos were taped up alongside the old, the result of several mind-numbing days of additional surveillance on Cross's movements. Not the most stimulating part of the process so far, but it had certainly paid off.

Here were Alex Cross and John Sampson, working the scene of that wonderfully twisted new case in Franklin Square.

And there was Alex with his son Ali, and the mother, Christine, who seemed to have brought quite a bit of Sturm und Drang of her own to the table.

It all came down now—every picture, every map, every clipping he'd collected since coming to Washington. None of it was necessary anymore. He'd committed it all to memory. And besides—now was the time to get the details out of his head and really start to fly!

Once upon a time, Kyle knew, he would have wanted—no, *needed*—to have this thing mapped out down to the finest details. But that wasn't true anymore. Now his options just hung there in the air, like so many pieces of fruit waiting to be picked.

Maybe the final narrative went something like this: Alex wakes up on the bathroom floor, the knife still in his hand. He gets up, disoriented, and stumbles into the bedroom to find Bree gutted in their bed. When he runs to check on the children, it's more of the same. The grandmother, too. Alex can't remember a thing, not even how he got home that night. Flash forward a year or two, and he's learning all about the unique hell that is maximum-security lockup, festering in his own innocence while the walls close in around him a little more every day.

Or—maybe not.

Maybe he'd take Alex out definitively, once and for all. Good old-fashioned torture and murder, not to mention getting to actually watch Cross die, had considerable appeal, too.

In the meantime, there was no specific hurry to decide the final option. His only job for now was to breathe Max Siegel's air, stay open to the possibilities, and focus on whatever was right in front of him.

And, at the present moment, that was Agent Patel.

When he went back to check on her, she was just starting to soften up around the edges. All well and good. By the time she started putting up any kind of smell, he'd be rid of her.

"Fun while it lasted, roomie," he said, and leaned down to give her a chaste good-bye kiss on the lips. Then he rolled his departing guest into a standard white body bag and zipped her up for transport.

Chapter 67

ANOTHER EARLY MORNING, and another phone call from Sampson. This time, I wasn't even out of bed. "Listen, sugar, I know you had a hell of a night out on the parkway, but I thought you'd want to know. We just got another body in this numbers case."

"Great timing," I said, still flat on my back with Bree's arm slung over my chest.

"I guess nobody's getting my memos about that. Listen, I can cover this if you need to take a pass."

"Where are you?" I asked him.

"The bus terminal behind Union Station. Seriously, though, you sound like the bad half of a hangover, Alex. Why don't you stay put, and forget I called?"

"No," I said. Every part of me wanted to stay attached to

that mattress, but you get only one first shot at a crime scene. "I'll be there as soon as I can."

Bree grabbed at my arm as I sat up and swung my feet to the floor.

"God, Alex, this is, like, the definition of 'early.' What's going on now?"

"Sorry to wake you," I said, and leaned back far enough to kiss her good morning. "You know, I can't wait to marry you, by the way."

"Oh yeah? How's that going to change any of this?"

"It won't," I said. "I just can't wait."

She smiled, and even in the semidark it was a beautiful thing to see. No woman I've ever known can look as good as she does in the morning. Or as sexy. I had to get up again fast before I started something I couldn't finish.

"Do you want me to come with you?" she asked, a little groggy but up on one elbow now.

"Thanks, no. I've got this. But if you could get the kids to school—"

"Done. Anything else?"

"A couple of quick, unspeakable acts before I leave?"

"Rain check," she said. "Sampson's waiting. Now go—before we both do something we won't regret."

I was gone a few minutes later, and had to wave off the security detail in the backyard when they saw me launch out the door. It had been only a few hours since I'd come dragging past them, moving in the opposite direction.

"Hey, guys. Regina's just getting up," I said. "Coffee'll be out for you soon."

"And biscuits?" asked one of them.

"I wouldn't doubt it," I said, and laughed.

This was getting out of hand, though. I knew about crazy hours as well as the next guy, but leaving the house before Nana Mama even gets her kitchen up and running for the day? *That* is the definition of "early."

Chapter 68

ALL OF THE EARLY-MORNING buses were lined up on the street outside Union Station when I got there.

Sampson had already shut down the rear terminal, and there were traffic cops in orange vests everywhere, pointing people to where they needed to go. One more colossal headache, but at least it wasn't mine.

I pulled around back and walked up from street level to the cavernous main deck of the parking garage. Sampson was waiting for me with a large coffee in each hand.

"I'm hating this one, sugar. Hating it real bad," he said, handing over my morning fuel.

We walked toward the back, where I could see a row of big brown Dumpsters against the wall on the H Street side. Only one of them was sitting open.

"Nude this time," Sampson said. "And the numbers are all

down her back. You'll see. Also, it looks like she was stabbed instead of beaten to death. All in all, a real nasty scene."

"All right," I said. "Let's do this. See what we've got." I slipped on my gloves and stepped up to survey the damage.

She was facedown on top of the refuse inside—mostly bags of garbage from the terminal. The numbers were etched into her skin in two parallel rows on either side of the spine. It wasn't an equation, though. This was something else.

N38°55'46.1598"

W94°40'3.5256"

"Are those GPS coordinates?" I said.

"Be curious to see where they point, if they are," Sampson said. "This guy's evolving, Alex."

"Anyone move the body?"

"ME still hasn't gotten here. I don't know what the holdup is, but I don't think we should wait anymore."

"I agree. What a way to start the day. Give me a hand here."

We both took a deep breath and climbed up into the Dumpster. It was hard to maneuver with the shifting bags underfoot, much less try to maintain the scene. As quickly as we could, we got a grasp of the victim and gently turned her over.

What I saw there knocked me right back on my ass. I leaned over the edge of the Dumpster and, for the first time in a long while, nearly lost the contents of my stomach.

Sampson was right there with me. "Alex, you okay? What's going on?"

The taste of metal filled my mouth; I felt dizzy from the rush of adrenaline, from being blindsided so badly.

"She's an agent, John. At the Bureau. Remember her? The DCAK case? It's Anjali Patel."

Chapter 69

POOR ANJALI.

And goddamnit! How did this happen? How the hell could it?

There's something inescapable about knowing the victim of a homicide, especially a killing as brutal as this. Unwelcome questions kept pushing to the surface: Did she see it coming? Did she suffer much? Was it over quickly for her?

I tried to remind myself that any precision knife work would have been postmortem, but that thought was cold comfort right now. Besides, the best I could do for Patel was to focus on my job and on this crime scene as objectively as possible under the messed-up circumstances.

Right away, I got on the phone to the ME's office. I wanted to make sure Porter Henning was assigned to this one, and also to find out what the hell was taking them so long. They should have been here by now. Hell, I was.

Sampson took down the numbers we'd found on Anjali's

back and got on his BlackBerry to see what he could find out about them in the short term.

By the time I'd spoken with Porter, who was caught in traffic on the Eisenhower Freeway, John was waving me back over to see something.

"I don't know, Alex. This is pretty random." He turned the screen around to show me the map he'd pulled up.

"It's an address in Overland Park, Kansas. This thing's just getting weirder and weirder. Maybe it's some kind of math formula after all."

"What about a reverse search on the address?" I asked.

"Working on it." It was slow going, though, with his man paws and that tiny keyboard. This is why Sampson almost never texts anyone.

"Here we go, I got it. It's a restaurant," he said. "KC Masterpiece Barbecue and Grill?"

Sampson was shaking his head as if it couldn't be right, but the name hit me like cold water. It must have shown on my face, too, because Sampson waved his hand in front of my eyes.

"Alex? Where'd you go?"

My own hands had tightened into fists. I wanted to hit something. Bad. "Of course," I said. "This is exactly how the son of a bitch works."

"How *who* works?" John said. "What are you—?"

But then he got it.

"Oh Jesus."

It all made sense now, in the worst possible way. There was the *Alex Rifle* reference from the night before, and now this—*KC Masterpiece.*

Kyle Craig's masterpiece.

He'd done this before, leaving tokens behind at crime scenes, always aimed at getting him credit where credit was due. Both of these murders were references to my own open cases—the sniper-style hit on Tambour, and the numbers so brutally etched into Anjali Patel's skin.

Obviously Kyle had killed them both. Or had someone do it for him.

Then, with a horrible kind of aftershock, I remembered something else: Bronson "Pop-Pop" James, my young client. He'd been shot trying to rob a store—a place called Cross Country Liquors. Of course. Why hadn't I come back to that fact until now?

It all added up—another ton of bricks dropped onto my shoulders. Kyle was circling me and closing in as he did it, wreaking as much havoc as possible in the process. This wasn't just blind savagery either. It was much more specific than that and, unless I was mistaken, much more personal.

It was all part of my punishment for catching him the first time.

Chapter 70

IN ONE PHONE CALL, I re-upped with Rakeem Powell for additional twenty-four-hour security coverage at the house. I'd take out a loan if I had to; cost was not my concern right now. I couldn't be sure what Kyle's endgame was, but I wasn't going to wait for him to come at me again.

I spent most of the day at the Hoover Building. With Anjali's sudden death, it was like a wake over there, except in the SIOC, which was buzzing like an air traffic control tower.

The Bureau director himself, Ron Burns, made his designated operations room available to us, and the manhunt for Kyle Craig was back on full steam. This wasn't personal for just me. Craig was already the biggest inside scandal in the Bureau's hundred-year history. And now he'd killed another agent, maybe to get back at the FBI, too.

Every seat in the operation center's double horseshoe of desks was filled. The five main screens at the head of the room showed alternating pictures and old video of Kyle, plus national and world maps with electronic markers for his known victims and associations, and past movements.

We were on the line all day with Denver, New York, Chicago, Paris—everywhere Kyle had been known to live since his escape from ADX Florence. And every field office in the country was put on high alert.

Even so, with all this flurry of activity, we had to accept the fact that nobody had any idea where Kyle was.

"I don't know what to tell you, Alex," Burns said, pacing. We'd just hung up after a marathon conference call. "We've got nothing useful here, no physical proof that Kyle killed Tambour or Patel, or even that he's been in Washington. And nothing on that Beretta you pulled out of evidence either, by the way."

The Beretta he was referring to was the one Bronson James had used in the armed-robbery attempt. My original idea had been that Pop-Pop had gotten it from a gang member off the street, but Kyle Craig could have just as easily put that gun in his hand. I knew that Kyle favored Berettas, and he knew that I knew.

"*I'm* the proof," I said. "He's called me on the phone. He's made threats. The man is obsessed with me, Ron. In his mind, I'm the only one who's ever beaten him, and Kyle Craig is nothing if not highly competitive."

"What about these disciples of his? Just for the sake of argument." Burns was talking to me but also to a dozen other agents who took notes and banged away on laptops as he spoke. "The man's got followers, some of them apparently ready to die on his command. It's happened before. How do we know he didn't commission one of them for these hits?"

"Because the hits were directed at me," I said slowly. "This is the part Kyle would want to do himself."

"Even so"—Burns stopped pacing and sat down—"we're getting off point here. Whether Craig made these kills or he didn't, our hand is pretty much the same. We keep scouring the crime scenes. We make sure that our radar's up and that our people are as ready as they can be the next time he strikes."

"That's not good enough. Goddamnit!" I said, and swiped my notes off the desk, taking with them a few other people's papers, too. Right away, I regretted it. "I'm sorry," I said. "Sorry."

Burns bent to where I was picking up the papers and put out a hand. He pulled me to my feet. "Take a breather. Go get some dinner. There's nothing else to do right now."

Like it or not, he was right. I was exhausted and a little embarrassed, and I definitely needed to go home for a while. Once I'd gathered up my stuff, I headed out.

Waiting at the elevator, I felt my phone vibrate for the umpteenth time that day. It had been a steady stream of calls from MPD, Sampson, Bree, Nana—

But this time, when I looked at the ID, it just said, "A. Friend."

"Alex Cross," I answered, and I was already heading back to the operations center.

"Hello, Alex," Kyle Craig said. "Really in the thick of things now, aren't we?"

Chapter 71

"THIS PHONE I'M CALLING ON is encrypted, so don't bother trying anything," Kyle went on. "Now, if I've timed this correctly, you're right in the belly of the beast. Is that right? And don't put me on speaker—or I'm hanging up."

I came into the conference room, gesticulating like crazy to let them know something was going on. Agents started scrambling, although there wasn't much they could do. I had no doubt Kyle was telling the truth about the encrypted phone.

Someone handed me a pad and pen, and Burns sat down with his ear close to the cell, until an assistant ran over with a laptop. He took the director's place and started transcribing as much as he could hear.

"You killed Anjali Patel and Nelson Tambour, didn't you, Kyle?"

"I'm afraid I did."

"And what about Bronson James?" I said. "Did you do that, too?"

"Remarkable little boy, wasn't he? Just vegetable soup, last I checked."

My big mistake the previous time with Kyle had been to lose my shit during the manhunt. I was determined not to let that happen again, but my heart was pounding with as much hate as I've ever felt for anyone in my life.

"Do you see the swath of destruction *you're* creating here?" he went on. "How much better off these people would be if you simply didn't exist?"

"What I see is a man with an obsession against me," I told him.

"Not true," he said. "I think you're fascinating, especially for a Negro. If you weren't, you'd be dead by now, and Tambour, Patel, and little Bronson James would all be wondering what to have for breakfast tomorrow. It's quite a compliment, really. Not many people are worthy of my time."

His voice sounded almost... playful? He appeared to be in an especially good mood. Killing seemed to do that for him. Kyle also loved to talk about himself.

"Can I ask you something?" I said.

"*Interesting.* You don't usually ask permission. Go right ahead, Alex."

"I'm curious about the way you killed Tambour and Patel. It's not like you to imitate anyone—"

"No," he said right away. "It's usually the other way around, isn't it?"

"But that's exactly what you did here. Twice."

"So what's your question, Alex?"

"Have you been in touch with them?" I asked. "The original killers. Are they *yours,* Kyle?"

He thought for a second, maybe trying to slow this down a little. Or maybe concocting a lie?

"I haven't, and they aren't," he said then. "This Patriot character is a bit pedestrian for me. But that other one, with the numbers? Much more interesting. I'll admit, I wouldn't mind a little tête-à-tête with that chap."

"So you don't know who either of them are," I said.

There was another long pause. Then he laughed, as heartily as I'd ever heard from Kyle.

"Alex Cross, *are you asking me for advice?*"

"You used to be a good agent," I said. "Remember? You used to advise me."

"Of course. They were the second-worst years of my life. The first being my time in that so-called Supermax out in Florence—which I have you to thank for." He stopped, and I heard another long, slow breath. "Which also brings us full circle, doesn't it?"

"Yes, it does," I said. "Your whole life seems to revolve around paying me back for that."

"Something along those lines."

"So why all the running around, playing games, Kyle? What are you waiting for?"

"The right inspiration, I suppose," he said without a trace of irony. "That's the beauty of creation and imagination. Remaining open to what comes. The more seasoned the artist, the more capable he is of responding in the moment."

"So you're an artist now?"

"I suppose that I always have been," he told me. "I'm just getting better at it, that's all. It would be foolish to quit while I'm in my prime. But I will tell you one thing, my friend."

"What's that?" I said.

"When the end comes—trust me—we'll both know it."

Book Four

FINAL TARGET, FINAL STRATEGIES

Chapter 72

LEAVING DC in the old white Suburban that morning, Denny had seen in the side mirror vapor trails coming out of the exhaust, but he didn't think too much about it. With a rig as old as this one, he couldn't bother himself over every mechanical hiccup.

Now, three and a half hours from home, the hiccup had turned into something more like a death rattle. There was a familiar dry clank coming from the engine.

As they pulled over to the side of Route 70, Mitch looked up from the *Penthouse* he'd nabbed off the rack at their last pit stop. "What's going on, Denny? That doesn't sound right."

"Can't you hear the head gasket going?" Denny said. It was amazing how observant Mitch could be with a rifle in his hand, considering how dim he was about most of the rest of his life.

A quick check under the hood told Denny what he already

knew, but he waited until they were limping back up the highway to say anything more about it to Mitch.

"Now, don't freak out or anything, buddy, but the old magic bus ain't going to make it back to DC. I think we're going to have to ditch it."

Mitch's face lit up like a little kid's. "I know where we can do it!" he said. "I used to go hunting around here all the time. It's the perfect place, Denny. Nobody ever goes back there."

"I'm thinking we stick it in long-term parking at the airport and walk away," Denny said. "By the time anybody figures out we ain't coming back..."

But Mitch wasn't having it.

"Come on, Denny. *Please?*" He was sitting sideways on the seat now and pulling at Denny's sleeve like some kind of little punk. "Let's just...drown this thing, man. Get rid of it once and for all."

Denny shouldn't have been surprised. Mitch had been getting more and more paranoid about the Suburban ever since their traffic stop on the last road trip. It was all getting real old, real fast.

At the same time, though, this might be a chance to calm Mitch the fuck down, Denny realized. He needed his boy focused, and that could be worth a lot in the long run.

"Yeah, all right," Denny said finally. "We can dump most of this stuff. It's garbage anyway. The rest, we can pack out. Then we'll do what any other self-respecting American patriot would do."

Mitch was grinning at him, ear to ear. "What's that, Denny?"

"Trade up, my man. You ever hot-wire a vehicle before?"

Chapter 73

WHEN IT WAS DONE, they stopped to wash up in a Mobil bathroom and stole a cone of tulips from a bucket outside the convenience store. Denny would have liked for them to be wearing ties, too, but it was getting late.

In fact, it was after dark when they finally pulled up to the tidy little Cape on Central Boulevard in Brick Township. It was a quiet street, with big trees arching over from both sides to meet in the middle, and you could smell the salt of the ocean in the breeze.

"You grew up here?" Denny said, looking around. "Man, why'd you ever want to leave?"

Mitch shrugged. "I don't know, Denny. I just did."

When they got to the front door, Denny unscrewed the porch lightbulb and then rang the bell. A middle-aged woman came to answer. She had Mitch's same girth and round face, and she squinted out into the dark to see who it was.

"Is that... Mitchell?"

"Hey, Mom."

The dish towel dropped out of her hand. "Mitchell!" The next second, she was pulling him inside and wrapping her saggy sausage arms around him. "Lord, Lord, you brought my boy home for a visit, and I *thank you!*"

"Quit it, Mom." Mitch squirmed under the kisses, but he was smiling as he detached himself, the tulips half crushed in his hand. "This is Denny," he announced.

"Nice to meet you, ma'am," Denny said. "I'm real sorry about just dropping in like this. We should have called first. I know we should have."

Bernice Talley waved it away like so many flies in the air. "Don't you give it a second thought. Come in, come in."

As she reached past Denny to close the door, her eyes lingered on the Lexus ES parked at the curb.

"I'll bet you boys are hungry" was all she said, though.

"Yes'm," Mitch answered.

"Mitch is always hungry," Denny said, and Bernice laughed like she knew it was true. Her right hip rode up badly when she walked, but she limped right on past the cane hooked over a doorknob in the hall.

"Mitchell, offer your friend something to drink. I'll see what I can shake out of this fridge."

Denny hung back as they passed through the living room. It was all matching furniture in here, but old stuff. "Grandma on a budget" stuff. It was the kind of place where he could imagine his old man trying to sell his vacuums, or knives, or whatever had been paying for the whiskey bottles back then.

He couldn't have been too good at it, though. The son of a bitch never drank anything better than Old Crow.

On a side table, Mrs. Talley had three gold-framed pictures arranged in a perfect little arc. One was of Jesus, with his eyes raised up to God. One was of Mitch, looking young and doofy in a suit and tie. And the third was a military portrait of a middle-aged black man, in full uniform with a decent show of ribbons on his chest.

Denny stepped into the kitchen, where Mrs. Talley was busying herself while Mitch sat at the old Formica table with a couple of open Heinekens in front of him.

"Hey, is that Mr. Talley in the picture out here?" he asked.

The old woman stopped short. Her hand floated halfway to her bad hip before she reached over and opened the fridge instead.

"We lost Mr. Talley two years ago," she said without looking around. "God rest his soul."

"I'm real sorry to hear that," Denny told her. "So it's just you here by yourself, huh?" He knew he was being a shit, but it couldn't be helped.

She mistook it for concern. "Oh, I'm fine. There's a boy who mows the lawn and shovels the snow, and my neighbor Samuel comes over if I got something heavy needs moving."

"Well, I'm sorry to have brought it up, Mrs. Talley. I didn't mean to—"

"No, no." She waved away more of the invisible flies. "It's perfectly all right. He was a good man."

"A good man who left behind a fine son," Denny added.

Mrs. Talley's face eased into a smile. "You don't have to

tell me that," she said, and ran a hand over Mitch's broad shoulder as she passed from fridge to counter with a bag of onions.

Denny could see that, under the table, Mitch's knee was just starting to bounce up a storm.

Chapter 74

EVEN WITHOUT ADVANCE NOTICE, Bernice Talley managed to pull together a fast New England–style clam chowder, some good bread, a salad, and a couple of microwaved potatoes with everything on them, from butter to sour cream to Canadian bacon. It was the best dinner Denny had eaten since he'd started this whole mess, living in the shelters and that godforsaken Suburban, which he was glad to be rid of now. He contentedly filled himself while Mrs. Talley chattered on about people he'd never heard of. Mitch mostly listened.

Finally, after seconds of Edy's French Vanilla with gobs of chocolate sauce, Denny pushed back and stretched his arms and legs.

"Ma'am, that was spectacular," he said.

Mrs. Talley beamed. "Wait until you try my waffles," she told him.

"We ain't staying the night, Mom," Mitch said, more into his ice-cream bowl than to her.

Right away, the woman's face fell. "What do you mean? Where are you going to go at nine thirty at night?"

"We're just coming back from a conference in New York," Denny put in quickly. "Mitch thought it would be nice to drop by, but we've got to be back in Cleveland tomorrow morning. We'll be driving all night just to get there for work."

"I see," she said quietly, but the heartbreak in her voice was hard to miss.

"Tell you what"—Denny got up and started clearing dishes—"why don't you two go talk in the living room for a while? I'll clean up in here."

"No, no," she started in, but he eventually wheedled her out of the room.

When she was gone, he put on the woman's yellow Playtex gloves and washed all the dishes by hand. He wiped down the sink, the counter, the table, the fridge, and the two bottles of beer he'd drunk. Then he pocketed the gloves.

Half an hour later, he and Mitch were on their way down the front walk.

"Nice lady, sweet lady, great cook," Denny said. "Sorry we couldn't stay any longer."

"That's okay," Mitch told him. "We got things to do back in DC."

Denny gave him a fist bump on that one. It seemed maybe Mitch was getting focused again, back to his old self.

Once they reached the curb, Denny stopped short and snapped his fingers. "Hang on. I left my wallet on the counter. I'll be right back."

"I'll get it," Mitch said, but Denny put a hand out to stop him.

"Bad idea, Mitchie. You saw your mom's face just now. Don't want to make her cry all over again, do you?"

"I guess not," Mitch said.

"Of course you don't. Now just sit tight in the car, and don't come inside. I'll be back before you know it."

Chapter 75

I WAS SPENDING as many hours at the house as I could, including all of my desk time. Between Kyle Craig, the Patriot snipers, and these new homicides with the numbers, my attic office was as stuffed with case materials as it had ever been. That meant a lot of crime-scene photos, so I told the kids that Dad's office was off-limits for the time being, which explained the phone call I got from Jannie that afternoon.

"Hello, Alex, this is Janelle the Banished, calling from the faraway land of the second floor."

My daughter's always been one to put the "smart" in smart aleck. I just try to keep up. "Hail thee well, Janelle. How goes it in the nether regions?"

"You have a visitor, Daddy," she said, back to business. "There's a man named Mr. Siegel at the front door. He's an FBI agent."

At first I thought I'd heard wrong. What could Max Siegel

be doing at my house? The last time we'd tangled had been the worst so far.

"Daddy?"

"I'm coming right down," I said.

When I got to the second floor, Jannie was still waiting there. She trailed after me down the stairs, but I told her to stay inside.

Then I closed the front door behind me on the way out.

Siegel was on the front steps, looking very Brooklyn in jeans and a black motorcycle jacket. He also had a black helmet in one hand and a brown paper bag in the other.

One of our security guys, David Brandabur, had positioned himself on the stoop, between Max and the door.

"It's fine, David," I said. "I know him."

We both waited for David to go back to his car before either of us spoke.

"What are you doing here, Max?" I asked.

Siegel came up another step, just far enough to hand me the bag. Right away, I could see on his face that something had changed.

"I wasn't sure what you liked," he said.

I pulled out a fifth of Johnnie Walker Black. Some kind of a peace offering, I supposed, but with Siegel, I really didn't know what to think.

He shrugged. "I know, I know. Agent Schizo, right?"

"Something like that," I told him.

"Listen, Alex, I realize what I'm like to work with. I take all this shit very personally. I shouldn't, but I do. I'm passionate as hell. Maybe it's part of what makes me good at my job, but I can also be a real asshole sometimes."

I wanted to say, "Sometimes?" but I just listened to what Siegel had to tell me.

"Anyway," he went on, "I just came by to say I know you've got your hands full these days, and if there's anything you need, you should let me know. Anything at the Bureau, or even just security backup here at the house—someone to pull an overnight or whatever."

He looked up at my blank face and finally smiled. "Really. No tricks. No bullshit."

I wanted to believe Siegel. It certainly would have made things easier. But my instinct was still to distrust him. I couldn't just shake that off because he came over with a peace offering.

Then the door opened behind me, and suddenly Bree was there. "Everything okay out here?" she asked.

Siegel chuckled. "I guess my reputation precedes me."

"Actually, we've got a teenage news service sitting on the stairs inside," Bree said. She put out her hand, ever the peacemaker. "I'm Bree Stone."

"Detective Stone," he said. "Of course. Good to meet you. I'm Max Siegel, Alex's nightmare from the Bureau. We occasionally see things a little differently."

"So I've heard," she said, and they both laughed. It was a little surreal actually. This was a side of Siegel I'd never seen before, the friendly, interested-in-anyone-but-himself side. And it seemed to have come out of nowhere.

"Max was just dropping this off," I said, showing her the bottle of scotch.

"Right." Siegel took a step down toward the sidewalk. "So, anyway, mission accomplished. Nice to meet you, Detective."

"Stay for a quick drink," she said, and gave my hand a squeeze. "It's the afternoon. I'm sure we could all stand to wind down a little."

There was no pretense here; we all knew what she was trying to do. Siegel looked up at me and shrugged. This was my call, and honestly I would have liked to have said no, but that seemed as if it could just create more trouble than it was worth.

"Come on in," I said, and led the way. "*Mi casa es su casa,* Max."

Inside, Jannie had fallen back as far as the kitchen table. Nana and Ali were there, too, in the middle of a game of Go Fish. It was Ali's latest obsession these days, but they all stopped and looked up as we came in.

"Max, this is everyone. Regina, Jannie, Ali, this is Agent Siegel."

Ali's eyes bugged out at the motorcycle helmet, and Siegel put it down in front of him. "Go ahead, little guy. Try it on if you want to."

"It's fine," I said to Ali.

I took out some glasses and ice, and a couple of Smart-Waters for the kids. Nana went to open the cabinet where we keep the chips and crackers, but I shook my head no just enough for her to see.

"You've got a nice place here," Siegel said, looking out the window at the backyard. "Great setup in the middle of the city."

"Thanks." I handed him a short pour of the scotch, and then one for Bree and myself, and one with water for Nana.

"So here's to fresh starts," Bree said pointedly, and raised her glass.

"Here's to summer coming!" Ali chimed in.

Siegel smiled down at him and put a hand on his shoulder.

"And here's to this good family," he said. "It's really nice to meet you all."

Chapter 76

SOMETIMES THE BREAKS in a murder case come out of the blue—like a phone call on a Sunday morning, from somewhere you never expected.

"Detective Cross?"

"Yes?"

"This is Detective Scott Cowen from Brick Township PD, in New Jersey. I think we may have a line on your sniper problem up here."

MPD had been fielding literally hundreds of tips every week on a newly dedicated sniper hotline. More than 99 percent of those calls were fantasy fiction or dead ends, but whatever Cowen was sitting on, it had gotten him past Dispatch. He now had my attention.

I turned my newspaper sideways and started writing in the margin next to the crossword. *Cowen. Brick Township.*

"Go ahead," I said.

"Yesterday afternoon, we pulled a white ninety-two Suburban out of the water over at Turn Mill Pond near here. The plates were already gone, no surprise, but I don't think whoever put it there expected us to find it, at least not this fast. The thing was, we had an ultralight air show going on at the airport this weekend, and a couple of guys flying over saw something down there and called it in—"

"Yes?" I said. Cowen seemed to talk without taking any breath at all.

"Yeah, so it couldn't have been in the water more than forty-eight hours, I'm thinking, because we still managed to pull some damn good prints off of it. Six of them had a dozen or more points each, which was great in theory, until none of them came up on my first pass through IAFIS—"

"Detective, I'm sorry, but can you explain to me how this connects to my case?"

"Well, this is the thing. I'm thinking we've got a dead end here, too, but then this morning I get a call from the state—apparently one of those six prints is a match for your UNSUB down there."

Now we were getting somewhere. I stood up off the couch and started toward the attic, double time. I needed my charts and notes right now.

UNSUB stands for Unknown Subject, which was the only designation we had for our phantom gunman. The print he'd left behind on the night of the first sniper hit, and then again at the National Law Enforcement Officers Memorial, had been deliberate, like a calling card. This new print sounded a lot more like a mistake to me, and at this point in the game, I loved a good mistake.

I wondered whether all of the remaining prints from the car belonged to the same guy, or if maybe we'd just gotten a line on both members of our sniper team.

That thought, I kept to myself for the time being.

"Detective Cowen from Brick Township, you may have just made my month. Can you send me everything you have?" I asked.

"Give me your e-mail," he said. "They're all scanned and ready to go. We've got six full prints, like I said, plus another nine partials. It was really just a lucky break that we found that vehicle so fast—"

"Here's my e-mail," I said, and spit it out for him. "Sorry to rush you, but I'm a little eager to see what you've got."

"No problem." I heard typing in the background. "Okay, they're on the way. If you need anything else, or want to come take a look around, *or whatever*, you should just let me know."

"I will," I said.

In fact, I'd already mapped out the route to Brick Township, New Jersey, on my laptop while he was talking. If this turned out to be what it seemed, I'd be meeting Detective Cowen face-to-face before the day was out, and he and I would be taking a look around—*or whatever.*

Chapter 77

THE LIMITATION ON THESE new prints from New Jersey was that I had nothing to compare them to. No criminal records anyway. Accordingly, there was no way to know whether they'd all come off the same person or not.

I thought about Max Siegel's offer of help the other day. With the Bureau's resources, he probably could have gotten further with these than Detective Scott Cowen had. But I just wasn't ready to jump in there.

Instead, I put in another request with my Army CID contact in Lagos, Carl Freelander. Better to go with a known quantity, I figured, even if he was halfway around the world and maybe getting sick of my calls.

"Twice in one month, Alex? We're going to have to get you one of those punch cards," he said. "Tell me what I can do for you people."

"Meantime, I owe you another drink," I told him. "And,

for what it's worth, I may just be chasing the same ghost as the last time, but I need to be sure. I've got six more prints I want to run through the civil database. Maybe all from the same person, and maybe not."

Cowen had been right about the quality of the prints. MPD's standard is thirteen points, meaning anywhere a ridge or line ends, or intersects with another ridge or line. If two prints line up in thirteen or more of those places, it's a statistical match, and I had half a dozen viable scans to work with.

Carl told me to send them along and leave my line open for an hour or so.

True to his word, he called me back fifty minutes later.

"Well, it's a good news/bad news kind of thing," he said. "Two of the six prints you sent me came up military. You got the left index and middle fingers on a guy named Steven Hennessey. U.S. Army Special Forces, Operational Detachment–Delta, from nineteen eighty-nine to two thousand two."

"Delta Force? There's a red flag," I said.

"Yeah, the guy saw action in Panama, Desert Storm, Somalia—and get this: he ran long-gun training for ground forces in Kunduz. Sounds a hell of a lot like a sniper to me."

I felt as if my slot machine had just come up bar-bar-bar. We'd almost certainly just found our second gunman, and this one had a name.

"What about a last known address?" I said. "Do we know where Hennessey is now?"

"Yeah, that's the bad news," Carl said. "Cave Hill Cemetery in Louisville, Kentucky. Hennessey's been dead for years, Alex."

Chapter 78

THE THREE-AND-A-HALF-HOUR DRIVE to New Jersey flew by. Probably because my mind was running the whole time. It was too bad I was so pressed, because I would have liked to have visited my cousin Jimmy Parker at his Red Hat restaurant along the Hudson in Irvington. God, I needed a break, and a good meal.

Maybe someone was buried down there in Louisville, but I was willing to bet that it wasn't the real Steven Hennessey. Not with his prints on that Suburban.

The question was, who had Hennessey become in the last several years? Also, where was he now? And what were he and this phantom partner of his doing in New Jersey?

My plan was to meet Detective Cowen at Turn Mill Pond, where the car had been pulled out of the water. I wanted to catch that scene while there was still daylight, then follow him back to the impoundment lot to see the vehicle itself.

But when I called Cowen to tell him I was almost there, he didn't pick up.

The same thing happened when I got to the meeting point at the south end of the pond. I was pissed, but there was nothing to do now except get out and take a look around.

Turn Mill was one of several bodies of water in the Colliers Mills Wildlife Management Area, which encompassed thousands of acres. From this spot, all I could see were trees, water, and the dirt road I'd just driven in on.

Plenty of privacy for dumping a car anyway.

The ground at the edge of the waterfront was heavily rutted and tamped down, presumably where the police had pulled the Suburban out. It looked to me as though the vehicle had been pushed into the water from the edge of a wooden bridge where the pond narrowed into a channel.

Looking down from above, one would assume the water was plenty deep enough, but it obviously wasn't. In any case, it wasn't the kind of thing you could undo.

Once I'd taken all of that in, I headed back to my car. I figured it couldn't be too hard to the find the police station in town, but that's when I saw a cruiser coming up the road, *fast.*

It sped along the pond a ways, curved into the woods, and then came back out again. It stopped right behind where I'd parked.

A uniformed officer, a blond woman, got out and waved as I came over.

"Detective Cross?"

"That's me."

"I'm Officer Guadagno. Detective Cowen asked me to drive out here and bring you back as quickly as possible.

There's been a homicide in town, a woman by the name of Bernice Talley."

I assumed she just meant that Cowen had been pulled away from my case.

"Do we need someone else to let us into the impoundment lot, or can you do that for me?" I asked Guadagno.

"No," she said. "I mean, you don't understand. Cowen wants you to come to the scene. He thinks Mrs. Talley's murder may be related."

"To the Suburban?" I said. "To my sniper case?"

The cop fiddled with the brim of her hat. She seemed a little nervous. "Maybe both," she said. "It's nothing conclusive, but this same woman's husband was found shot dead two years ago, right over there." She pointed to a patch of woods about a hundred feet up the shore. "The ME called it a hunting accident at the time, but nobody ever came forward. Cowen figures whoever dumped that Suburban didn't just stumble onto this place, and frankly we don't get too many homicides around here. He's naming the son, Mitchell Talley, as a person of interest in all of it, both deaths."

She stopped then, her hand on the open car door, and looked at me more directly than before.

"Detective, this may be none of my business, but do you think this guy could be your shooter down in Washington? I've been following the case since it broke."

I demurred. "Let me go take a look at that scene before I say anything," I told her.

But, in fact, the answer to her question was yes.

Chapter 79

THE POLICE VEHICLES in front of Bernice Talley's home were two-deep when we got there. They had a tape line around the house, while the neighbors watched from the fringes. I had no doubt that all of them would be locking their doors and windows that night and for many nights to come.

My escort officer walked me inside and introduced me to Detective Scott Cowen, who seemed to be running the show. He was a tall, barrel-chested guy, with a shiny bald head that caught the light as he talked—and talked.

Just like on the phone, he briefed me with a long but mostly informative monologue.

Mrs. Talley had been found dead on her kitchen floor by the boy who mowed her lawn every Sunday. She'd been shot once at close range through the temple, with what looked like a nine millimeter. They were still working on time of death, but it was sometime within the last seventy-two hours.

The woman was believed to have been living alone, ever since the son, Mitchell, had moved out two years earlier—just a short while after the father was killed. Also, there was some word through the grapevine that the elder Mr. Talley had been known to knock his wife around over the years, and maybe to strike Mitchell, too.

"That could go to motive, at least on the father's death," Cowen added. "As to why he'd want to come back here and kill his poor mother, I wish to hell I knew. And then, of course, there's all of these."

He showed me a shelf in the living room, crowded with trophies and ribbons. They were all shooting awards, I saw—New Jersey Rifle and Pistol Club, Junior NRA, various fifty- and three-hundred-meter competitions, target skill awards. Most of them were first place, some second and third.

"The kid is an ace," Cowen said. "Some kind of prodigy or whatever. Maybe also a little . . . you know. Simple."

He pointed at a framed photo on one of the side tables. "This is him, maybe ten years ago. We're looking for something more recent we can use."

The boy in the picture looked to be about sixteen. He had a round face, almost cherubic, except for the dull look in his eyes and the half-assed attempt at a mustache. It was hard to imagine anyone taking him too seriously at that age.

The guns are his power, I thought. *Always have been.*

I looked back over at all the trophies and awards. Maybe this was the one thing Mitchell Talley had ever been good at. The one thing in his life he'd ever known how to control. On the face of things, it seemed to make sense.

"When was he last seen around here?" I asked. "Did he ever come to visit?"

Cowen shrugged apologetically. "We're still not sure. You're catching us right at the beginning of this thing," he said. "We don't even have prints on the house yet. We just found the mother. You're lucky that you're here."

"Yeah, lucky me."

I had the impression that the high profile on this sniper case was making people nervous around here, too. Everyone seemed to know who I was, and they were all giving me a wide berth.

"Don't worry about it. You aren't any further along than I would have expected," I told Cowen. "But I do have some ideas about how we might handle things from here."

Chapter 80

SEVERAL THINGS HAPPENED really fast in Brick Township, mostly because I needed them to.

I worked my contacts with the Field Intelligence Group in Washington to get hold of the FIG coordinator up in the Newark field office. Because it was a Sunday night, and because we had sufficient reason to believe Mitchell Talley had crossed, or would cross, jurisdictional lines, we were able to get an immediate Temporary Felony Want. Cowen would have forty-eight hours from there to secure an actual warrant, signed and issued. In the meantime, Newark could get word out to law enforcement up and down the eastern seaboard right away.

The idea for now was to leave off any mention of Steven Hennessey, or any accomplice at all. The Want specified only that Mitchell Talley was being sought for questioning in the deaths of Bernice and Robert Talley. Wherever our presumed snipers were, I didn't want them knowing we'd connected any of this to DC until I had more information.

Cowen agreed to give me some cover on that front. In the meantime, I got his people hooked up with Newark in the search for their suspect. Someone found a more recent snapshot in one of his mother's photo albums, and they used a scan of it for the local and regional BOLO—Be On The Lookout.

Realistically speaking, no one expected Talley to be in the area. The larger effort was focused on looking at stolen-car reports, monitoring transportation hubs, and tracking down surveillance tapes at area airports and bus and train stations. With luck, someone would be able to turn up an eyewitness or maybe even a relevant piece of video somewhere.

The closest thing to a lead so far had come from an elderly neighbor of Mrs. Talley's. She'd seen a sedan of some kind parked in front of the house a few nights ago but couldn't say what kind it was, or what color, or even how long it had been there.

For whatever that was worth, I forwarded the information down to Jerome Thurman, who had been tracking vehicle-related leads on this case for me from the start.

By now, I was beginning to feel like I'd been away from DC for too long. Maybe Talley and Hennessey had no plans to return to Washington, if that's where they'd even come from in the first place. But I had to assume otherwise. For all I knew, they were already back there and planning their next hit.

The minute I got things wrapped up with Detective Cowen, I was in the car and headed for home. And I was moving fast, using a siren all the way.

Chapter 81

AT EIGHT THIRTY the next morning, Colleen Brophy turned off of E Street and into the churchyard, where I was waiting outside the *True Press* office. She had a bulging backpack on her shoulders, an armload of newspapers, and a nearly finished cigarette in the corner of her mouth.

"Oh God," she said when she saw me. "You again. Now what do you want?"

"I wouldn't come if it wasn't important, Ms. Brophy. I'm well aware of how you feel about all this," I said. Still, after my long Sunday on the road, I was in "no mood for 'tude," as Sampson likes to say.

The *True Press* editor set down her load of papers and sat on the stone bench where I'd just stood up.

"How can I help you?" she asked, her sarcasm still intact. "As if I have a choice."

I showed her the picture of Mitchell Talley. "Have you ever seen this man?"

"Oh, come on," she said right away. "You think *this* is the guy who sent me those e-mails?"

"I'll take that as a yes. Thank you. When was the last time you saw him?"

She took out a new cigarette and lit it off the last of the old one before she answered.

"Do you really need me to participate in this?" she said. "The trust I have with these people is so tenuous."

"I'm not trying to bust a shoplifter, Ms. Brophy."

"I understand, but it's the shoplifters I'm worried about. A lot of the homeless people I work with *have* to break the law from time to time just to get by. If any of them see me talking to you—"

"This can stay a private conversation," I told her. "Nobody has to know about it. That is, assuming we can get on with this. Do you know this man?"

After another long pause and a few more drags, she said, "I guess it was last week. They picked up their papers on Wednesday, like everyone else."

" 'They'?" I asked.

"Yeah. Mitch and his friend Denny. They're kind of like a—"

She stopped short then and turned slowly to look at me. It seemed maybe she'd just put two and two together about something. Or maybe I should say one and one.

"Oh God," she said. "They're kind of like a team. They're the ones, aren't they?"

I could feel that mental click, when something falls into place. Had I just found my Steven Hennessey?

"What's Denny's last name?" I asked her.

"I honestly don't know," she said. "He's white, tall, and thin. He's got lots of stubble, and kind of a—" She waved her hand under her jaw. "Like a sunken chin, I guess you could call it. He sort of leads Mitch around."

"And you say they pick up papers on Wednesday?"

She nodded. "Sometimes they come back for more if they sell out, but I haven't seen them lately. I swear. I know this is serious now."

"I believe you," I said. Everything about her demeanor had changed. Now she looked more sad than anything. "Any idea where I might look for the two of them?"

"All over. Denny has this old white Suburban he drives around, when he can get gas. I know they sleep in there sometimes." The Suburban was a dead end now, but I didn't say anything about it to Ms. Brophy.

"And you can try the shelters. There's a list of them in the back of the paper." She took a copy off the top of her stack and handed it to me. "God, you know, I hate myself for telling you all this."

"Don't," I said, and paid her a dollar for the paper. "You're doing the right thing."

Finally.

Chapter 82

AFTER A LONG DAY of canvassing homeless shelters and soup kitchens, I wasn't any further along than I'd been that morning. For all I knew, Talley and Hennessey were still in New Jersey. Or gone to Canada. Or up in smoke.

But when I went back to the office for some files to bring home, Jerome Thurman caught me at the elevator with some news.

"Alex! You heading out?"

"I was," I said.

"Maybe not anymore."

He held up a page from some kind of printout. "I think maybe we've got something here. Could be good stuff."

Normally, Jerome works out of First District, but I'd gotten him a space in the Auto Theft Unit down the hall, where he could monitor vehicle leads for me. And by "space," I mean a stack of crates in their Records Room where he could set up his laptop, but Jerome's never been a complainer.

What he had was a list of hot license plate numbers from an NCIC database. One of the entries was circled in blue pen.

NJ—DCY 488.

"It's a Lexus ES, reported stolen from an apartment complex in Colliers Mills, New Jersey," he said. "That's, like, two, three miles down the road from where your white Suburban went into the water."

I risked a half smile. "Tell me there's more, Jerome," I said. "There's more, right?"

"Best part, actually. An LPR camera picked up the same plate number coming into long-term parking out at National on Saturday morning at four forty-five."

LPR stands for License Plate Reader. It uses optical scanning software to read the tag numbers on passing cars and then compares those numbers against lists of wanted and stolen vehicles. It's an amazing bit of technology, even if all the kinks haven't quite been worked out yet.

"Any reason we're just finding out about this now?" I asked. "That's well over forty-eight hours ago. What was the problem?"

"The system isn't live at the airport," Jerome said. "There's a manual download once a day, Monday to Friday. I just got this a few minutes ago. But, bottom line, Alex? I'm guessing your little birdies came home to roost."

"I'm guessing you're right," I said, and turned back toward the office.

Even before I got to my desk, though, my excitement started turning into something else. This was a double-edged sword, at best. Considering the heat on Talley and Hennessey right now, I couldn't imagine too many reasons why they'd come back to DC. Chances were, if we didn't find at least one of them soon, some other fox in the henhouse was going to get a bullet in the brain.

Nothing like a little pressure to help you do your best work, right?

Chapter 83

IT WAS JUST after midnight when Denny approached the black Lincoln Town Car parked on Vermont Avenue and got in. The man he knew only as Zachary was waiting for him. Zachary's usual nameless driver/goon was sitting face front at the wheel.

"The clock's winding down on this thing," Denny said straight-out. "We need to put it to bed before it all blows up."

"We agree," Zachary said. Like it was his decision. Like the big man in the ivory tower, whoever he was, didn't pull the strings, write the checks, and call the shots here.

Zachary took a plain manila folder out of the seat pocket and handed it to him. "This will be our last arrangement," he said. "Go ahead. Take it."

Arrangement. The guy was too much.

Inside the folder were two dossiers, if that's what you could call them—a couple of pictures, a few paragraphs, and some Google maps slapped together on copy paper, like somebody's shitty little school project. Wherever the boss man spent his billions, it sure as hell wasn't on document prep.

But as for the names on those dossiers? Now *they* were impressive.

"Well, well," Denny said. "Looks like your man wants to go out with a bang. That's a pun, little joke. No extra charge."

Zachary pushed his pretentious horn-rims a little higher on his nose. "Just . . . focus on the material," he said.

It would have been nice to go upside this guy's head one time. Nothing major, just enough to put some kind of expression on his face. Any expression at all would be a big improvement.

But this was no time to start coloring outside the lines. So Denny kept his mouth shut and took a couple of minutes to absorb the information. Then he slid the manila folder into the seat pocket and sat back again.

This part was all rote by now. Zachary reached over the seat, took the canvas pouch from Mr. Personality in the front, and put it on the armrest. Denny picked it up.

Right away, he could feel it was light.

"What the hell is this?" he said, and dropped it back on the armrest between them.

"That," Zachary said, "is one-third. You'll get the rest afterward. We're doing things a little differently this time."

"The hell we are!" he said, and just like that, the driver was up and over the seat with a fat .45 shoved halfway up Denny's nose. He could even smell traces of gunpowder. The weapon had been used recently.

"Now listen to me," Zachary said. More like purred.

"You're going to be paid in full. The only change here is our terms of delivery."

"This is bullshit!" Denny said. "You shouldn't be messing around with me now."

"Just listen," Zachary told him. "Your incompetence up in New Jersey was not appreciated, *Steven*. Now that the authorities know who you are, this is just good business practice. So, are we going to have a smooth finish to this thing or not?"

It wasn't a real question, and Denny didn't answer. What he did was reach down and take back the canvas pouch. That spoke for itself. The .45 was dislodged from his face and the driver pulled back, although he didn't turn around.

"Did you see the car parked behind us?" Zachary asked softly, as if they'd been sitting here having a friendly chat the whole time.

And, yes, Denny had seen it, an old blue Subaru wagon with Virginia plates. His spotter's radar wasn't something he turned on and off.

"What about it?" he said.

"You need to get out of the city. We've got too much exposure here. Take Mitch and go somewhere discreet—West Virginia, or whatever you think is best."

"Just like that? What am I supposed to tell Mitch?" Denny said. "He's already asking too many questions."

"I'm sure you'll think of something to handle him. And take this." Zachary handed over a silver Nokia phone, presumably encrypted. "Keep it off, but check it at least every six hours. And be ready to go when we tell you."

"Just out of curiosity," Denny said, "what's this 'we' shit anyway? Do *you* even know who you're working for?"

Zachary reached across and opened the door to the side-walk for him. They were done here.

"This one's your big payout, Denny," he said. "Don't blow it. Don't make any more mistakes either."

Chapter 84

FOR THE SECOND DAY of canvassing at homeless shelters, I did what I already should have and pulled in more of my team, including Sampson. I even called in that favor with Max Siegel, to see if he could spare any warm bodies.

Max surprised me by showing up himself, along with two eager young assistants. We split up the list and agreed to come together at the end of the day to check out mealtime and evening sign-in at one of the larger facilities.

At five o'clock that afternoon, we were all at Lindholm Family Services when they opened their doors for dinner. The shelter served more than a thousand meals a day, to a clientele that was everything you might expect, and some things you might not.

There were families with kids, and people who talked to themselves, and folks who looked like they just came from an office somewhere, all eating shoulder to shoulder at long cafeteria tables.

For the first hour or so, it was a frustrating repeat of the day before. None of the people who were willing to talk to me recognized Mitch's picture or the old file photo I'd pulled of Steven Hennessey, aka Denny. And some people wouldn't talk to the police at all.

One guy in particular seemed to be in his own world. He was sitting at the end of a table, turned away from everyone else, with his tray balanced on the corner. He mumbled to himself as I came over.

"Mind if I talk to you for a second?" I said.

His lips stopped moving, but he didn't look up, so I held the picture down low where he could see it.

"We're trying to get a message to this guy, Mitch Talley. There's been a death in the family he needs to know about."

This is the kind of half-truth you have to be comfortable with to get things done sometimes. We were all in street clothes today, too. Jackets and ties can be counterproductive in a place like this.

The man shook his head. "No," he said, too fast. "No. Sorry. I don't recognize him." He had a thick accent that sounded eastern European to me.

"Take another look," I said. "Mitch Talley? Usually hangs out with this guy named Denny. Any of it ringing a bell? We could use your help."

He looked a little longer and ran a hand absently over his salt-and-pepper beard, which was matted halfway to dreadlocks.

"No," he said again, without ever looking up. "I'm sorry. I do not know him."

I didn't push it. "All right," I said. "I'll be around for a while if you think of anything."

As soon as I stepped away, he went right back to the mumbling, and on a hunch, I kept an eye on him.

Sure enough, I'd barely started talking to the next person before the mumbler got up to leave. When I looked over, his tray was still there—along with most of his dinner.

"Excuse me, sir?" I called out loudly enough that a few people around him turned their heads.

But not him. He just kept going.

"Sir?"

I was moving now, and that caught Sampson's attention. The mumbling guy was clearly making a beeline for the exit. When he finally did look back, realizing we were coming after him, he broke into a run. He shot straight out the double doors and onto Second Street ahead of us.

Chapter 85

OUR RUNNER WAS HALFWAY to the corner by the time Sampson and I got outside. He'd looked maybe early fifties to me, but he was moving pretty well.

"Damnit, damnit, damnit—"

Foot pursuit sucks. It just does. Never mind all the variables—it's nothing you want to be doing at the end of a long day. But here Sampson and I were, tearing ass down Second Street after a crazy man.

I shouted a few times for him to stop, but that obviously wasn't in his game plan.

The rush-hour traffic on D had bunched up enough that he made it across the street fairly easily.

I cut right behind him between a taxi and an EMCOR truck, while a couple of guys on lawn chairs outside the shelter shouted after us.

"Go, buddy! Go!"

"Dig, dig, dig, dig, dig!"

I was guessing they weren't talking to me.

He ran straight on, into the little park by the Labor Department. It cut a diagonal between the high-rise buildings toward Indiana Avenue, but he never got that far.

The ground was terraced here, and when he lurched up and over the first retaining wall, it slowed him down just enough. I got one foot on the wall and both my hands on his shoulders, and we came down hard in a patch of ground cover. At least we weren't on the sidewalk anymore.

Right away, he started scrabbling with me, trying to pull free, then trying to bite me. Sampson got there and put a knee down on his back while I stood up.

"Sir, stop moving!" John shouted at him as I started a quick pat down.

"No! No! Please!" he yelled from the ground. "I haven't done anything! I am an innocent person!"

"What's *this?*"

I had pulled a knife out of the side pocket of his filthy barn coat. It was sheathed in a toilet paper roll and wrapped in duct tape.

"You can't take that!" he said. "Please! It is my property!"

"I'm not taking it," I told him. "I'm just holding on to it for now."

We got him up on his feet and walked him back over to the wall to sit down.

"Sir, do you need medical attention?" I asked. There was an abrasion on his forehead from where we went down. I felt a little bad about that. Trembling here in front of me, he just seemed kind of pathetic. Never mind that he'd been holding his own until a minute ago, trying to bite off one of my fingers.

"No," he said. "No."

"You're sure?"

"I am not required to talk to you. You have no reason to arrest me."

His English was good, if a little stilted. And he obviously wasn't as out of it as I'd thought, although he still wouldn't look at us.

"How about this?" I said, indicating the knife. I handed it to Sampson. "Look, you just ran away from your dinner. You want a hot dog? Something to drink?"

"I am not required to talk to you," he said again.

"Yeah, I got that. Coke okay?"

He nodded at the ground.

"One hot dog, one Coke," Sampson said, and headed over to the carts on D Street. I could see Siegel and his guys on the sidewalk, waiting to find out what had happened. At least Max was keeping his distance; that was a welcome change.

"Listen," I said. "You notice I haven't asked for your name, right? All I want is to find the guy in the picture, and I think you know something you're not saying."

"No," he insisted. "No. No. I am just a poor man."

"Then why did you run?" I said.

But he wouldn't answer, and I couldn't force him. He was right about that. My hunch wasn't enough to detain him.

Besides, there were other ways to get information.

When Sampson came back with the hot dog, the guy ate it in three bites, downed the soda, and stood up.

"I am free to go, yes?" he said.

"Take my card," I said. "Just in case you change your mind."

I gave it to him, and Sampson handed back the knife in the cardboard sheath. "You don't need money for a call," I said. "Just tell any cop on the street you want to talk to me. And stay out of trouble with that blade, okay?"

There was no good-bye, of course. He pocketed the knife and headed straight up D Street while we stood there watching him go.

"Talk to me, Sampson," I said. "Are we thinking the same thing here?"

"I think we are," he said. "He knows something. I'm just going to let him get around the corner first."

"Sounds good. I'll ask Siegel to finish up at the shelter. Then I want to get this Coke can over to the lab, see if it tells us anything."

Our mystery man had just reached First Street. He turned left and continued on out of sight.

"All right, that's my cue," Sampson said. "I'll call if there's anything to tell."

"Same here," I said, and we split up.

Chapter 86

WALKING AWAY from the police detectives, Stanislaw Wajda could feel his heart still bucking in his chest. This wasn't over yet. *No. No. Not at all.*

In fact, when he reached the corner and chanced a quick look back, they were still watching. They'd probably follow him, too.

It had been a mistake to run like that. It only made things worse. Now there was nothing to do but keep moving. *Yes.* Figure it out later. *Yes.*

The grocery cart was right where he'd left it, in an alcove at the back of Lindholm. You weren't supposed to use the back door here. In fact, very few people seemed to even know about it.

The alcove was just big enough to tuck the cart away—out of sight of the street—when he couldn't keep an eye on it himself. He pulled it out now and proceeded up the road, slowly and cautiously, but ready to run again if he had to.

It felt good to move. The walking eased his mind. And the sound of the cart rattling and shimmying over the sidewalk was a kind of white noise that blocked out the other sounds of the city. It created a space where he could think clearly and focus on his work, and what to do next.

Now, if he could just remember where he'd been when he left off.

Mersenne 44, was that it? *Yes*. That was it. Mersenne 44.

It came back slowly, shimmering into his mind as if out of the shadows, until he could see it clearly.

See it and speak it.

The words tumbled out of him when they came, but quietly, in nothing more than a mumble. Nothing anyone would overhear, just enough to help make the number real once again.

"Two to the thirty-two million, five hundred eighty-two thousand, six hundred and fifty-seventh," he said.

Yes. That was it precisely. Mersenne 44. *Yes. Yes. Yes.*

He picked up his pace now and continued up the street without looking back again.

Chapter 87

IT WAS QUIET at the Fingerprint Analysis Section when I got there. The only person in the lab was one of the civilian staff, an analyst named Bernie Stringer who usually went by "Strings." I could hear the heavy metal on his iPod blaring away while he worked.

"I hope that's not priority!" he shouted, and then pulled out an earbud. "Narcotics is already kicking my ass here." There were two full boxes of slides on the bench next to him.

"I just need some prints off of this," I said, holding the Coke can up by the lip.

"Tonight?" he said.

"Yeah, actually. Now."

"Knock yourself out, man. Cyanoacrylate's in the drawer by the fuming chamber."

That was fine by me. I like working in the lab every once in a while. It makes me feel smarter, even if printing is Forensics 101.

I went over to the fuming chamber and set the can upright inside. Then I put a few drops of cyanoacrylate, which is really just superglue, on a dish and sealed it all up to heat for a while.

In about fifteen minutes, I had a nice four-print set standing out on the surface of the can. Sampson's paw print was there, too, but it was easy enough to differentiate, sizewise.

I dusted the ones I wanted with black powder and took a few pictures, just in case.

After that, it was only a matter of lifting them with clear tape and laying them back down on a card for scanning.

"Hey, Strings!" I shouted over. "Can I use your system?"

"Knock yourself out! Password's B-I-G-B-U-T-Z."

"Of course it is," I said.

"Huh? What's that?"

"Nothing."

Once I got the prints onto the computer, it took IAFIS about half an hour to spit out four possible matches. A lot of the time, the final comparison is done by eye, which is good. It helps keep the process human.

And it didn't take long for me to confirm one of the four.

The tented arch pattern on our man's index finger was fairly distinctive, even as these little puzzles go.

With a few keystrokes, I had his name and record right there in front of me.

He was Stanislaw Wajda.

That explained the accent anyway. He'd been arrested just once, on a domestic assault charge in College Park, Maryland, a year and a half earlier. It didn't seem like too much to go on.

But, in fact, I'd just stumbled onto a killer.

Chapter 88

AN INITIAL ONLINE search for "Stanislaw Wajda" brought up all kinds of different results. When I filtered for news reports, I got a whole slew of year-old stories about a missing-persons case.

That seemed promising, and I clicked on the first one, from the *Baltimore Sun*.

Questions Persist in Professor's Disappearance

April 12, College Park—The search continues for University of Maryland professor Stanislaw Wajda, 51, who was last seen leaving the A. V. Williams Building on the university campus the evening of April 7.

Wajda's mental state at the time of his disappearance has since become a matter of widespread speculation. While local police and UM officials have declined to comment on the issue, the professor's erratic behavior over the last six months is a matter of public record.

In October, police were summoned to Wajda's home on Radcliffe Drive for a domestic-disturbance call. Wajda, who had no previous criminal record, was charged with aggravated assault and held overnight, until the charges were dropped.

On campus, Professor Wajda has been brought before the university provost two times in the past year, once for unspecified aggressive behavior toward a graduate student, and a second time following what one eyewitness described as an explosive episode in the university library over a missing periodical.

Wajda, a professor of mathematics, came to the United States from Poland in 1983 to study at Boston University, where he won several top academic prizes in his field. More recently, he was featured in the PBS NOVA documentary "Ones to Watch" for his study of prime numbers, and specifically his pursuit of a proof for what many consider to be the holy grail of mathematics today: Riemann's hypothesis. . . .

I stopped reading right there, got up, and dialed Sampson's number on my way out the door.

"Strings, thanks much."

"No problem. Glad to help out."

Chapter 89

"WHERE ARE YOU, JOHN?"

"I'm outside of the damn shelter, if you can believe it. I can't. Guy pushed a shopping cart around the block a few times and then checked back in for a bed before Siegel and the others were even gone. I've got Donny Burke coming to take the overnight for me."

"We need to pull the guy out of there," I said.

"Why do you sound like you're running?"

"He's a math professor, John. An expert in prime numbers. And Riemann's hypothesis."

"What?"

"Yeah. His name's Stanislaw Wajda, and he's been missing for a year. Wait for me. I'll be right there."

It was faster to run over to the shelter than get my car. I was already down the back stairs and cutting across Judiciary Square.

"I've got this," Sampson said. "I'll have him out by the time you get here."

"John, don't—"

But he'd already hung up. Sampson can be just as stubborn and pigheaded as I am sometimes, which is why it's hard to hold it against him.

I picked up the pace.

From Judiciary Square, I came out on Fourth Street and cut around the block toward Second. Before I got there, though, I saw Sampson coming right toward me as if he'd just been around the back of the building.

"He's gone, Alex! His cart's not there anymore, and there's a goddamn door in the back. He duped me! He's out!" Sampson turned away and kicked a garbage bag off the curb, sending a shower of trash into the street.

Before he could take another swinging kick, I pulled him back. "Hang on, John. One thing at a time. We don't know anything for sure yet."

"Don't even start with that," he told me. "It's him. I put that damn knife back in his hand, and then I let him get away."

"We both did, John," I said. "We *both* did."

But Sampson wasn't hearing me. I could tell he was going to blame himself no matter what I said, so I stopped trying and switched to action.

"He can't be far," I said. "It's not like he hopped into a cab or something. We'll walk the neighborhood all night if we have to. I'll get this out on WALES right away. Put some more eyes on the street. Maybe get someone from Warrant Squad in the morning, if it comes to that. Those guys are bloodhounds. We'll get him."

Sampson nodded and started up the street without another word. No time like the present.

"What'd you say the name was?" he asked as I came up alongside him.

"Stanislaw Wajda," I told him.

"Stanislaw...?"

"Wajda."

"Screw it. I'll learn to say it after we find the son of a bitch."

Chapter 90

IT WAS THREE DAYS BEFORE we got anywhere even close to some forward movement. No Talley. No Hennessey. No Wajda.

And then the worst happened.

On Friday morning, for the third time that month, I got an early call from Sampson about a dead body. Another junkie had been beaten to death, with more of the same numbers gibberish carved into his forehead and across his back.

But one thing was different this time, and it changed everything.

"They found Stanislaw's shopping cart next to the body," Sampson told me. "At least, I'm pretty sure it's his. Hard to tell one from another, you know?" His voice was hoarse. I wasn't sure how much sleep he'd gotten since Wajda had disappeared. "This poor kid doesn't look like he was much more than eighteen, Alex."

"Sampson, are you going to be okay?" I asked. "You don't sound like yourself."

"I sure hope so."

"This isn't your fault, John. You know that, right?"

He still wasn't ready to answer that one. All he said was "You don't have to come down here."

"I'm coming," I said. "Of course I am."

Chapter 91

THE SCENE AT Farragut Square was depressingly familiar when I got there. I'm never sure which is worse—the shock of something I've never seen before, or the weight of seeing it one too many times.

"The cart's definitely his," Sampson told me. "We just found *this*."

He held up an evidence bag with my own smudged business card inside. It felt like a hard kick to the head. What a mess this was.

"There's also visible blood spatter on the frame, and a sawed-off sledgehammer on the bottom rack. Presumably our murder weapon."

"I've been thinking about this," I said. "There's a long underpass right by Lindholm. Homeless people sleep there all the time. That may be where he's been hunting for his victims."

"Maybe so," John said. "But then why cart them all the way over here? I don't get this at all. Why K Street?"

Not counting Kyle Craig's fake-out with Anjali Patel, all three victims in this case had been left somewhere along K, each one near the intersection of a prime-numbered street—Twenty-third, Thirteenth, and now Seventeenth. With two incidents, it had been harder to see, but with three, the pattern popped right out. I wondered if the letter "K" represented something specific in mathematics, but I wasn't sure. And, moreover, "The man's insane, Sampson. That's the one constant. We may not get very far looking for motive here."

"Or for him," John said, and thumbed over at the cart. "Whatever made him leave his stuff behind, something's changed, Alex. I don't know what it is, but I have a feeling we may never see this guy again. I think he's history."

Chapter 92

STANISLAW WAJDA BLINKED AWAKE. It was hard for him to see at first. A chiaroscuro of vague forms filled his vision. Then, slowly, things began to distinguish themselves. A wall. Concrete blocks. An old boiler on a cracked cement floor.

The last he remembered, he'd been in the park. *Yes.* The boy. Was it just last night?

"Hello," someone said, and Stanislaw jumped. His heart lurched into a gallop as he suddenly knew enough to be scared.

A man was there. Dark hair. Vaguely familiar.

"Where am I?" said Stanislaw.

"Washington."

"I mean—"

"I know what you mean."

His hands were unbound, he realized. His feet, too. No chains, no handcuffs. He'd almost expected otherwise. He looked down and saw that he was sitting, half slumped, in an old wooden chair.

"Don't get up," the man said. "You're still going to feel a little bit groggy."

He'd seen this man's face before. At the shelter. *Yes.* With the two black detectives. *Yes. Yes.*

"Are you the police?" he said. "Am I arrested?"

The man chuckled low, which was very odd indeed. "No, Professor. May I call you Stanislaw?"

Even as the situation began to take shape, none of it made any sense to him.

"How do you know my name?" he said.

"Let's say I'm an admirer of your work," the man told him. "I saw what you did in Farragut Square last night, and I don't mind telling you, it was a thrill. Definitely worth the effort for me to get all the way over there."

Wajda's stomach lurched. He felt as though he might vomit. Or even faint.

"Oh Jezu—"

"Not to worry. Your secret's safe with me." The man pulled another chair over and sat down across from him. "But tell me something, Stanislaw. What's with the prime numbers? The police reports say it's something about Riemann's hypothesis. Is that accurate?"

So he knew. This strange fellow knew what he'd done. Stanislaw could feel tears warming the corners of his eyes.

"Yes," he said. "Riemann's. Yes."

"But what about it, specifically? Enlighten me, Professor. I'm dying to know."

It had been a long time since Stanislaw had seen curiosity in a young person's eyes. Years and years. A lifetime ago...

"The Riemann zeta function zero, as you know, lies on the critical line with real part between zero and one, if the zeta function is equal to zero—"

"No," the man said. "Listen to me carefully. Why do you kill for it? What does it mean to you?"

"Everything," he said. "To understand it is to grasp infinity, do you see? To conceive of a framework so vast as to transcend ideas of size or even limitation—"

The man slapped him hard across the face. "I don't want one of your stupid college lectures, Professor. I want to know why you kill those boys in the way that you do. Now, can you answer that for me or not? You're intelligent—it should be simple."

He could, Stanislaw realized suddenly. *Yes. Yes.* The outcome had been taken from his hands. There was no longer room for anything but the truth.

"Those boys are better off dead," he said. "There is nothing here for them but misery and suffering. Don't you understand? Don't you see?"

"I do see."

"They have fallen out of God's reach, but I can still help them. I can give them that which is infinite," he said. "I can give them back to God. Do you understand?"

"I think I do," the man said, and stood up. "This is very disappointing. We might have—" He paused and smiled. "Well, never mind about what might have been. Thank you, Professor. It's been an education."

"No," Stanislaw said. "Thank *you*."

He saw the ice pick then, and followed it with his eyes as the man raised it up and to the side until it disappeared into silhouette against a bare bulb in the ceiling. Then Stanislaw lifted his own chin high, opening himself as widely as possible so that no matter what happened, the man would be sure not to miss.

Chapter 93

I'M SO USED to my own phone going off at all hours that I was reaching for the nightstand before I realized it was Bree's cell ringing, not mine. The clock by the bed said 4:21. *Oh, good God Almighty, what now?*

"This is Stone." I heard her in the dark. "Who's this?"

Right away, she sat up. When she turned on the light beside the bed, the phone was pressed against her chest, and she whispered so low that she practically mouthed the next words to me.

"It's Kyle Craig."

Now I was up, too. When I took the phone, I could hear Kyle still talking on the other end of the line.

"Bree, sweetheart? Are you there?"

If he'd been in front of me, I honestly believe I could have killed him without thinking twice. But I kept my head as best I could. I grabbed control of my emotions.

"Kyle, it's Alex. Don't ever call this number again," I said, and hung up.

Bree's jaw literally dropped. "What was that?" she said. "Why did you do that?"

"My line in the sand. It doesn't do me any good to let him keep setting the rules."

"Do you think he'll call back?"

"Well, if he doesn't, we'll both get a little more sleep," I said.

Something had changed in me. I wasn't going to keep playing this game forever. I couldn't.

And, in any case, my own cell phone rang a few seconds later.

"*What?*" I answered.

"Bree never answered my question," Kyle said. "About how the wedding plans were coming along. I figured that was more her department than yours."

"No," I said. "You wanted to make yourself seem more threatening."

He laughed almost congenially. "Did it work?"

"I'm hanging up, Kyle."

"Wait!" he said. "There is something else. It's important, or I wouldn't be calling so early."

I didn't ask what it was. In fact, I was about to hang up anyway when he went on.

"I got you an engagement present," he said. "Of sorts. Since I'm allowing you to get married and all. A little something to free up your schedule, so you can focus on that pretty little bride to be."

Now my heart sank. I had to know. "Kyle? What have you done?"

"Well, if I told you, that would spoil the surprise, wouldn't it?" he said. "Twenty-ninth and K, northeast corner. *And you might want to hurry.*"

Chapter 94

BY SUNRISE, we had a full tactical team in place at the corner of Twenty-ninth and K. There was very little I'd put past Kyle, and while it could be a mistake to show up when and where he specified, I couldn't just ignore the phone call. So we took precautions, as much as we possibly could.

The location was at the edge of Rock Creek Park, with the Whitehurst Freeway running overhead. We put officers with MP5s on the overpass, and a barrier of armored SWAT vans hugging the corner to block as many sight lines as possible.

Our nerve center was a coffee shop on K, where the SWAT unit commander, Tom Ogilvy, could stay in radio contact with his team. Sampson and I listened in on headsets.

EMS was on standby, with patrol units barring the street a block away in each direction. All personnel were outfitted with Kevlar and helmets.

And maybe it was all for nothing. Was Kyle actually

watching? Was he armed? Ready with something up his sleeve? Or maybe none of the above. I think that's exactly what he wanted me to wrestle with now.

In any case, it didn't take long for the entry team to find something. Less than five minutes after they'd snaked into the park from Twenty-ninth, their lead man radioed over.

"We've got a body here," he said. "White male, middle-aged. Looks like it could be a homeless guy."

"Proceed with caution," Ogilvy radioed back. We'd already briefed everyone about the possibilities here. "I want a full visual check around that body before anyone touches it. B Team, I need you on high alert."

Three more minutes of silence ticked by until the "all clear" came back—such as it was. When I reached for the coffee shop door, Sampson grabbed my arm.

"Let me do this one, Alex. If Kyle's here, it could be you he's waiting for."

"No way," I told him. "Besides, if Kyle ever comes for me, it's going to be face-to-face, not from a distance."

"Oh, because you know everything there is to know about that maniac?" he said.

"I know that much," I said, and headed outside.

Even before we got close to the body in the park, I recognized Stanislaw Wajda's filthy barn coat. He'd been left on his side, shoved under a clump of bushes, just like his own victims before him.

There was no carving this time. The only visible injury was a single puncture wound to the throat, similar to the one we'd seen on Anjali Patel.

The skin on his neck was a solid stain of dried blood, and

it continued down under his shirt. That meant he'd most likely been sitting up when he was stabbed. Probably when he died, too.

We'd already run prints on the shopping cart and sledgehammer from Farragut Square. There was no doubt anymore that Wajda was our Numbers Killer. Still, whatever he'd done when he was alive, I felt a wave of pity for him now.

"What's this?" Sampson pointed at something in Wajda's hand. I pulled on some gloves and knelt down to take whatever it was from between the clenched fingers.

It was a small greeting card—the kind you usually send with flowers. This one had a picture of a wedding cake on the front, with an African-American bride and groom at the top.

"It's my engagement present," I said. I felt a little sick to my stomach.

When I opened the card, I instantly recognized the precise block letters of Kyle's handwriting.

To Alex:
You're welcome.
—K.C.

Chapter 95

AFTER FIVE DAYS of lying low with Mitch in the West Virginia woods, Denny got the call he'd been waiting for. Then it was another several days for reconnaissance in DC before they were good to go. It wouldn't be much longer now, just a little while and he'd be a free man. A very *rich,* free man.

The door banged open behind him as they came out onto the roof of the National Building Museum.

He turned around, and Mitch held up a hand.

"My bad," he said.

"Just shut the damn thing and come on," Denny said, harsher than he meant to.

It wasn't as if the noise really mattered. The museum was closed for the night, and the nearest threat risk was the twenty-something mope sitting downstairs at a ground-floor security desk, watching horror movies on his laptop. It was more about having spent one too many nights sleeping elbow to elbow in the old Subaru with Mitch, living off of canned food and listening to him yammer on about the "mission."

He shook it off and walked over to the southwest corner of the roof to look out.

Traffic on F Street was light for a Friday. There was a slight breeze, with the promise of showers for later, but so far everything was quiet. The first limos would start pulling up in front of Sidney Harman Hall—or just "the Harman," to the locals—in about fifteen to twenty minutes.

Mitch came along and waited silently behind Denny as he unrolled the canvas tarp. Then Mitch set out his gear and started assembling the M110.

"You mad at me or something, Denny?" he said finally. "We got a problem?"

"Naw, man," Denny said right away. There was no sense in making him uptight tonight. *Especially* not tonight. "You're doin' great. I'm just ready to get this one done, you know? A little overeager. *My* bad."

That seemed to satisfy him. Mitch nodded once and went right back to business. He flipped down the bipod, set the rifle on the ledge, and put his eye up to the scope. Once he'd adjusted the buttstock against his cheek, he could start dialing in.

"We're working in a range tonight," Denny said, keeping his tone nice and easy now. "Cars are going to be stopping all up and down the block."

Mitch swept left and right a few times, getting a feel for the sidewalk in front of the theater. "You said these crumbums are a couple of judges?"

"That's right," Denny said. "Two of the most powerful fuckers in the country."

"What'd they do?"

"You know what an activist judge is?"

"Not really. What's that?"

"Well, let's just say that the good old U.S. of A.'s better off without them," Denny said. "I'll spot 'em and you drop 'em, Mitchie, but it's going to be fast. You've got to be ready, okay? One, two—then we're out of here."

Mitch held his position like always, but the corners of his mouth turned up just a hair. It was the closest thing to a cocky little smile Denny had seen on him in a while.

"Don't worry, Denny," he said. "I won't miss."

Chapter 96

BY SEVEN THIRTY, F Street was one long line of black cars.

The event tonight was "Will on the Hill," an annual fundraiser for arts education in DC. Two dozen Capitol Hill movers and shakers were all set to perform an "inside-baseball" version of Will Shakespeare's *Twelfth Night* for an audience of more of the same—congressmen, senators, Hill staffers, and half of K Street, probably.

Denny watched the road through his sighting scope. "No shortage of foxes in the henhouse tonight, am I right?"

"I guess," Mitch said, still eyeing over the crowd. "I thought this was going to be a bunch of famous people. I don't recognize none of them down there."

"Yeah, well, you're kind of famous now, too, and nobody knows what you look like," Denny said.

Mitch smiled. "Point."

Rahm Emanuel and his wife were just arriving. The House

minority leader and Senate president pro tempore had shown up together a minute ago, grabbing a much-needed photo op in the middle of a contentious legislative session.

Each one got out of his car and crossed the redbrick sidewalk, maybe six paces, until he was under the cantilevered glass wall that hung over the theater's main entrance. This was definitely going to be tight when it happened.

Finally, at ten minutes to eight, Denny spotted who he was looking for. A short Mercedes limo stopped at the curb.

The driver got out and came around to open the door, and the Honorable Cornelia Summers stepped into view.

"Here we go, Mitch. Ten o'clock. Long blue dress, getting out of the Mercedes."

Right behind her, Justice George Ponti stood up. They stopped long enough to wave self-consciously at the press and the gawkers gathered behind police lines on the sidewalk. Even from a distance, Denny noticed that these two looked out of their element.

"Number two's in the tux, with the gray hair."

Mitch had already adjusted his stance. "I'm there."

"Shooter ready?"

Summers took Ponti's arm, and they turned to go inside, just a few steps away now.

"Ready," Mitch said.

"Send it."

The M110 gave off a familiar sharp pop as the bullet passed through the suppressor at three thousand feet per second. In virtually the same moment, Cornelia Summers collapsed to the ground with a small red blossom just above her left ear.

Justice Ponti stumbled as she came off his arm, and the second shot missed. A glass door about ten feet from the man's head shattered into a million pieces.

"*Again,*" Denny said. "Now."

The Supreme Court justice had turned back toward the car. He already had one hand on the door.

"Do it, Mitchie."

"I got him," Mitch said, and there was another sharp pop.

This time Ponti went down for real, and the entire block in front of the Harman was thrown into full-blown pandemonium.

Chapter 97

DENNY WATCHED THE STREET while Mitch broke down. A steady rain had started to fall, but that didn't stop hundreds of people in very nice evening wear from scattering like cockroaches up and down the block.

"What's going on, Denny?" Mitch had already packed the scope, stock, and magazine away.

Denny motioned Mitch over. "Come here. You should see this. It's amazing what you've done."

Mitch seemed torn, but when Denny waved him over again, he set down his gear and duckwalked back to the ledge. Then he peered at his work.

The Harman looked like some kind of glass-fronted insane asylum. Police flashers were already rolling in the street, and the only people not moving down there were the two bodies laid out on the sidewalk.

"You know what that's called?" Denny said. "That's mission accomplished. Couldn't have gone better."

Mitch shook his head. "I messed up, Denny. That second shot—"

"Don't mean nothing now. You just soak this shit up for a minute and enjoy it. I'll get us ready to go."

Denny stepped back and started securing the clasps on Mitch's pack while Mitch watched, transfixed.

"Not bad for a night's work, right, Mitchie?"

"Yeah," Mitch said, only half out loud, more to himself than anything. "Kind of awesome, actually."

"And who's the hero of the story, bro?"

"We are, Denny."

"That's right. Real live American heroes. Nobody can ever take that away from you, no matter what. Understand?"

Mitch didn't even answer this time, except to nod. It was as if, once he'd gotten a glimpse, he couldn't tear his eyes from the scene.

A second later, Mitch was dead—with a bullet in his head.

The poor guy probably didn't even hear Denny's muzzled Walther go off, it happened that fast. Just as well. It was a goddamn awful business sometimes; the least Denny could do for him was make it quick and professional.

"Sorry, Mitchie. Couldn't be helped," he said.

Then he picked up Mitch's pack, left everything else, and headed for the stairs without looking back at the evening's third homicide.

Chapter 98

I'D BEEN WORKING at the Daly Building when the first terrible report came in, and this time I was on the scene within minutes of the gunfire. I tried hard to ignore the chaos in the street, tried not to think about the victims—not yet—and focused on the one thing I needed to know most.

Where did the shots come from? Was it possible they'd made a mistake this time?

An MPD sergeant on the sidewalk had an initial report that Cornelia Summers had gone down first, and that she'd been on George Ponti's left as they headed into the Harman. Two Supreme Court justices—even now, it seemed unbelievable!

I looked to the left, down F Street. The Jackson Graham Building was a possibility, but if I'd been the gunman, I would have gone for the National Building Museum. It was a couple of blocks up, well clear of the scene, and had a flat roof with plenty of cover.

"Get me three more uniforms," I told the sergeant. "Right away. I'm going to that building—the National."

Within minutes, we were down the street and pounding on the museum's front doors. One very alarmed-looking security guard came running to let us in. The Federal Protective Service had jurisdiction here, but I'd been told it would be a good half hour before they could get a team on-site.

"We need to get to the roof," I told the guard. His tag said DAVID HALE. "What's the fastest way up there?"

I left one patrol officer behind to radio in for a full lockdown of the building, and the rest of us followed Hale through the museum's central hall. It was a huge, open space with Corinthian columns all the way to the ceiling, which was several stories overhead. That's where we needed to go.

Hale brought us to an emergency exit at the far corner. "Straight up," he said.

We left him there and took the stairs in rough formation, leapfrogging one flight at a time, with flashlights and weapons drawn.

At the top, we came to a fire door.

It should have been alarmed, but the metal housing was on the ground and the mechanism itself was hanging loose by a couple of wires.

My heart was already pounding from the run. It notched up again now. We'd come to the right place.

When I opened the door, an empty expanse of roof was in front of me, with the top of the Accountability Office visible across G Street beyond that. The rain was coming down hard, but you could still hear the sirens and shouting coming from the Harman.

I signaled for one officer to go right and the other to follow me out in the direction of the street noise.

As we came around toward the southwest corner, a row of raised skylights was blocking our view.

I saw the shadow of something by the farthest one—a pack of gear, or maybe just a garbage bag—and pointed it out to the cop next to me. I didn't even know the guy's name.

We worked our way along the roof with our lights off, staying low just in case.

Once we got close enough, I could see that someone was still there. He was on his knees, facing the Harman and not moving.

My Glock was up. "Police! Freeze!" I aimed low for his legs, but there was no need, as it turned out. As soon as the other officer hit him with a flashlight beam, we saw clearly the dark hole at the back of his head, washed clean by the rain. His body had lodged in the corner of the half wall that ran around the roof, holding him up that way.

One look at his face, and I recognized Mitch Talley. Now, suddenly, my legs were like Jell-O. This was too much, it really was. Mitch Talley was dead? How?

"Jesus." The patrol officer with me leaned in for a better look. "What is that, nine millimeter?"

"Call it in," I told him. "Get an APB on Steven Hennessey, aka Denny Humboldt. He couldn't have gotten far yet. I'll call CIC. We need to shut this neighborhood down—now. Every second counts."

Unless my instincts were way off here, Hennessey had

just broken up the Patriot sniper team, for whatever reasons of his own.

If I were him, I would have been running like hell. I would already be out of Washington and I'd never look back.

But I wasn't Hennessey, was I?

Chapter 99

DENNY DROVE AROUND for hours. He stayed north and stopped at a couple of different drugstores in Maryland. He bought a Nationals ball cap, a shaving kit, a pair of weak reading glasses, and a box of chestnut-brown hair dye. *That should do it.*

After another stop, in a Sunoco bathroom in Chevy Chase, he made his way back down to the city. He parked in Logan Circle and walked the two blocks over to Vermont Avenue, where the familiar black Town Car was waiting.

Zachary gave a rare unguarded smile as Denny slid into the backseat.

"Look at you," he said. "All set to fade into the woodwork. I'll bet you're good at it, too."

"Whatever," Denny said. "Let's get this done. So I can fade away, as you say."

"It sounds as though things went off well enough, assuming the news reports are to be believed."

"That's correct."

Zachary stayed where he was. "They didn't say anything about an accomplice, though. Nothing about Mitch."

"I'd be surprised if they did," Denny said. "This lead investigator, Cross, likes to keep his cards close to the vest. But, believe me, it's taken care of. And I don't really want to talk about Mitch anymore. He did his job well."

The contact man studied Denny's face a little longer. Finally, he reached over the front seat and took the pouch from the driver. It seemed right this time, but Denny unzipped the bag and checked, just to be sure.

Zachary sat back now and seemed to actually unclench a little. "Tell me something, Denny. What are you going to do with all that money? Besides getting a new name, I mean."

Denny returned the smile. "Put it somewhere safe, for starters," he said, and tucked the pouch into his jacket as if to illustrate the point. "Then after that—"

There was no rest of the sentence. The Walther fired from inside his pocket and caught the driver in the back of the head. A spray of blood and gray matter hit the windshield.

The second shot took care of Zachary, right through those pretentious horn-rims of his. He never even got to reach for the door. It was over in a matter of seconds—the two most satisfying shots Denny had ever taken.

Except, of course, not Denny. Not anymore. That was a pretty good feeling, too. To leave this all far behind.

No time for celebrations, though. The car had barely gone quiet before he was out on the sidewalk and back to doing what he'd always done best. He kept moving.

Chapter 100

THE TWENTY-FOUR HOURS following the hits at the Harman were a full-court press like I'd rarely seen in Washington. Our Command Information Center had traffic checks going on all night; Major Case Squad put both units on the street; and NSID was told to drop all nonessential business, and that was just inside the MPD.

Details were operating out of Capitol Police, ATF, and even the Secret Service.

By morning, the hunt for Steven Hennessey had gone from regional to national to international. The Bureau was fully activated and looking for him everywhere it was possible for the Bureau to look. The CIA was involved, too.

The significance of these murders had really started to sink in. Justices Summers and Ponti had been the unofficial left wing of the Supreme Court, beloved by half the country and *foxes in the henhouse,* basically, to the other half.

At MPD, our late-afternoon briefing was like a march of the zombies. Nobody had gotten much sleep overnight, and there was a palpable kind of tension in the air.

Chief Perkins presided. There were no introductory remarks.

"What are we looking at?" he asked straight-out. Most of the department's command staff were there, too. Every seat was taken, and people were standing around the edge of the room, shifting on their feet.

"Talk to me," he said. "Anyone."

"The hotline and website are on fire," one of the district commanders, Gerry Hockney, reported in. "It's all over the place, literally. Hennessey's a government operative. He's holed up in a storage facility in Ohio, he's in Florida, he's in Toronto—"

Perkins cut him off. "Anything credible? I need to know what we *have*, not a lot of useless bullshit."

"It's too early to say, to commit to anything. We're overwhelmed, sir."

"In other words, no. Who else? Alex?"

I waved from where I was. "Waiting on a weapons report from that double homicide on Vermont Avenue last night. Two John Does found shot dead in a car, with cash on them but no IDs.

"It was definitely nine millimeter, but we don't know yet if it was the same weapon that killed Mitch Talley."

A huge buzz went up around the room, and I had to shout to get everyone's attention back.

"Even if it was," I went on, "the most it can tell us about Hennessey in the short term is that he was in the city sometime between twelve and four a.m."

"Which means he could be anywhere by now," Sampson said, giving the shorthand version for me. "Which means we should wrap this shit up and get back out there."

"Do you think Hennessey was working for the two dead guys in the car?" someone asked anyway.

"Don't know," I said. "We're still trying to track down who they were. It does seem like he's cleaning house, though. Whether or not he's finished is another question we don't have an answer for."

A lieutenant in the first row spoke up. "Do you mean finished cleaning house, or finished with these sniper killings?"

The questions were natural, but they were starting to get on my nerves. I held my hands out in a shrug. "You tell me."

"So, in other words," Chief Perkins cut in, "we're nearly twenty-four hours out and we know less than we did before these murders, is that it?"

Nobody wanted to answer. There was a long silence in the room.

"Something like that," I said finally.

Chapter 101

TWO MORE DAYS of nerve-rattling quiet went by without much progress or any sign of Steven Hennessey or even anyone who might know him. Then, finally, there was some movement over at the Bureau. Max Siegel called me himself to tell me about it.

"We got something over the Web," he said. "Anonymous, but this one checked out. There's a guy going by Frances Moulton, supposedly fits Hennessey's description down to the toenails. He's got an apartment over on Twelfth, except nobody's seen him for approximately two months. Then, this morning, someone spotted him coming out of there."

"Someone—who?" I asked.

"That's the 'anonymous,'" he said. "The super at the building backed it up, though. He hasn't seen this Moulton character in months either, but he gave me a positive ID on Hennessey's picture when I brought it over."

Either this was huge or it just felt that way given the zeros we'd racked up until now. Sometimes it's hard to tell the difference, when you're desperate.

"What do you want to do with this?" I asked. Whatever it meant, it was still Siegel's lead, not ours.

"I'm thinking you and I might sit up on this place for a while, see what happens," he said. "If you want, I'm game. See? I can change."

It wasn't the answer I'd expected, and my own pause spoke for itself.

"Don't bust my balls, here," Siegel said. "I'm trying to play nice."

In fact, it seemed like he was. Did I love the idea of spending the next eight hours or more in a car with Max Siegel? Not really, but more than that, I didn't want to be on the outside of this investigation for a second.

"Yeah, okay," I said. "I'm in. Where can I meet you?"

Chapter 102

I EVEN BROUGHT coffee.

Siegel brought some, too, so there was plenty of caffeine to go around. We parked in a Bureau-issue Crown Vic on the east side of Twelfth Street between M and N. It was a narrow, tree-lined block with a lot of construction going on, but not at the Midlands. That was Frances Moulton's place and, if we were on the right track, Steven Hennessey's address as well.

The apartment in question was on the eighth of ten floors, with two large windows facing the street. They were both dark when we got there. Max and I settled in for the long haul.

Once we'd said everything there was to say about the case, it got a little awkward—long silences set in. Eventually, though, the conversation loosened back up. Siegel threw me a softball, the kind of thing Bureau guys ask when they don't have something better to say.

"So, why'd you get into law enforcement?" he asked. "If you don't mind my asking."

I smiled into my lap. If anything, he was trying too hard to do the buddy-buddy thing.

"Hollywood just didn't work out. Neither did the NBA," I deadpanned. "What about you?"

"You know. The exotic travel. The great hours."

For once, he got a laugh out of me. I'd decided before coming that I wasn't going to just sit there and hate him all night. That would have been like torture.

"I'll tell you this much," he said. "If things had gone differently? I think I could have been a pretty good bad guy, too."

"Let me guess," I said. "You have the perfect murder in your head."

"Don't you?" Siegel said.

"No comment." I popped the lid on my second coffee. "Most cops do, though. Perfect crime anyway."

After another long pause, he said, "How about this: if you could take someone out—someone who really deserved it—and you knew you could get away with it, would you be torn?"

"No," I said. "That's too slippery a slope for me. I've thought about it."

"Come on." Siegel laughed and leaned back on the car door to look at me. "Say it's just you and Kyle Craig alone in some dark alley. No witnesses. He's all out of ammo and you've still got your Glock. You're telling me you don't pull the trigger now and ask questions later?"

"That's right," I said. The Kyle reference was a little weird, but I let it slide. "I might want to, but I wouldn't do it. I'd take him in. I'd like to bring him back to ADX Florence."

He looked at me, grinning as if he were waiting for me to break.

"Seriously?" he said.

"Seriously."

"I don't know if I believe you."

I shrugged. "What do you want me to say?"

"That you're a human being. Come on, Alex. You can't get by in this business without at least a little walk on the dark side."

"Absolutely," I said. "Been there, done that. I'm just saying, I wouldn't pull the trigger." Whether or not it was true, I really wasn't sure. I just didn't want to go there with Siegel.

"Interesting," he said, and turned back to face the front door of the Midlands. "Very interesting."

Chapter 103

ALEX WAS LYING through his teeth. He was a good liar, but he *was* lying. If he had any idea he was sitting across from Kyle Craig right now, that Glock would be out in a heartbeat, and one round shy a second later.

But that was the whole point, wasn't it? Cross didn't have a clue. Any doubts about that were well behind them. This couldn't possibly be more delicious, could it? No, it could not.

Kyle sipped his coffee and went on. "That's what this is all about, isn't it?" he said offhandedly. *Interesting*—Siegel's speech and inflection were now more natural to him than his own.

"What do you mean?" Cross asked.

"The whole 'foxes in the henhouse' thing. The good guys and the bad guys, all mixed in together. The line between good and evil isn't so clear anymore."

"That's true," Cross said. "More for the Bureau than the PD, though."

"I mean everywhere," Kyle said. "The crooked congressman. The greedy son of a bitch CEO who just can't get by on that first ten million. Hell, embedded terror cells. What's the difference? They're all out there, right under our noses, living next door. It's as if the world used to be black and white, and now it's all just gray, if you squint a little."

Alex was staring now. Right into his eyes. Was he finally tuning in?

"Max, are you talking about Steven Hennessey here? Or yourself?"

"Huh-oh," Kyle-Max answered, and shook a finger at him. "I didn't even see you switch hats. Very slick, Dr. Cross."

And Alex just laughed. It was amazing, really. Kyle had managed to make Cross hate Max Siegel, and now, with the turn of a few screws, Kyle was well on his way to making Alex into a true-blue fan of the smart but obnoxious agent.

Who knows—Siegel might have gotten all the way to an invitation for family dinner or some such thing, at the rate this was going. But then something happened that even Kyle hadn't expected.

A bullet came through the windshield.

Chapter 104

SIEGEL AND I were both out on the pavement and behind our doors at the same time. I heard another shot hit the grille, and then a sickening thud as one hit Siegel's side of the car.

"Max?"

"I'm okay. Not hit."

"Where's it coming from?"

My Glock was out, but I didn't even know where to point it. My other hand was dialing 911 while my eyes scanned the buildings around me.

"One of those two," Max said, pointing at the Midlands and the place just north of it.

I looked up at Hennessey's apartment again—still dark, with the windows closed. Rooftops were his thing anyway. Wasn't that true?

"Hello? Are you there?" said someone on my phone. "This is Nine-One-One Emergency. Can you hear me?"

"This is Detective Cross, MPD. We have an active shooter at Twelve Twenty-one Twelfth Street Northwest. I need immediate assistance, all available units!"

Another shot exploded a planter and a second-floor window directly behind me, one after the other. I heard a scream come from inside an apartment.

"Police!" I shouted for anyone who could hear. "Stay down!" At least half a dozen people were still out on the sidewalk, scrambling for cover, and there was no way to keep more from coming along the walkway on the road.

"We've got to do something. We can't just stay here. Someone's going to get shot," said Max.

I looked at him across the driver's seat. "If he's using a scope, and we move fast, he might not be able to keep up."

"Not with both of us anyway," he said grimly. "Take the Midlands. I'll get the next one up."

This was completely outside of protocol. We should have waited for backup, but with the potential for so much collateral damage, we weren't willing to delay any further.

Without another word, Siegel came out of his crouch and sprinted across the street. I wouldn't have thought he had it in him.

I counted to three to put some space between us, then started running with my head down. Another window shattered somewhere behind me. I barely noticed. My only focus right now was on getting to the other side of that apartment building's front door—and then getting inside after Hennessey.

Chapter 105

ONCE INSIDE, I took the stairs. It was ten flights to the roof, but I'm in pretty good shape. Adrenaline did its job, too.

A few minutes later, I was coming out on top of the Midlands. It was a strange déjà vu—a lot like the other night at the museum.

I swept my Glock left and right—nothing. No one behind the door either.

I'd come out through a utility room, and the walls were blocking my view of the Twelfth Street side of the building. That's where Hennessey would have been shooting from if he was here.

Sirens were wailing in the distance; with any luck, they were headed my way.

I pressed my back against the wall and moved slowly to the corner, weapon first.

The street side of the roof, though dimly lit, looked deserted to me. There were a couple of folding lawn chairs and a steel barrel lying on its side.

No sign of Hennessey, though.

I came to the edge and looked out. Twelfth Street was quiet down below. Other than the Bureau car with its doors open and a patch of broken glass on the ground, there wasn't any indication of what had just happened.

A few people were even walking by, oblivious to the damage.

Then, as I leaned out for a better look, my foot hit something that made a small, metallic clinking sound. I took out my Maglite and pointed it at the ground to see what it was.

Shell casings. Several of them.

My pulse spiked, and I turned around—right into the barrel of a Walther nine millimeter.

The man with his finger on the trigger, presumably Steven Hennessey, held the pistol up about an inch from my forehead.

"Don't move," he said. "Not a goddamn muscle. I won't miss from this distance."

Chapter 106

HE'D DONE A pretty good job of changing his appearance—glasses, dark hair, clean-shaven. Enough to let him move around the city anyway.

And probably enough to walk away from here unrecognized, too, I realized. It was all starting to fall into place.

"Hennessey?"

"Depends who you ask," he answered.

"You left that anonymous tip at the Bureau yourself, didn't you?" I said. This whole thing was a setup, I felt sure, and we'd given him exactly what he wanted—a quiet surveillance detail by the people who knew the most about him. Whether he'd been trying to kill us in the car or draw us closer, I still didn't know.

"And look what I caught," he said. "Now, I want you to reach back slowly and drop that Glock right off the roof."

I shook my head. "I'll throw it over there. I can't put this thing in the street."

"Sure you can," he said. The tip of his Walther was cool when he pressed it into my forehead. Presumably he'd been using something bigger a few minutes ago.

I reached back and let the Glock fall. When it smacked onto the concrete below, my stomach clenched.

He took a step back then, out of arm's reach.

"To tell you the truth, I just wanted you dead and out of the way. But now that you're here, I'm giving you thirty seconds to tell me what you've got on me," he said. "And I'm not talking about what's already in the papers."

"No, I don't imagine you are," I said. "You want to know how deep you need to go before you can disappear again."

"Twenty seconds," he said. "I might even let you live. Talk to me."

"You're Steven Hennessey, aka Frances Moulton, aka Denny Humboldt," I said. "You were with U.S. Army Special Forces until two thousand two, most recently in Afghanistan. There's a grave in Kentucky with your name on it, and I'm assuming you've been running freelance off the radar since then."

"What about the Bureau?" he said. "Where else are they looking for me?"

"Everywhere," I said.

He adjusted his grip and locked his elbows. "I know who you are, too, Cross. You live on Fifth Street. No reason I can't make a stop there tonight, too. Understand?"

I felt a rush of anger. "I'm not messing with you. We've

been grasping at straws. Why do you think we don't have a whole team here?"

"Not yet you don't," he said. The sirens were definitely getting closer, though. "What else? You're still alive. Keep talking."

"You killed your partner, Mitch."

"Not what I'm asking about. Give me something I can use," he said. "Last chance, or you won't be the only Cross to die tonight."

"For God's sake, if I had something, I'd tell you!"

The first police cruiser came screaming up the block down below.

"Looks like your time's up," he said.

A gun fired—and I flinched before I realized it wasn't Hennessey's. His eyes opened wide. A line of blood rolled onto his upper lip, and he collapsed straight down in front of me, as if someone had just dropped his strings.

"Alex?"

I looked to the right. Max Siegel was standing on the roof of the next building, lit from behind by a small shaft of light from the stairwell. His Beretta was still up and pointed my way, but he lowered it when I turned to him.

"You okay?" he called.

I stepped on Hennessey's wrist and took the Walther out of his hand. There was no pulse at the neck, and his eyes were like blank saucers. He was gone. Max Siegel had taken him out and saved my life.

By the time I stood up again, the street was filling fast. Besides the sirens, I could hear doors slamming and the squawk of police radios. The block was locked down, but I still needed to go and find my Glock.

Siegel appeared to stare after me as I headed for the door. I owed him a thank-you, to say the least, but the street noise would've swallowed my words, so I just flashed a thumbs-up for now.

All good.

Chapter 107

IT RAINED THE NEXT MORNING. We had planned to do our big press briefing outside but ended up moving it to the Daly Building lineup room instead. A hundred reporters, maybe more, had shown up for this thing, and we put a live audio feed in the lobby for the spillover and also for any latecomers.

Max and I sat at a table at the front with Chief Perkins and Jim Heekin from the Directorate. The sound of camera shutters was everywhere, most of them pointed at Max and me. We were most definitely the odd couple.

This was one of my famous moments. I'd had a few before. There would be a couple of weeks of constant interview requests, maybe a book offer or two, and definitely some number of reporters waiting outside my house when I got home that night.

The briefing started with a statement from the mayor, who took about ten minutes to explain why all of this meant we should vote for him in the next election. Then the chief gave a rundown of the basics of the case before we opened up the floor to questions.

"Detective Cross," a Fox reporter asked right out of the gate, "can you walk us through the events of what happened on that roof last night? A real blow-by-blow? Only *you* can tell that story."

This was the "sexy" part of the case—the stuff that sells papers and ad space as well. I gave an answer that was short enough to keep things moving along but detailed enough to keep them from spending the next hour hounding me about *how it feels* to come *face-to-face* with a *cold-blooded killer*.

"So, would you say that Agent Siegel saved your life?" someone followed up.

Siegel leaned into his mike. "That's right," he said. "Nobody takes this guy out but me." They gave him a good laugh for that one.

"Seriously, though," he went on, "we may have had our bumps in the road, but this investigation is a perfect example of how federal and local authorities can work together in the face of a major threat. I'm proud of what Detective Cross and I accomplished here, and I hope the city's proud of us, too."

Apparently even Siegel's good side had a huge ego. But I was in no mood to be picky or small. If he wanted the face time, he could have it.

I held back for the next several questions, until inevitably someone asked, "What about motive? Can you tell us definitively at this point that Talley and Hennessey were operating on their own? And for what reason?"

"We're looking into all possibilities," I said right away.

"What I can tell you is that the two gunmen responsible for the Patriot sniper killings are now deceased. The city should go back to normal. As to any open aspects of the investigation, we have no comment at this time."

Siegel looked at me but kept his mouth shut, and we moved right along with our dog and pony show.

The full truth, which we would never share with the press, was that we had plenty of reasons to believe Talley and Hennessey had been following someone else's game plan. Maybe we'd find out whose, and maybe we wouldn't. If I'd had to guess that morning, I would have said this case was as closed as it was going to get.

It happens. A lot of police work is about skimming the bottom layers off things without ever getting to the top. In fact, that's exactly what the people at the top count on. The ones who work for them—the guns for hire, the thugs, the street criminals—those are the ones who absorb most of the risk, and all too often they're the only ones who take the fall.

Something about "foxes in the henhouse" comes to mind.

Chapter 108

AFTER TWO MORE DAYS of boring and exhausting paperwork, I took a long weekend and spent some time playing what the kids like to call Ketchup. Mostly it's just me turning off my cell and hanging out with them as much as possible, although Bree and I did sneak away for a few blessed hours on Sunday afternoon.

We drove up to a place called Tregaron, in Cleveland Heights. It's a huge neo-Georgian mansion on the Washington International School campus, available for rentals in the summer months. We got a tour from their tightly wound community relations director, Mimi Bento.

"And this is the Terrace Room," she said, walking us in from the grand foyer.

It was a parquet-floored hall with brass chandeliers, open to a canopied patio at the back. Beyond that were the pristine gardens and a view of the Klingle Valley. Not too shabby. Beautiful, actually. And classy.

Ms. Bento checked her leather folio. "It's available August eleventh, twenty-fifth, or... next year, of course. How many guests were you thinking?"

Bree and I looked at each other. It seemed weird that we hadn't thought about this in much detail, but we hadn't. We wanted to keep it somewhat small, I guess. It was all kind of new for us.

"We're not sure yet," Bree said, and the corners of the woman's mouth turned down almost imperceptibly. "But we definitely want the ceremony and reception in the same place. We'd like to keep everything relatively simple."

"Of course," she said. You could just see the dollar signs getting smaller in her eyes. "Well, why don't you look around a little more, and I'll be in the office if you have any questions."

Once she was gone, we walked outside to see the terrace. It was a perfect spring day, and easy to imagine a wedding happening here.

"Any questions?" Bree said.

"Yes." I took her hand and pulled her in. "Is this where we'd have our first dance?"

We started swaying right there while I hummed a few bars of Gershwin in her ear. *No, no, they can't take that away from me....*

"You know what?" Bree said suddenly. "This place is absolutely gorgeous. I love it."

"Then it's settled," I said.

"Except I think we should skip it."

I stopped dancing and looked at her.

"I don't need to spend the next few months thinking about what color the invitations are going to be or who's going to sit next to who," she said. "That's someone else's wedding, not mine. Not ours. I just want to be married to you. Like now."

"Now?" I said. "Like—*now?*"

She laughed and reached up to kiss me. "Soon anyway. After Damon comes home from school. What do you think?"

I didn't have to think. All I needed out of this wedding was for it to be exactly what Bree wanted—fancy mansion or Washington courthouse, I didn't care. As long as she was there.

"After Damon comes home, then," I said, and sealed the deal with another kiss. "Next question: do you think we can sneak out the back, or do we have to tell Mimi?"

Chapter 109

THE BACKYARD WAS BEAUTIFUL, the way everyone did it up for us. Sampson, Billie, and the kids had put little white lights in the trees, and candles everywhere you looked. There was jazz in the air, and a dozen high-backed chairs arranged on the patio for the friends and family we'd invited on short notice.

The kids stood up with us for the ceremony—Ali, with the rings; Jannie, beaming in the beautiful white dress we'd let her splurge on; and Damon, looking like a taller and much more self-aware and confident version of the kid we'd dropped off at Cushing last fall.

As for Bree, no surprise, she was stunning in a simple white strapless dress. Simple and perfect in my eyes. She and Jannie had the same little white flowers in their hair, and Nana sat proudly in the front row with a single hibiscus tucked over her ear and a sparkle in her eyes that I hadn't seen in the last few years.

At six thirty sharp, our pastor from St. Anthony's, Dr. Gerry O'Connor, nodded to Nana that it was time to start the proceedings. She'd made one request for today—that she be allowed to offer up a convocation of her own sort.

"I believe in marriage," she said, standing up to address the group. You could hear the church in her voice already. "More specifically, I believe in *this* marriage."

She came over to where Bree and I were standing and took each of us by the hand. "You two haven't asked me for this, but I'm giving you to each other tonight and I am so honored to do it.

"Bree, I never knew your parents, God rest their souls, but I have to believe they'd be pleased as punch to see you marrying my grandson. This man is a good man," she said, and I could see a few rare tears brimming in her eyes. "He's my one and only, and I don't share that lightly.

"And you," she said, turning to me. "You have hit the jackpot here, mister."

"Don't have to tell me that," I said.

"No, but when did that ever stop me? This woman is love, Alex. I can see it on her face when she looks at you. I can see it when she looks at the children. I can even see it when she looks at loquacious, silly old me. I've never known a woman more generous with her spirit. Have you?" she asked the larger group, and they all came back with a decisive "No!" or, in a few cases, "No, ma'am!"

"That's right," she said, and leveled a bony finger at me. "So don't ever mess it up!"

She sat back down while everyone else was still laughing, many of us through our own tears. Just a few words, but she seemed to have covered everything beautifully.

"All yours, Pastor," she said.

And when Dr. O'Connor opened his book to begin, and I took in that circle of smiling faces around me—my best friend, John Sampson; my grandmother; my beautiful children; and this amazing woman, Bree, whom I'd come to realize I couldn't even imagine trying to live without—I knew that his first two words could not have more perfectly captured everything that was in my heart and mind at that exact moment.

Those words were "Dearly Beloved."

Chapter 110

THE BEST PARTY EVER lasted long into the night. We didn't skimp on the food, bringing in a friend's catering company for endless amounts of jerk pork, coconut rice, fried plantains, and something Sampson had decided to call a Breelex. It was two kinds of rum, pineapple, ginger, and a cherry—or just pineapple, ginger, and a cherry for the kids, although Damon sampled the adult beverage once, that I know of.

Jerome Thurman jammed with his combo, Fusion, in the backyard, where there was plenty of dancing under the stars and even a little bad singing from me, after a Breelex or two. Or three. The kids said I was "pitchy" and "absolutely dreadful."

We were all up bright and early the next morning, though. A cab took us to the airport for a flight to Miami, and then on to Nassau. At the other end, a limo picked us up and whisked us off to the aptly named One&Only Ocean Club.

Bree and I had seen this place in my favorite James Bond

movie, *Casino Royale,* and I swore I'd get her here one day. The Bond jokes started as soon as we pulled into the familiar teardrop-shaped driveway, with the drool-worthy cars everywhere you looked.

"Cross," she said as I helped her out of the limo. "*Bree* Cross."

She'd surprised a lot of people, I think, by taking my name. It was entirely up to her, but I loved that she did. I liked hearing it as much as saying it.

"*Dr. and Mrs. Cross,* checking in," I told the gracious, very welcoming woman at the front desk. Bree squeezed my hand, and we laughed like a couple of kids. Or maybe just a couple of newlyweds. "How soon do you think we can be out in that ocean in your backyard?"

"I'd say about three and a half minutes," the woman told us, and slid our keys across the desk. "You're all set here. That's one double suite in the Crescent Wing and one ocean-side villa. Enjoy your stay."

"Oh, we will!" Jannie had just come up behind us. Nana, Damon, and Ali were still outside ogling the white sand beach and turquoise water. It really was turquoise.

"Here you go, Miss J." I handed her the suite key. "I'm officially putting you in charge of that, and we'll see you guys for lunch tomorrow."

"Daddy, I still think you're crazy for bringing us," she said, and leaned in as if she had a secret to tell. "But I'm really glad you did."

"Me, too," I whispered back.

Besides, it would still be a honeymoon. That's what DO NOT DISTURB signs are for.

Chapter 111

OUR VILLA WAS the pièce de résistance. Just like in the movies, as they say. There was a full wall of sliding louvered doors that opened up to a private terrace and infinity pool, with stairs leading down to the beach. The staff had placed fresh flowers everywhere, inside and out, and the mahogany California king bed alone probably cost a year's salary.

"Yeah, this will do," I said, closing the door to the outside world behind us. "Good enough for Double Oh Seven, and all that."

"Oh, James, James," Bree joked some more, pulling me down onto the bed. "Ravish me, James, as only you can."

And that's what I did. One thing very quickly led to another, and our immediate beach plans got moved to sometime in the future. Still, we did manage to work up an appetite. By the time we were on our feet again, the sun was dipping down and we were both ready for a great meal.

I'm not sure which was better that evening—the French-Caribbean food at Dune, the amazing bottle of Pinot Noir we ordered, or just the feeling of having nowhere else I needed to be for a change, nowhere else I wanted to be either.

We made a full night of it, too, and stopped at the casino at the Atlantis Resort after dinner for some blackjack. Bree was up for a while, then I was, but we left around midnight a few dollars in the hole. And who cared? Not us.

We walked back to our place the long way, holding hands along the beach.

"Happy?" I said to Bree.

"Married," she said. "Happily married. It doesn't even feel real yet. This *is* the real world, though, isn't it? I'm not dreaming this, am I, Alex?"

I stopped to put my arms around her, and we stood watching the moon's reflection bouncing off the ocean.

"You know, we still haven't been in that blue, blue water yet," I said. My fingers started in on the top buttons of her shirt. "Up for a night swim, Mrs. Cross?"

Bree looked around. "Is that a dare?"

"Just an invitation," I said. "But I'd feel a little silly, all naked and alone out there." She was already working on my pants.

We left our clothes on the sand and swam out. I could hear steel drums coming from the hotel somewhere, but it was as if we had the whole ocean to ourselves. We kissed in the water for a while and then ended up making love again, right there on the shore. It was a little risky, and sandy, but just the kind of danger I'll take any day of the week.

Chapter 112

WE SLEPT IN LATE the next morning and took our time getting ready for the day. Bree was just looking over the room-service menu and I was pulling on a T-shirt when the phone rang. It was still early for the kids to be calling, but I didn't mind. Actually I was looking forward to taking some razzing from them.

"Good morning!" I answered.

"Yes, it is." Kyle Craig's unmistakable voice wormed into my ear. "And how was the wedding?" he said.

I should have seen it coming. Should have taken more precautions. These calls had become a signature of Kyle's.

Before I said another word, a plane roared overhead—and I realized with a sudden jolt that I could hear it over the phone, too.

I ran to the front window to look out. "Kyle? Where are you? What's going on?"

"Did you notice I kept my promise?" he said. "I told you I'd let you get married, and I did."

"Let me?"

There was no sign of him outside, but that didn't mean anything, did it? He could have been hiding anywhere. Clearly, he was here. And close, too.

"And do you want to know why?" he asked.

My breath was heavy in my chest as I continued to check out the grounds. "No," I said. "I don't."

"Because *I believe in marriage,*" he said, aping Nana's voice. "Isn't that what she said the other night?"

Suddenly I couldn't breathe at all.

"And besides," he went on, "a wife's so much more fun to take from a man than a girlfriend. I've been patient, Alex, but it's time to move on."

"Move on? What the hell are you talking about?" I said, but I was afraid I already knew.

"Enlightenment, my friend," he said. "Look down toward the water. See what you see."

I threw back the glass door and looked out. It took me a second, but then I saw them.

Jannie and Ali were down on the beach, waving my way. A few steps behind them, somehow, impossibly, stood Max Siegel. He was in shades and a loud shirt, with a beach towel covering his right hand and a cell phone in the other. He smiled when he saw me, and then as his mouth moved, I heard Kyle Craig's voice in my ear.

"Surprise," he said.

Chapter 113

IT FELT AS IF my heart stopped and then started up again. My mind was racing. Kyle must have had some kind of major procedure. *His face wasn't Kyle's at all.*

"That's right," he said. "Everything you're thinking right now is true. Except for the part where you save everybody. That's not happening."

Farther up the beach, Nana was watching from under an umbrella. Damon, the only one not to have met Max Siegel, was on a lounge chair beside her, listening to his iPod.

"What do you think, kids?" Kyle said, putting some Siegel back into his voice. "Want to go give your dad a good-morning kiss?"

He pocketed the phone and took up Ali's hand, making sure to show me a flash of whatever was under that towel. A gun of some kind.

God, no. This wasn't happening.

We'd left our own weapons back in DC, very much on purpose. Now that seemed like a horrible mistake. I'd have to improvise. But how? Using what as a weapon?

I whispered fast and low to Bree as they came across the beach. There was no time to consider options. There was just my instinct, and a quick prayer that we got this right.

"Hey, Daddy!" Ali called out as they came toward the terrace stairs. He tried to pull ahead, but Siegel—Kyle!—kept hold of his hand. It was everything I could do to stay where I was.

Jannie ran ahead of them. "Can you believe Mr. Siegel is staying here, too?" she said, and kissed me on the cheek. "Is that crazy or *what?*"

"Unbelievable," I said. Neither she nor Ali seemed to notice how hollow my voice sounded.

"Sorry to drop in like this," Kyle said, as Max. He was grinning at me, daring me with his eyes, obviously wanting me to make some kind of move. And the voice—it wasn't Kyle's, but it *was* Kyle's. How could I have missed the similarities before? It's amazing how the brain follows what the eyes see—or don't see.

"No problem," I said. I kept the charade up for the kids' sake and moved back inside. "Come on in. Bree's taking a shower, but she'll be right out."

Kyle put a hand on Ali's shoulder, and my stomach turned. "Why don't you go and get her?" he said, smiling. "I'll wait here with the kids. I'm sure she'd like to know I was here. What a coincidence. Is this crazy?"

Something like an electric charge passed between us—something a lot like hatred. "Bree?" I called out. I moved toward the bathroom with my eyes still on Kyle. "Can you come out here?"

For just a second, I poked my head in. "Max Siegel just dropped by," I said, loud enough for his benefit.

Bree was slipping out of her T-shirt and sticking her head under the running water while we stared helplessly at each other.

"Be right there!" she called back.

I turned to face Kyle again. He was still holding on to Ali.

Jannie was sitting on the edge of the unmade bed, but now she was watching me intently. I think she had started to sense that something was wrong.

"She'll be right out," I said, as naturally as I could.

"Good," Kyle said. "Then I'm going to take you all for a drive. Kids, you up for a little adventure?"

"Sure!" Ali said. Jannie stayed quiet. The whole time, Kyle kept his right hand covered with that towel, his gun out of sight.

When Bree came into the room, she was in bare feet and wearing one of the resort's robes. You'd never know from watching her that she was just as scared and pumped up as I was.

"Max, good to see you," she said, and extended a hand as she came toward him.

"Not as good as it is to see you," he said, without hiding his pleasure anymore.

But then as they went to shake, Bree's free hand whipped a small canister out of the pocket in her robe — the hair spray from the complimentary kit in the bathroom. She sprayed it in Kyle's eyes. He yelled in pain, and with a second fluid motion, Bree kneed him in the groin.

At the same time, I took a glass decanter off the bar, where I'd positioned myself. I crossed the floor in three fast steps and swung as hard as I could. The heavy container smashed into Kyle's jaw and nose. He crumpled to the floor. Shards of glass flew everywhere.

Ali screamed, but there was no time for explanation or soothing. Bree scooped him up as if he were weightless, grabbed Jannie's arm, and got them out the door.

And I fell onto Kyle with everything I had.

Chapter 114

KYLE SWUNG HIS FIST and caught me square in the jaw. A shock ran through my head, but I couldn't swing back. I now had one hand on his wrist and the other on the gun he'd carried in.

I head-butted him instead, hard, where he'd already been cut. It was enough to wrench the weapon free. *A Beretta nine millimeter. Max Siegel's gun.*

I scrambled backward on the floor, aiming it between his eyes, which he was rubbing at furiously, trying to see.

"Roll over!" I told him, getting to my feet. "Face down on the floor, hands away from your body!"

Kyle smiled. His eyes were practically bloodred, running with tears, but I knew that he could see me again.

"This is ironic," he said. "I could have sworn you were lying that night in the car, but you really can't pull that trigger, can you?"

"Not without a reason," I said. "So either give me one, or roll over and kiss the floor—right now! Do it!"

"You know I don't say this lightly, Cross, but fuck you."

Suddenly, he did roll, too fast, and a shard of glass clenched in his hand crossed the space between us. I felt the muscle in my calf tear. My knee buckled. I was halfway to the ground before I knew what happened.

And Kyle was up on his feet.

He stumbled on his way out, and it probably saved his life. The one shot I managed to get off splintered the sliding door instead of his head, just before he jumped off the terrace and disappeared outside.

Chapter 115

I FIRED ONCE into the air as I came onto the beach. Anyone who wasn't already moving out of Kyle's way started scattering now. His gait was erratic. It was possible he had a concussion, but my leg wasn't doing me any favors either. I had never seen a chase like this one.

Some people were screaming; others were pulling their kids out of the water. Then, without a clear shot, I could only watch as Kyle reached down and plucked a small boy, maybe two or three years old, off the ground before his mother could get to him.

The woman ran right at them, but Kyle clutched her boy over his torso like a shield.

"Get back!" he screamed. "Get back, or I'll—"

"Take me!" The mother was on her knees, unable to come closer or turn away. "Take me instead!"

"Kyle, put him down!"

He turned to look at me then, and I was close enough to see the calm coming back into his eyes. He had the bargaining chip he needed, and he knew it.

"You came here for me, not this boy," I said. "Let him go! *Take me.*"

The poor boy was sobbing and reaching out for his mother, but Kyle just hitched him up a little higher and held on even tighter.

"I'll need that gun back first," he said. "No more talk. Just set the gun down and back away. Three. Two—"

"Okay." I started kneeling slowly. My leg was seizing up, and I could barely move it now. "I'm putting it down," I said.

But I didn't trust that boy's life to Kyle's word. So I took the chance I had to take. I turned the gun at the last second and fired low. The boy wasn't big enough to shield Kyle top to bottom. My shot caught him just below the kneecap.

He howled like a wild animal. The boy dropped to the sand and then scrambled for his mother. Kyle tried to stand, but he could get up only on one leg—and only until I shot that one, too.

He flew back into the sand, his chest heaving with pain. His legs were a bloody mess now, and it felt good. I especially liked taking him down with his own weapon.

I saw Bree then, running toward us with two uniformed officers. She pointed Kyle out to them as they came, and then ran straight over to me.

"Oh my God." She put an arm around me to take some of the weight off my leg. "Are you all right?"

I nodded. "He'll need an ambulance."

"It's on the way," one of the police officers said.

Kyle's eyes were closed, but he opened them when my shadow crossed between the sun and his face.

"It's over, Kyle," I said. "For good this time."

"Define 'over,'" he wheezed. His breath was ragged, and he was shaking with pain. "You think you've won something here?"

"I'm not talking about winning," I said. "I'm talking about putting you away where you can't hurt anyone ever again."

He tried to smile. "Didn't stop me the last time," he said.

"Well, you know what they say. The only thing worse than going into solitary is going back," I said. "But maybe it's just an expression."

For possibly the first time ever, I saw something like fear in Kyle Craig's eyes. It lasted only a second before he snapped back to the same rigid demeanor.

"This isn't over!" he croaked, but he was already talking to my back.

The ambulance was just pulling up to where we were, and I wanted to warn the EMTs.

"Take care of him first," I said, "but you need to be careful. This man is extremely dangerous."

"We've got this, sir," one of the policemen told me. "And I need you to surrender that weapon."

I handed it over a little reluctantly, and Bree helped me down onto a lounge chair, where I could still keep an eye on things. In the meantime she grabbed a towel and wrapped it tightly around my leg.

Kyle didn't bother to resist as the med techs gave him a drip and an oxygen mask, then cut away his pant legs. He'd lost a lot of blood. His face was paper white. I think the reality of going back to ADX Florence was really starting to sink in.

They got him onto a gurney and put the IV bag and oxygen tank between his legs so that they could lift everything up into the ambulance.

"You need to cuff him," I called over to the cops. "And don't let those EMTs ride alone!"

"Just calm down, sir," one of them told me in an angry voice.

"I'm a police officer, and I know what I'm talking about," I said. "This man's wanted by the FBI, and you need to restrain him. *Right now!*"

"Okay, okay." He motioned to his partner, and they walked over toward Kyle.

Almost as if the scene were in slow motion, I watched as the first cop stepped into the back of the ambulance. The cuffs came up—and then I saw Kyle reach for them, with the kind of channeled strength only a psychopath like him could muster in that condition. He used the cuffs to pull the officer down to him and, in a second, had the man's gun in his hand.

Bree stood up instinctively to help, but I rolled off the lounge chair and pulled her down with me.

There was a gunshot, and then another.

Then the first of two loud explosions. We would find out later that a bullet had pierced Kyle's oxygen tank.

It burst into a ball of flame inside the confines of the ambulance, followed quickly by the fuel tank.

The entire vehicle imploded with a blast that stunned my eardrums. Glass and metal flew more up than out, and a shower of sand rained down over us. People were screaming again.

When I raised my head, I saw that there was no question of survivors. The ambulance was a black carcass, with flames and dark smoke still rising into the air. Both police officers and both EMTs were dead.

And so was Kyle. By the time the fire was out and we got close enough to see his body, we realized that it was charred from top to bottom.

The face he'd invested so much in was completely unrecognizable, just a featureless black mask where the man used to be. In fact, not that much of him was even there anymore.

As to whether Kyle fired into that oxygen tank on purpose, I have to wonder. Maybe going back to solitary confinement was more than he could bear. Prison might have easily killed him in the end, and maybe Kyle knew that.

Maybe he was even trying to take me out with him as he went—one last effort to finish the job that, for whatever reason, he'd turned into his life's work.

Actually, I think I know what the answers to all those questions are, but of course I'll never know for sure. And maybe someday I won't care anymore either.

Epilogue

SUMMER

Chapter 116

THE MEDIA STORM WAITING for me when I got home topped what I'd left behind, if that was possible. Kyle Craig had been the most famous wanted person in the country, and everyone clamored for a piece of the story. I had to hire Rakeem Powell's security service for several more days just to keep the gawkers at bay and give my family some semblance of privacy.

I thought Nana would blow a fuse over what happened in Nassau, but she didn't. We all quietly settled back in as best we could.

Over the next several days, I started the slow and steady process of talking to the kids, together and separately. I wanted them to know that while what happened was very real, it was also the end of something.

I think each got that in his or her own way. By the time my two weeks' vacation was up, everyone was doing pretty well.

But I'd also come to a decision. I needed to be around more than I'd been, at least for a while. I put in for an unpaid leave from work through the end of the summer and just hoped they'd accept it. If not, then not. I'd find something else to do.

In fact, I was thinking seriously about writing another book, this one focusing on Kyle Craig and the Mastermind case. Not only had Kyle been the toughest challenge of my career, he'd also been a friend of mine—once. I felt as if I had a story to tell, and it would be a powerful one.

Meanwhile, there were sunflowers to plant and movies to see. Boxing lessons to catch up on in the basement, baseball games, trips to the Smithsonian. Long dinners to linger over until after dark, with good conversations or games of Go Fish. There was my new wife to lavish with all the love I could give.

And, of course, a new life to start together.

Chapter 117

IF ONLY THINGS could have stayed that way—the endless summer.

It was just after Fourth of July weekend when I got that call from MPD, the call that everyone over there swore they wouldn't make, no matter what the circumstances.

A detective in Austin, Texas, had been calling around looking for me. He was dealing with a multiple down there, a baffling and grisly one. But it wasn't just the murders. The case was starting to show a striking similarity to one of my own—something I thought I'd put to bed years ago.

Even so, I made the appropriate referral to a detective I'd worked with in Dallas and stood my ground. I wasn't a cop right now. Not until September.

But then the next call came about two weeks later. This one was from a detective in San Francisco by the name of

Boxer. She had a strange one on her hands, and her case sounded familiar, too, a lot like the murders committed by a madman known as "Mr. Smith." I had caught Smith and watched him die. At least, I thought I had.

But that's a story for another day.

James Patterson

A NOVEL WRITTEN BY ALEX CROSS, NOW AVAILABLE IN PAPERBACK

Alex Cross's Trial

James Patterson
& Richard DiLallo

Alex Cross tells the incredible story – passed down through the generations – of an ancestor's courageous fight for freedom.

From his grandmother, Alex Cross has heard the story of his great-uncle Abraham and his struggles for survival in the era of the Ku Klux Klan. Now, Alex records the extraordinary tale in a novel he's written – a novel called *Trial*.

As a lawyer in early-twentieth-century Washington DC, Ben Corbett represents the toughest cases. When President Theodore Roosevelt asks Ben to return to his hometown to investigate rumours of the resurgence of the Ku Klux Klan there, he cannot refuse.

When he arrives in Eudora, Mississippi, Ben meets the wise Abraham Cross and his beautiful daughter, Moody. Ben enlists their help, and the two Crosses introduce him to the hidden side of the idyllic Southern town. Lynchings have become commonplace and residents of the town's black quarter live in constant fear. Ben aims to break the reign of terror – but the truth of who is really behind it could break his heart.

Written in the fearless voice of Detective Alex Cross, Alex Cross's *Trial* is a gripping story of murder, love, and, above all, bravery.

arrow books

If you enjoy following the Alex Cross series, you'll love James Patterson's newest bestselling series featuring Detective Michael Bennett.

THE *SUNDAY TIMES* NO. 1 BESTSELLING DETECTIVE MICHAEL BENNETT NOVEL, NOW AVAILABLE IN PAPERBACK

Worst Case

James Patterson

& Michael Ledwidge

Alex Cross has Washington DC. The Women's Murder Club have San Francisco. Detective Michael Bennett has New York City – chaos capital of the world.

The son of one of New York's wealthiest families is snatched off the street and held hostage. His parents can't save him, because this kidnapper isn't demanding money. Instead, he quizzes his prisoner on the price others pay for his life of luxury. In this exam, wrong answers are fatal.

Detective Michael Bennett leads the investigation. With ten kids of his own, he can't begin to understand what could lead someone to target anyone's children. As another student disappears, one powerful family after another uses their leverage and connections to turn up the heat on the mayor, the press, anyone who will listen, to stop this killer. Their reach extends all the way to the FBI, who send their top Abduction Specialist, Agent Emily Parker. Bennett's work life – and love life – suddenly get even more complicated.

Before Bennett has a chance to protest the FBI's intrusion on his case, the mastermind changes his routine. His plan leads up to the most dreadful demonstration yet – one that could bring cataclysmic devastation to every inch of New York.

arrow books

THE NEW NOVEL IN THE NO. 1 BESTSELLING DETECTIVE MICHAEL BENNETT SERIES, AVAILABLE FROM JANUARY 2011

Tick, Tock

James Patterson
& Michael Ledwidge

NYC's no. 1 detective, Michael Bennett, has a huge problem – someone is recreating the crimes of infamous killers from New York's history. The city has never been more terrified.

A rash of horrifying crimes tears through New York, throwing it into complete chaos and terrorising everyone living there. Immediately, it becomes clear that they are not the work of an amateur, but of a calculating, efficient, and deadly mastermind.

The city calls on Detective Michael Bennett, pulling him away from a seaside retreat with his ten adopted children, his grandfather, and their beloved nanny, Mary Catherine. Not only does it tear apart their first vacation since Michael's wife Maeve died – it leaves the entire family open to attack.

Bennett enlists the help of a former colleague, FBI Agent Emily Parker. As his affection for Emily grows into something stronger, his relationship with Mary Catherine takes an unexpected turn. All too soon, another appalling crime leads Bennett to a shocking discovery that exposes the killer's pattern and the earth-shattering enormity of his plan.

Turn the page for a sneak preview of

Tick, Tock

Chapter 1

LIKE ALL REAL ESTATE located on East 77th Street between Madison and Fifth Avenue, the parking garage was outrageously exclusive. Tucked side to side and bumper to bumper within its four dark underground levels were several vintage Porsches, a handful of Ferraris, even a pair of Lamborghini Diablos.

The car that squealed out of the garage's rising elevator door at three minutes past noon that Saturday was a glittering Mercedes. It was an out-of-the-box quartz-blue SL550 convertible with all the bells and whistles and a sticker price north of a hundred thousand dollars.

"With this heat, I figured you'd want the top down as usual, Mr. Berger," the half Spanish, half Asian–looking garage attendant said as he bounced out and held open the wooden inlaid door. "Have a good one, now."

Mr. Berger seemed as equally well suited to the exclusive

10021 zip code as his car: salt-and-pepper Beckham buzz cut, pressed khakis, navy silk golf shirt, the kind of deep golden tan that suggested even deeper pockets.

"Thanks, Tony," Berger said, deftly slipping the man a five as he slid behind the luxury sports car's iconic three-pronged steering wheel. "I'll try and give it a shot."

Fine leather slammed luxuriously into his back as he launched the convertible down East 77th Street and out onto Fifth Avenue with a high-torque snarl. The crisp, almost sweet smell of Central Park's pin oaks and dogwoods fused harmoniously with the scent of the hand-stitched leather.

After a few minutes, the park gave way to the ornate facade of the Plaza Hotel. Along both sides of the upscale street, glittering signs for Tiffany & Co., Zegna, Pucci, Fendi, and Louis Vuitton began to flick past like an issue of *Vanity Fair* come to life. Outside, swarms of summer Saturday tourists took pictures and stood gaping as if they were having trouble believing they were standing in the very center of the capital of the world.

But the world's most expensive avenue might as well have been a dirt road through a shitkicker's cornfield as far as Mr. Berger was concerned. Behind the mirrored lenses of his Persol aviators, he kept his gray eyes locked level and forward, his mind blank.

It was his one true talent. In his life, every victory had come down to a singleness of purpose—his ability to focus, to leave out everything but the matter at hand.

Even so he felt his pulse skitter minutes later when he arrived at his destination: the New York Public Library's main branch on the west side of 42nd and Fifth.

But even Laurence Olivier had stage fright, he reminded himself. Jack Dempsey. Elvis Presley. All men felt fear. What separated great and worthy men such as himself from the rest was the ability to manage it, to act despite feeling it breathing down his neck.

By the time he tucked the Merc into a spot in front of a Carvel ice-cream truck half a block east, down 43rd, he felt somewhat better. To completely ground himself, he watched the hard top hum into place over his head—precise, symmetrical, a glorious harmony of moving parts. Once it locked itself down, his fear was still there but he knew he could man it now.

Move it, Mr. Berger, he thought. *Now or never.*

He lifted the heavy laptop bag from the passenger-seat well and opened the door.

"Now" it was.

Chapter 2

ONCE UNDER THE grand arched portico and through the revolving door, Mr. Berger noticed immediately that the steely-eyed ex-cop who usually worked the cavernous front hall on Saturdays wasn't there. Instead, there was a young summer-hire slouch in an ill-fitting blazer. Even better, the bored-looking bridge-and-tunneler waved Berger through without lifting a finger to the laptop bag's zipper.

The hushed Rose Main Reading Room on the third floor was about the size of a professional soccer field—one rimmed with ten-foot caramel-colored wood shelves and lit by brass rococo chandeliers that hung down from its thirty-foot, mural-painted, coffered ceiling. Berger stepped past table after long table of very serious-looking thirty- and forty-somethings, iPod earbuds snug in their ears as they stared intently into laptop screens. Graduate students and ardent self-improvers. No summer weekend at the Hamptons for this studious bunch.

He found a seat at the last table along the wall, with his back to the door of the Brooke Russell Astor Reading Room. He pretended to play video Sudoku on his nifty new iPhone until the only other person at the study table, a pregnant Asian woman in a Juicy tracksuit, got up twenty minutes later.

As she waddled away, Mr. Berger slipped on a pair of rubber surgical gloves under the table.

Then he slid the bomb out of the laptop bag.

It looked exactly like a seventeen-inch Apple MacBook, except that in the hollowed-out space where the keyboard and mouse pad and computer guts had been, two kilograms of T4 now sat, the Italian version of the plastic explosive C4. On top of the vanilla-colored explosive stood a two-inch-thick layer of barbed stainless steel roofing nails, like a double helping of silver sprinkles on the devil's ice-cream cone.

There was a gel-like adhesive attached to the device's bottom. He pressed the bomb firmly down in front of him, gluing it securely to the library desk.

The detonator cap had already been inserted into the explosive and now merely awaited the final connection to an electrical charge, which would occur when someone discovered the laptop and made the mistake of folding open the closed front cover. Tied just inside the lid with a snug lanyard knot of fishing line was a mercury switch, an ingenious little thermometer-like glass tube that was used in vending-machine alarms. When the lid was closed, you could play

Frisbee with the IED. Once the cover rose two inches, however, the liquid mercury would spill to the switch's bottom, cover its electrical leads, and initiate instant detonation.

In his mind, Mr. Berger pictured the bomb's massive shock wave ripping through the crowded Rose Main Reading Room, blowing apart everything and everyone within forty feet and sending a killing wall of shrapnel in every direction at four times the speed of sound.

He peeled off his gloves and stood with the now empty laptop bag, careful not to touch anything. He crossed the room and stepped quickly out of the exit without looking back.

It has begun, he thought with a feeling of magnificent relief as he found the marble stairs. From here on out, it would be all about timing. A race against the clock, so to speak.

On your mark.

Get set.

"Blow," Mr. Berger whispered happily to himself, and took the stairs two by two.

Chapter 3

"UNDER THE BOARDWALK, down by the sea," I crooned in a high voice, really getting into it with my eyes closed. "On a blanket with my ten big fat babies is where I'll be."

It seemed to me like an appropriate song for walking along a sandy dirt road beside the blue-gray Atlantic. Unfortunately I was the only one who thought so. A fusillade of groans and boos and Bronx cheers sailed back from all ten of my kids.

Still I bowed, displaying my hallmark grace under pressure. Never let them see you sweat, even on summer vacation, which is really hard when you think about it.

My name is Mike Bennett, and as far as I know, I'm still the only cop in the NYPD living in his own private TLC show. Some of my more jovial coworkers like to call me Detective Mike Plus Ten. It is actually Detective Mike Plus Eleven, if you include my grandfather, Seamus. Which I do, since he is more incorrigible than the rest of my kids put together.

It was the beginning of week two of my humongous family's much-needed vacation out in Breezy Point, Queens, and I was definitely in full goof-off mode. The eighteen-hundred-square-foot saltbox on the "Irish Riviera," as all the cops and firemen who summer here call it, had been in my mom's family, the Murphys, for a generation. It was more crowded than a rabbit's warren, but it was also nonstop swimming and hot dogs and board games—and beer and bonfires at night.

No e-mail. No electronics. No modern implements of any kind except for the AC and a salt water–rusted bicycle.

The Bennett summer White House was open for business.

Time was flying, and I was another year older and even deeper in debt than usual, which I realized the last time I had the guts to peek at my 401K. As I watched Chrissy, the baby of the bunch, chase a tern, or maybe it was a piping plover, on the shoulder of the road, I still couldn't believe that she was going into first grade at the end of the summer.

But I was making the most of it. As usual. For a single father of double-digit kids, making the most of things pretty much went without saying.

"If you guys don't like the Drifters, how about a little Otis Redding?" I called to everyone. "All together now. '(Sittin' on) the Dock of the Bay' on three."

"Is that any example to them, Mike? We need to pick it up or we'll be late," Mary Catherine chided beside me in her brogue.

I forgot to mention Mary Catherine. I'm probably the only

cop in the NYPD with an Irish nanny as well. Actually, with what I pay her, she is more like a selfless angel of mercy.

And, as always, the young, attractive lass was right. We were on our way to St. Edmund's on Oceanside Ave for five o'clock Mass. Vacation was no excuse for missing Mass when you had a late-to-the-cloth priest for a grandfather. What else? Did I mention that all my kids were adopted? Two of them are black, two Hispanic, one Asian, and the rest Caucasian. Normal, our family is not.

"Would ya look at that?" Seamus said, tapping his watch from the sandy steps of St. Edmund's when we finally arrived. "It must be the twelve apostles. Of course not. They'd be on time for Mass. Get in here, heathens, before I forget that I'm not a man of violence."

"Sorry, Father," Chrissy said, a sentiment that was repeated eleven more times in rough ascending order by Shawna, Trent, Fiona, Bridget, Eddie, Ricky, Jane, Brian, my eldest, Juliana, Mary Catherine, and last but not least yours truly.

"Just to let you know, I'm offering Mass for Maeve today," Seamus said.

Maeve is my late wife, the woman who put together my ragtag wonderful family before falling to ovarian cancer a few years before.

"I wouldn't have it any other way, Monsignor," I said as the organ started.

COMING IN SEPTEMBER 2010

Postcard Killers

James Patterson
& Liza Marklund

James Patterson teams up with no. 1 bestselling author Liza Marklund to create the most terrifying holiday thriller ever written.

NYPD detective Jacob Kanon is on a tour of Europe's most gorgeous cities. But the sights aren't what draw him – he sees each museum, each cathedral, and each café through the eyes of his daughter's killer.

Kanon's daughter, Kimmy, and her fiancé were murdered while on holiday in Rome. Since then, young couples in Paris, Madrid, Salzburg, Athens, Amsterdam and Berlin have been found dead. Little connects the murders, other than a postcard sent to the local newspaper prior to each attack.

Now Kanon teams up with the Swedish reporter, Dessie Larsson, who has just received a postcard in Stockholm – and they think they know where the next victims will be.

With relentless logic and unstoppable action, *Postcard Killers* may be James Patterson's most vivid and compelling thriller yet.

Century · London

THE *SUNDAY TIMES* NO. 1 BESTSELLER

Swimsuit

James Patterson
& Maxine Paetro

Perfect models, beautifully executed

A supermodel disappears from a swimsuit photo shoot at the most glamorous hotel in Hawaii. Only hours after she goes missing, Kim McDaniels' parents receive a terrifying phone call. Fearing the worst, they board the first flight to Maui and begin the hunt for their daughter.

Ex-cop Ben Hawkins, now a reporter for the *LA Times*, gets the McDaniels assignment. The ineptitude of the local police force defies belief – Ben has to start his own investigation for Kim McDaniels to have a prayer . . . and for Ben to have the story of his life.

Swimsuit is a heart-pounding story of fear and desire, transporting you to a place where beauty and murder collide and unspeakable horrors are hidden within paradise.

'Patterson's annual summer thriller is another exceptional treat'
Mirror

'It terrifyied me rigid – but there was no way in a million years I could put it down . . . utterly compulsive'
Daily Express

arrow books

We support

I'm proud to support the National Literacy Trust, an independent charity that changes lives through literacy.

Did you know that millions of people in the UK struggle to read and write? This means children are less likely to succeed at school and less likely to develop into confident and happy teenagers. Literacy difficulties will limit their opportunities throughout adult life.

The National Literacy Trust passionately believes that everyone has a right to the reading, writing, speaking and listening skills they need to fulfil their own and, ultimately, the nation's potential.

My own son didn't used to enjoy reading which was why I started writing children's books – reading for pleasure is an essential way to encourage children to pick up a book. The National Literacy Trust is dedicated to delivering exciting initiatives to encourage people to read and to help raise literacy levels. To find out more about the great work that they do visit their website at www.literacytrust.org.uk.

James Patterson